FIre THE water

TIMOTHY KYLE

No is a full sentence. Bodies are sacred. Consent is everything.
Read this book to see what fuck around and find out truly
means.

Trigger Warnings

Other Books by Timothy Kyle

The Tree House
The Girl in the Red Wig

Chapter 1

POPPY

Present Day

January 17th, 2026

"My name is Poppy Rodriguez. I'm a statistic. A victim...to a *sickness*."

All at once, my next breaths are stolen from me. The words I was searching for vanish into silence. The only hint of white noise comes from the whirling fan blades above my head. Every now and again the pull chains on the fan will ping against the light fixture. But other than those slivers of noise, it's just me and my phone stuck in a staring contest.

My mind feels strangulated by so many swirling, horrific thoughts. The words I need to find are trapped on the inside, with no way out. It's hard to breathe. Hard to concentrate. Hard to do anything—let alone exist. But I have to keep going. I *need* to tell my story.

"I need your help," I pause to purse out a shuddering breath. "I think I've found a way to make something of my life—to help the voiceless find their voice."

I pinch my eyes shut for a moment. When I open back up, the first thing I notice is the red circle on my phone. The time ticking by. It's all a simple reminder that I'm still recording. But how can I talk when I don't even recognize my reflection?

It's this fucking ring light! It spotlights every single imperfection. The heavy bags under my eyes. Lips that look wired shut. I can even see the tension pulsing in my jaw.

My olive skin doesn't look the same either. It's fairer, with less of the bronze and caramel I can get from only a couple of hours in the sun. Even the light curls in my golden-brown hair look dead and brittle. They cascade down a couple inches past my shoulders, looking like wilted vines.

Everything I see is symbolic. This is the transformation from who I was, to who I am now. I've lived a life of opportunity. A life of heartbreak and hope. I even fell in love. But it all went to shit.

I continue to watch my mute self, imagining the proverbial angel and devil sitting on my shoulders. The fiery side is telling me revenge is a necessary evil. The angel side is telling me to follow my gut, no matter how lost and hollowed out I feel on the inside.

There's only one singular truth that keeps me going. It's Nina and Jet. I'm here because of them. They give me the willpower to push forward. The power to be brave in spirit and actions.

Actions! Yes! That's why I'm here!

This may only be a first step, but it's a terrifying one—like a skydiver with no parachute. No safety net. But it all makes sense. These feelings. After all, I went off social media for good reasons. *Really good reasons!* And yet, I'm so tired of being afraid. No more. Not today. This is my time to be courageous—to tell my story to the world—and let fate guide what happens next.

I reach with shaky hands, grabbing the wallet-size picture between my thumb and index finger to hold it up in plain view to my phone. Then I grab the lighter.

"A wise person once told me to fire the water. Well, today, I choose *fire*."

CHAPTER 2

zane

ONE DAY LATER

JANUARY 18TH, 2026

My grip tightens around the metal railing, squeezing harder and harder until it squeaks against my clammy hands. Then I let my body lean into it, feeling like Jack and Rose from *Titanic*.

The railing presses against my mid-section like a block of ice, cutting through layers of fabric without mercy. The bone-chilling cold is sharp, yet strangely cathartic. Maybe it's because I'm finally able to feel something inside of me. What that something is, I don't know yet.

I am feeling brave though, so I walk around the railing. Then, I slowly slide my feet closer to the edge. One *very* gradual inch at a time, they crunch through the Sedona red dirt. Then I stop, feeling a fluttering inside of me when my toes reach the edge.

A deep exhale helps me be in the moment. My eyes oscillate over the grandeur before me. There's so much to see in the chasm below, but it's the early morning skyline that has my eyes enamored. The sun's light barely peeks over the horizon. The clouds look like little bits of cotton candy. Each one has their own unique palette of pink, lavender, and orange.

It's a canyon that's more than just grand. It's Mother Nature at her most masterful, beauty so raw it feels otherworldly, like something pulled from a dream. But within it is something deeper, far beyond a 277-mile-wide hole in the earth.

I breathe in the scenery as the breeze slowly forms into a whipping gust. I love the way it feels, especially when a few loose, curly tendrils tickle their way across my face. It causes my teeth to chatter as the chill seeps deeper into my bones. But I like it. I'm desperate to feel anything at this point in my life.

I step back around the railing to take a quick glance at my phone. It's 5:29 a.m. I'm right on time—just as she requested. I glance behind me to see if she's here. There are only a few visitors minding their own business around me. None of them are the wildflower that lives in my thoughts and dreams.

Twenty-four! Fucking! Seven!

I begin to people-watch the few strangers around me. Each person seems lost in their own world of tranquility. Like me, they look out in wonderment. It's just what you do when you visit a wonder of the world—you begin to wonder.

I wonder about a lot of things in my life. What if I never fell in love with her? What if I never fought for her? What if Kitty never found her? What if I didn't drive? What if the balance of tiny objects didn't fall through the cracks? It's all one big fucking game of what-ifs, I guess.

The baffling part is how it all comes down to control. Sometimes we want it. Other times we don't. Then fate leads us down different winding roads. But life is nothing but a collection of choices we make. Most are meaning-less, but some alter our destinies forever.

A car door shuts behind me. I can't explain it, but I just know it's her. A quick glance confirms what I'm feeling—my wildflower has arrived. The pressure inside has me hyper-aware of each breath—like I'm reminding myself to breathe. The thought of her walking next to me on this journey has my mind spiraling into so many dark thoughts and memories.

I'm too much of a coward to turn around. What would I say anyways? Greet her with a hello? Maybe a simple head nod with some eye contact would suffice. Or, maybe I can just walk away and pretend I never came here. That would be the easy way out. But I know I'm here for a reason. A *really* good reason.

It's also how my brother, Nick, would want it. He wants me here just like Poppy's sister needs Poppy to be here. It's like this was their grand plan all along. Us. *Back to-gether.* The only problem is, together never felt possible.

When the scent of lavender and vanilla hits my nostrils, I glance across my shoulder. She stops at my side, giving me a quick side glance before looking down at her feet.

I swear the corner of her lips twitched the slightest bit. Maybe she was trying to smile but couldn't. If it was a smile, it was gone in the blink of an eye.

I do a double take over my shoulder. She's bundled up in winter wear like me. She's also wearing a green bandana in her hair. It's tied like a headband, instantly bringing our inside joke to mind. I'm also reminded of how short she is. Especially when I'm next to her. The top of her head is barely even with my shoulders.

The one thing I didn't forget is her hair. The way it cascades down just past her shoulders, doing it's own little dance in the breeze. Or the way those wavy curls of caramel and bronze shimmer in the sunlight. It has that perfect hint of gold to match her hazel eyes. There's even a subtle hint of reddish-orange that I could never forget when the sun hits it just right.

But what I remember most is the way Poppy feels up close. The way I once inhaled her scent in those brief moments of bliss. Those are the memories that have imprinted into the core of my brain. The kind I wish I could turn off to avoid the constant rippling pain in my chest. But turning that off is impossible when it comes to my obsession with Poppy Rodriguez.

She finally turns to face me.

"Hey."

That one syllable leaves her out of breath. As for me, it's her eyes that steal mine. Right now, they are the perfect mix of amber, green, and glinting gold. The power they hold over me is magnetic. It's a beauty that stirs something in the furthest depths of me, making me yearn for so many things I cannot have.

"Hey," I finally murmur, swallowing the tension noosing tighter around my throat. It's the first words we've shared since the funeral—not counting her text inviting me on this trip.

"Did you bring it?" she asks, tucking a few curly strands behind her ear. Her eyes can only land on mine for a fleeting moment. Then she's looking away, avoiding the pain that devours our insides anytime our eyes meet.

"Yeah, I got it," I tell her, patting the side of my backpack. The slight pinging noise tells her I no doubt have it.

"How about you?"

Poppy nods softly, releasing a long breath through pursed lips. Then she pats her backpack so I can hear the same sound.

We gaze past one another in silence, not knowing what else to say. All we have is this hike. It's our *only* purpose for being together. Well, it was our only purpose, until I saw the video she posted on Instagram. She doesn't know it yet, but that video played a role in my decision. A *very* big role.

Nevertheless, I still know my purpose for being here. Our priority is saying goodbye to my brother and her sister, Nina. However, the elephant in the room is all the things left unsaid between us. And while neither of us is anywhere near ready to talk, it's a long hike down and out.

"You ready?" she asks, fitting her gloves onto her dainty hands.

"Let's go."

We head down the Bright Angel Trailhead into the Grand Canyon. There'll be no phone reception. It's just the two of us, together. We'll be shoulder to shoulder the whole way down to a resting place called Indian Gardens. It'll be a nine-mile round trip to say goodbye to our favorite people. It's how her sister apparently wanted it, which means, it's how my brother would want it, too.

CHAPTER 3

POPPY

FOUR YEARS EARLIER

2022

"Fuuuuck! I want that sweet pussy! Spread those fucking legs for me, baby. Come on, be a good girl."

The sound suddenly dies out in my earbuds.

"Fuck, really," I mutter, taking a long sigh. I'm so frustrated I forgot to charge them this morning.

There's something about listening to a smutty romance novel when you're surrounded by a crowd of people. Everyone else is living their own superficial lives while I'm getting all riled up and fucked raw in my fictional one.

Oh well. I guess it's back to reality.

I check my phone for the third time in the last 10 minutes. Fuck! She should've been out here by now. What the fuck is she doing talking to him anyways?

The mere thought of my best friend getting back with her ex has my mouth already tasting like stomach acid. Lonny's always had a thing for bad boys. I still remember her first boyfriend in kindergarten, Tommy. That boy stabbed her in the ear with a crayon and called her a poop nugget. The next day they were holding hands and dating.

Ha! Some things never change!

I stifle a chuckle thinking about all the shit we've been through. Now, here we are, sophomores in college, and she's in the Student Recreation Center contemplating another try with John—the Karen of Frat Boys.

The funny thing is she knows I'm going to call her on her shit. We've been best friends forever, so it's allowed. But I don't think it matters to her. She loves to be chased. It's always been that way with her. But to be fair, what girl doesn't like a little pursuit? I sure would envy knowing what that feels like.

The snickering and giggles get louder from behind me. I turn around and look up from my phone to see a group of sorority girls. They're strutting towards me like a scene straight out of *Mean Girls*.

Sororities are a big thing at most colleges and universities. However, I'm beginning to feel like Arizona State University grows them on trees. Nina and Lonny had warned me about it when I booked my ticket out here to visit them. It's just funny to see it firsthand because it's so not my vibe.

I take a seat on an open bench. It's the perfect spot—far enough away from all the foot traffic and getting nothing but sunlight. It feels good to soak in this desert heat. I sure am going to miss it when I have to head back to San Diego.

My phone dings.

Lonny

Be out in five minutes. Sorry, pookie bear!

The sudden sensation of licking on the back of my leg has me jumping off the bench. The next thing I know, I'm face planting into the ground.

I start to get up, then I freeze at the feeling of wet sandpaper slopping over my face. My entire mood shifts in an instant. It's a dog, but not just any dog. It's a puppy!

The golden retriever couldn't be much bigger than a volleyball. His puppy energy has me instantly floating on cloud nine. Even the puppy yelping has my heart melting on the inside.

I sit up on both knees and cradle her in my arms. "Hi, girl. You okay? Oh, yes! Oh, yes! I love it when you lick my face. Where's your owner?" I ask, noticing the leash still attached to its collar.

"Hi."

A large shadow casts over me like an eclipse. I look up at the gruff sounding voice. The first thing I notice are the golden-brown messy curls on his head. The bits of freckles spattered along his razor-sharp jawline and cheekbones. And the eyes. I can't think straight because the shade of aqua blue doesn't look real with the way the sun cascades light around his body.

"Fuck," I blurt out without thinking.

He laughs quietly. "You...o-okay?"

"I'm fuh, f-fine." I stumble over my words.

"Are you sure?"

"Yeah, I'm good." I stop to clear my throat as I stand up. But even when I'm standing, my eyes still have to arch their way up to see the top of him. "Can I help you?"

"Yeah, I just came for Kitty here," he says, reaching to snag the leash out of my hand.

I pull it away from his grasp, stepping back. "Wait! What?"

"Um, that's my dog…Kitty."

"Kitty? Like, here kitty-kitty?"

I'm unable to hide my disbelieving tone. I mean, is this a fucking joke? "How do I know you're not some fraternity douchebag that stole a dog, named it Kitty as a conversation starter, and now you're parading it around to pick up girls?"

The lines crinkle in his forehead. "That's actually a good idea, but no. No…that's really my dog," he says more sternly.

He seems sure. But why is the corner of his mouth beginning to curl up in a smirk? Did he see me eat shit a second ago? Is he fighting back laughter? Whatever it is, I feel the need to hold my ground. Be stubborn. It's always been a strength of mine.

"Sorry. I don't trust people that name dogs this cute after a pussy…cat."

Wait! What! Really, Poppy! Pussy!

"Did you just say pussy? That's very unbecoming?"

I scoff at his retort. "Did you just say unbecoming. I mean, are we in an etiquette lesson with Queen Elizabeth?"

"Now you're cracking jokes about dead people. Hhhmmm, good one," he says, nodding his head with a mocking grin.

I put Kitty down because she's getting restless. My hand stays on the leash. I should just hand it over and call it a day. But I'm in the mood to be extra stubborn. And perhaps stare at him a little longer.

I let the awkward silence drag on between us. The longer it goes, the more I feel my cheeks heating up as my brain recalls my use of the word pussy.

His poker face finally cracks and he starts laughing. It quickly builds into a full-on belly laugh, loud and snorty enough that I feel passersby staring at us. For some reason it's both annoying and funny. Maybe it's because his cackling oddly reminds me of Jet.

"Ow!" I step back from the stinging on my knee. "Kitty, you can't lick the blood off my legs. That hurts, sweetheart."

I lean down to pick up Kitty and cradle her back into my arms. I rub my nose against hers as she gives me wet kisses.

"I'm so sorry someone named you after a completely different species," I say in my best baby voice.

"Oh, man. You're funny." He takes a deep breath to recover from his laughing spell. Then he goes down on one knee to dig into his backpack.

"What're you doing?"

"Well, you won't give me my dog back. I think that's a crime. Theft, maybe? Kidnapping? Hell, I don't know. But I'll hold off on calling campus police."

He pulls out what looks like a first aid kit. From this angle I can't believe how broad his shoulders and upper back muscles are. It's like he's wearing armor underneath his skin-tight white tee.

He brings his eyes back to mine when he has gauze in one hand and a spray bottle in the other. "May I?"

I cock my head to the side, feeling befuddled by so many things. But it's his height that suddenly has me. He's almost as tall as me on his knees. And he's fucking gorgeous!

"Come on. Have a seat right here," he invites me with a pat on the bench I was just sitting on. "My name is Zane."

"Poppy."

"Excuse me?"

"That's my name. I mean, my real name is Paulina. But everyone calls me by my middle name."

"Okay, well, Poppy. How about you take a seat? I'll bandage you up, and in exchange, you'll give me my dog back. Like a ransom deal?"

I begrudgingly sit down while another smirk cracks through those lips. I'm still unsure of what to say as I cradle a puppy in my arms. It's so cute it doesn't even feel real.

Zane goes right to work, meticulously cleaning my wound. I watch on and try my best to not make my ogling look too obvious.

His hands are massive. But they're not just long. They're thick. And the way his fingers work in a delicate fashion is how I'd imagine a surgeon working. There's also a certain tenderness in his eyes. He keeps glancing at me and asking if it hurts. It's like he somehow already knows that I have the pain tolerance of a 1st grader.

"So, how did this happen?"

"Kitty snuck up on me from behind. It scared the shit out of me, and I tripped as I got up from the bench."

"Tripped?" he says, looking around with a smirk. "On what? Air?"

"Ha, ha, ha. The lip of my flats caught something."

I watch as he tries to look away from me, licking his lips to fight away another grin. It's super annoying but also insanely sexy.

I get up after he tapes on the last bandage. "Here's your baby girl," I say, handing over his dog. "And thanks."

"You're welcome. It's the least I can do for making sure Kitty didn't wander off."

I suddenly notice Lonny staring at me from behind him. She gives me a 'skeeze or no skeeze' look. I give her a discreet head nod and half smile to let her know I'm okay.

Zane looks over his shoulder then back at me. "So…"

"Thanks again," I mutter, awkwardly stepping around him.

"Wait! Do you have somewhere you need to be?"

"Um, class." *Liar!* "I mean, no. But I was just headed back to the dorms."

"Can I walk with you?"

I pause, not knowing what to say. The translucent blue in those eyes leaves me out of breath.

"Um, I guess."

"You guess?"

"Well, as long as you're not a kidnapper or a frat boy."

He puts his hand over his mouth to stifle a chuckle.

I point my finger at him. "Wait! You're a frat boy! Aren't you?"

"No, I'm not. But I used to be. Is being in a frat somehow worse than being a kidnapper?"

I look up, pretending to be deep in thought while also trying to keep my flirtatious grin not overtly obvious.

"They're pretty equal. But I'll make an exception because you have a cute dog."

We start walking side by side. He seems comfortable with silence, whereas I feel the need to speak up.

"So, why do you walk around with a first aid kit?"

"Oh, I, uh, just got out of my Athletic Trainer's class."

"That's cool. Is that what you're studying?"

"No, I'm a pre-med studying biology. It's just an elective juniors take. But to be honest, it's probably my favorite class. And it's useful because I'm a swimmer."

"Of course!" I shout, probably sounding way too excited.

"Of course, what?"

"Well, you're uh, uh, uh..." My brain has left me without words. All I have are my hands gesturing like a mime. "You're, uh—"

"Tall. Big. Strong. Good looking."

Another sexy smile. Fuck!

"Well, yeah. I mean, at least the first three," I lie. "But you've got that swimmer look. You know the kind of limbs that are long and gangling."

I put my arms at my side because I was just moving my arms like a monkey.

"Gang...ling? What does that even mean?"

"Maybe that's the wrong word, but you just have really long arms and defined shoulders and upper body—you know, like a swimmer."

His grin gets a little wider. "You talk with your hands a lot, don't you?"

I don't know what to say. I've always been someone that talks with their hands. And the more nervous I am, the more I'm apt to start flapping my wings around like a wounded pigeon.

The flush of heat in my face comes quickly. I clear my throat because I suddenly forgot how to breathe. He also keeps smiling at me, which isn't helping matters.

"So, how good a swimmer are you?"

He runs his hand through his wavy curls and cocks his head to the side, flashing a half smile. "I'm pretty good."

I bite my fingernail while trying to read the smirk on his face. "You're a liar. I get the feeling that you're more than pretty good."

"Fair enough. Are you from the Phoenix area?"

"No. I grew up in San Diego. I go to San Diego State University. I'm just out here visiting my best friend and my sister for the weekend. How about you? Where ya from?"

"Born and raised right here in Phoenix. But I love San Diego. I've competed up there quite a few times."

He runs his hand back through his hair. I can't tell if it's a nervous tic or if he's just clearing a few loose tendrils from his eyes. It's such a little thing, but it's sexy as hell.

"So, this is the dorm," I tell him as we stop in front of the entrance. Kitty starts nuzzling against my leg. I lean down to pick her up. She licks my cheeks as I give her a goodbye kiss.

"Bye, Kitty."

He pulls out his phone. "Hey, can I get your Insta?" he asks, taking a step closer to me.

The pit in my stomach is immediate. It was a harmless request. A very normal question. But he doesn't know me, or what I've been through.

"Oh, I'm uh..." I stop to clear my throat. "I'm not on socials. It's a long story."

"Then, I'll take your number."

He angles his gaze into my eyes. My mind is suddenly swimming in those ocean blue orbs of his. There's a calmness in them. I can't explain it. It's just something I feel. Or maybe it's something I envy to feel—like the calm before the storm.

"Oh, I don't know about that." I stop to catch my breath. I want to be honest, but I also don't want to say anything stupid. "I don't live here. I don't look or act like most girls either. I just have no filter when things come out of my mouth. It's uh—"

"Honest. Real. Fun."

"Um, I guess you can call it that."

"It's better than fake, right?" He looks away as a group of ogling sorority girls begin eye fucking him. Then his eyes tip down to mine. "I feel like there's a lot of that around here. It's refreshing to meet someone that says what they're thinking. I like it."

"Even if they say the word pussy thirty seconds into meeting them."

"Yes, definitely if they say the word *pussy!*" He pops the p with his lips.

We share a nervous laugh. Then I finally give in, sharing my phone number. He repeats it back slowly, with a smile that has my heart swimming in happiness.

Is he actually interested? In me?

It doesn't make sense. I'm half his size. Not as cute as 90% of the twig-like supermodels out here. And I clearly demonstrated how to say the weirdest shit at the most inopportune times.

Zane calls it honesty. Refreshing. Fun. All words that should stave off my insecurities, but they don't. Not even close! But there's something about Zane. He's not like any college boy I've ever met. He's a man. And this man feels way out of my league.

"Well, it was nice meeting you," I tell him, awkwardly extending my hand.

He squeezes so tightly I hear my knuckles crack. "Take care, Poppy. And treat those cuts before you go to bed tonight."

I nod and wave goodbye. I don't want this to be the last time I talk to Zane. But I know it probably will be.

CHAPTER 4

POPPY

"You said what?!" Lonny shrieks again. Then she pegs me with another throw pillow.

I recall the pussycat beginnings of our conversation. The embarrassment as I retell the story a second time still makes me want to bury myself alive. Lonny spends most of the time laughing at my expense. Then I explain how attractive and kind he was.

"Bluest eyes I've ever seen. A swimmer's body, but like, holy fuck, Lonny! It was like a sculpture of muscles on top of muscles. He even thought I was funny. And he was so sweet. I mean, what kind of man cleans a cut on some random stranger?" I stop because I'm fantasizing about his fingers and hands. The way they delicately worked along my skin has me hot and bothered all over again.

"Lonny, it was...it was—"

"Fucking hot!" she shrieks, chucking another pillow that barely misses my head. "And you missed your chance."

"Maybe. But there was something more to him. I can't put my finger on it. He seemed genuinely attracted to me. I'm not used to that."

"You're gorgeous, Poppy. That doesn't surprise me. You just don't give guys a chance. Here, give me your phone. I want to see if he texted you yet." Lonny snags it off my lap. I'm too busy daydreaming to care.

"Nothing yet, but you should text him. Come on, it's your last night here."

I vigorously shake my head. "No. No. No. When he finds out about...you know...I just...I can't imagine going through those conversations."

My eyes dart away from Lonny. But I can still hear her let out an exasperated breath. She wants to encourage me. It's what she's tried doing many times before. But she knows this is a topic I *cannot* be pressed on.

"Can I at least stalk him on his socials?"

I shrug my shoulders. "I don't know, but I'm not texting him."

I get up from Lonny's bed and walk to her mirror. I feel the need to critique my body and downplay my chances of ever being with a guy like him.

Surprisingly, the shape of my ass looks pretty good in these jeans. But it has to be the right angle in the mirror. When I breathe in to elevate my chest, my breasts have a little extra perk in them. They look okay with the extra padding in my bra. They're not small, but they're not big either. As for my waist, I can still grip a good chunk of my love handles in my hand. Lonny swears that most boys like something they can hang onto, but the extra fat just makes me feel insecure and a bit bloated.

Fuck this!

This is only making me sadder. I glance back at Lonny, who's busy scrolling on my phone. She's a perfect ten in every way except for her taste in men. And she knows she's gorgeous. She's never been bashful about it. It's not that I'm jealous of her long legs, shapely ass, and long blond hair. I'm just jealous of the feeling of being wanted. I've felt it at times. But not like today.

The way Zane looked at me today was something completely different than what I'm used to. It was more than just interest and intrigue. It's like he sensed that there were deeper layers to me that he gently wanted to peel back.

"Oh shit! Oh shit! Oh fucking pussycat shit!"

I hurry to Lonny's side as she hides my phone in her chest. "Poppy, please don't freak out."

"What! What! Just show me!"

She cringes with uncertainty as she slowly rotates the phone to my eyes. I blink back what I'm seeing because I can't believe it. He texted me to come over.

Tonight!

Chapter 5

zane

A SMALL GROUP OF people file into our house. I don't know them and it's bugging the shit out of me. I scowl at my best friend, Trey.

"Who the fuck are these people?"

Trey takes a long drag from his blunt, speaking as he blows it out.

"Don't look at me. Kevin must've invited that group. I said we should just kick back tonight, but he only thinks with his dick. I'm over that fucking alcoholic."

All I can do is shake my head. "I don't like having people I don't know in our house. He fucking knows that."

"Me too. What time are you getting up tomorrow?"

"Four fucking thirty," I mumble, tapping my foot incessantly. I can't sit still so I start pacing on the front porch.

I look at my phone again. It's a little past 11. I can train on five hours of sleep, but any less and I'll see it in my times—along with an earful from coach.

"You good, man?"

I ignore Trey's question as my phone vibrates.

Poppy

Pulling up. Sorry we're late.

The nauseating feeling in my stomach is a mix of nervous excitement and my stomach growling. Then it hits me, I never had my third dinner.

Fuck!

"Yo, Zane!"

"What?"

"What's up with you?" Trey asks, his eyes lingering on me.

"This girl, man. Something about her. I don't know what it is. But she finally pulled up. Please don't be a douche."

"Whatever you say, Mr. pussycat."

I give Trey the don't-fuck-around-with-me look. "Seriously?"

He scoffs and playfully drives his shoulder into mine. I push him back and he almost eats shit.

"Chill out, fucker! Don't get all pissy with me over a girl."

I walk down the front porch a couple steps ahead of Trey, trying to ignore his comment.

"Hey! Thanks for coming!" I give Poppy a side hug—the awkward kind you give the girl cousins in your family.

Great! Already off to an awkward start.

"Yeah, of course, this is my friend Lonny. Lonny, this is Zane."

Everyone exchanges pleasantries. I notice how her friend's eyes linger on Trey after they shake hands.

"Can I offer you guys a drink?"

Poppy looks down at her feet. "I'm fine, thanks."

"What about you, Lonny? There's a Keg inside." I turn to ask Trey. "What is it tonight?"

Trey didn't hear a word. He's in a smiley trance because Poppy's friend is a blonde. It's his biggest weakness.

"Trey!" I slap him on the shoulder.

"Sorry. It's, uh, it's basically horse piss," he says. His eyes don't break from Lonny as he tries to play it cool.

"Horse piss it is," Lonny says with an extra warm smile directed right at Trey.

"Poppy, you sure you're okay?"

She holds up her water bottle. "I'm driving. I'm good. But thank you."

Trey and I guide the girls through the house for a quick tour. Then we introduce them to Trey's sister, Lisa. She's also in town visiting because it was her 19th birthday a couple of days ago.

Lisa and Poppy hit it off right away. They're both apparently majoring in Non-Profit Leadership, which gets them talking. I try to listen in on their conversation. However, I'm quickly distracted when Trey gives a head nod to the two guys on the couch.

"Is that them?" I ask.

"Yep."

"Why the fuck would Kevin invite them?"

"Because he's a dick."

Kevin's our roommate, or at least he is until his lease is up in a month. He's going to move out, which is a good thing because he's a slob and an asshole to both of us.

"Should we kick them out? I'll fucking throw them out. Full stop, man. Just say the word."

Trey knows I've never been one to back down from a fight. And with what these pricks did, it's taking so much restraint to not go over there and pummel the shit out of their smug faces.

Trey let's out a long sigh, shaking his head while talking. "No. They're just minding their business. I don't want to start any more drama with Kevin. He'll be gone soon anyways. Then we won't have to deal with his prick friends and prick cousins. But you better believe I'm not leaving Lisa's side tonight."

I give them both the stink eye from across the living room. One of the guys is Kevin's cousin. I don't even remember his name. The other guy I've never seen. He just looks like trouble with his mean mugging, resting bitch face.

Kevin's cousin was whistling at Lisa two nights ago. Lisa later told us how he was also checking her out in a way that made her feel uncomfortable. And when she tried to walk away from his advances, he cornered her in a hallway and put his hands on her hips. I wasn't there, but apparently Trey got in the guy's face only for Kevin to get in between them and break up what would've been a fight.

I've known Trey since he was in the 3rd grade. His sister's two years younger than him, so it wouldn't be the first time he's had to defend her against some prick. And since we're best friends, Lisa is like a sister to me as well. All he'd have to do is say the word, and I'd have both of their backs in a heartbeat.

"You sure, Trey?" I give him a questioning stare. I can tell he's thinking it over.

"Yeah. I'm good. We'll just keep our distance."

When the girls are done gabbing, we spend a few minutes playing with Kitty. After that I put her in the kennel for the night. Then Lonny, Lisa, and Trey head out to the dining room to play beer pong. I can tell Poppy's not interested in drinking, so the two of us head out to the back porch.

"So, why the chocolate milk?" she asks as I shut the sliding glass door to drown out the noise from inside.

"Oh, I had my afternoon training session. It was pretty intense, so this helps me re-energize for tomorrow. I'm also not a big drinker."

"Hhhmm, me either."

Poppy props her arms on the railing of the back porch, looking up at the sky. There's an undeniable nervous tension in the air when neither of us talks. Then her gaze goes over her shoulder to me as we share a brief smile.

Our porchlight gives just enough illumination to see the effervescent hint of green in those hazel eyes. I can even see that shimmer of gold in her brown hair as a light gust of wind has it fluttering off her shoulders. She is insanely gorgeous, but also incredibly unique in how she presents herself.

I don't have a type. I have dated a couple Latina girls, but it was never anything serious. Poppy just has this different vibe about her. She doesn't look or act like any of the girls I've ever been with. For one, she's tiny. I'm guessing maybe a hair over five feet tall. But she carries herself with confidence and spunk. She seems less worried about trends, outfits, and material things.

She's wearing blue overalls with a tight white sports bra showing underneath. Her wavy, golden-brown hair cascades down just a couple of inches past her shoulders. It's tied back by a velvety green headband with a white bow on top. I don't know what you call it when girls have those bows tied up into their hair, but whatever it is, it looks so good on her.

She's also curvy in all the right places. But she's not trying to flaunt it like most girls. And the way her shy smile is curling in my direction makes me feel like I forgot how to talk. I need to say something. The silence has been dragging on for far too long. But I don't know what to say.

Come on, Zane! Say anything!

"I like your little, uh..." I'm miming a halo over my head, not knowing how to say it because I can't think of the word. "Your little green headband, dipsey-doo-bow-thingy in your hair."

"Uh, dipsey what?" She chuckles.

My cheeks warm with embarrassment as I try to find the words. "Sorry, I don't know what it's called. But uh—" I pause to clear the nervous tension in my throat. "What

I'm trying to say is, you look really nice. I mean it. You just look, *really, really,* nice."

Every feature in her face seems to shift at once. Her eyes dilate, looking suddenly glossy as her smile rises higher, lighting up her now rosy cheeks. I can't help but admire how she looks so touched by my compliment. It's as if I can feel her gratitude warming in my chest—like there's this electricity flowing between us.

"Thanks, Zane."

"Of course."

Poppy looks away for a brief moment. It feels like we're both trying to slow our racing hearts and catch our breath.

"So..." she breathes out a long exhale. Then she turns her eyes to mine. "When were you going to tell me who you really are?"

"What do you mean?" The words leave my mouth, feeling like a feeble attempt at playing dumb.

Poppy chuckles under her breath with her eyebrows shooting up. "Really? Mister pretty good swimmer. You know...there's this thing called Google."

"Aaahhh, I guess you found me. Does any of what you read change your mind about me? Or maybe scare you?"

"Why would I be scared?"

I watch her eyebrows scrunch inwards. I hesitate, figuring she'd know by now. But maybe she doesn't. All I see is genuine curiosity that's morphing into anxious creases in her forehead. When her hands start to fidget, I huff out a hefty exhale while rubbing a hand along the back of my neck.

"I got in a couple fights my junior year of high school. One was small, just me being a hot head. The other was defending Lisa from some prick that tried to hurt her. That one made the local news and almost got me kicked out of school. I lost swimming scholarships because of it."

"Oh...okay." Poppy brings a closed fist to her mouth as she clears her throat. "Well, uh—"

"The guy deserved it, Poppy," I raise my voice, feeling confident—not an ounce of regret. "He put a hand on her. I did it so Trey didn't kill the guy. And I don't regret hurting him."

The tension in the air feels like balloons bursting beneath our chests. All the air is gone as we hold each other's gaze. Her eyes remain contemplative, studying me, trying to figure me out.

I don't have anything else to say on the topic. And I'm worried that I've just scared the shit out of her—made her think I'm some hot head that looks for a fight. But that's not me anymore. Defending Lisa was pure necessity. I'd do the same for Trey without blinking.

"I didn't know about any of that," she finally murmurs. "I'm also not a big sports person. And I didn't want Lonny to go through your Insta, but she did it anyways. Most of that stuff is fake though. If I'm being honest, I was just surprised you texted me."

"Why? Shouldn't guys make the first move?"

"Not necessarily. I mean, I'm not afraid to make the first move. But then again, I'm not looking for a guy."

"You're not, eh. But here you are on your last night in town, spending it with me."

"Lonny made me come. She says I need to take more risks."

"I'm a risk?"

"All guys are," she quickly shoots back with heightened tension in her voice. Poppy looks down at her trembling hand, white-knuckling the railing until she covers it with her other hand.

All guys are.

Those three words begin to stick to my insides. Her tone was so assured and rigid. Even the way she looked away from me after saying it, staring off into space, looking suddenly desolate and lost.

Maybe this is why she has no social media accounts. I contemplate trying to dig for more back story, but she's clearly not wanting to go there.

"Fair enough," I concede.

Poppy primps at her hair. Then she tips her eyes up to the stars, releasing a pent-up breath that clouds into the cold night air.

"Sooooo...you didn't want to see me tonight?" I ask.

"I wanted to see Kitty. Besides, it's hard to believe that guys like you are single. In fact, I made a bet with Lonny that you aren't single."

"Hhhmmm, I see," I acknowledge her while lightly bobbing my head.

She stands up a little taller and turns her accusatory eyes to me. "Yeah, guys like you typically fall into two categories. You either choose to be single so you can sleep around with different girls, which is fine. I got no hate with that. Girls can do the same if they want."

"And the other category?"

"Well, it's less likely. But maybe you're the type of guy that falls in love hard and can never let go of that one person. Then you become obsessed with what you can't have."

"I guess you got it all figured out. So, which one am I?"

Poppy looks down at her feet, sighing a heavy breath. Then she props her arms back on the porch railing. She looks down at her hair, barely draping over her shoulder. Her fingers delicately glide through it as she speaks.

"That's the thing. You're hard to read because you seem interested in me. But not in the douchebag kind of way. It's sincere, yet confusing. I just feel like there's more things you're not telling me."

"Well, maybe I'm not a douchebag. Maybe I'm just my own person. And maybe I'm not hiding anything. Come on, ask me anything."

"Are you seeing someone right now?"

The question knocks the wind out of my sail. I'm not going to lie to her, but I also don't know how to explain it without already sounding like an asshole.

"Well, define what you mean by—"

"Okay you're seeing someone," she cuts me off with a cold tone. "But you're just looking for a good time because you know I'm leaving tomorrow and probably desperate. Which I guess would make you desperate, too."

Her interjection has me tongue tied. I hold my hand up to defend myself. "Wait one second. Let me explain. I was seeing someone, recently, but we're not official. We never were. For all I know, she's seeing someone else right now."

"I'm never going to be anyone's back up or hookup. That's just not me."

"And neither am I. Hence, here we are."

Poppy rubs her hand along her temple as her forehead crinkles. "Unbecoming. Hence. Do you always speak in 19th century tongue?"

I chuckle under my breath. "My mom's an English teacher. She made me read all that classic shit when I was younger. But let me ask you something. Do you always assume the worst in people?"

"I have my reasons."

Those four words puncture the air out of my chest. I watch her eyes wilt before she looks away. Then her hands start to shake again. She tries to hide it by fidgeting them together.

It seems like more than just discomfort. She seems haunted. And the tone in her voice felt empty, like a dried-up barren well in the middle of nowhere. Lost and alone.

I want to know more about these *reasons*, but I also feel the need to tread lightly.

Very lightly.

CHAPTER 6

zane

WE SHARE ANOTHER LAUGH, and I can feel her loosening up. All it took was changing the subject a moment ago to talk movies and TV shows. It turns out we both share a love for the TV show, *The Office*.

Seeing her giggle and become more relaxed gives me the confidence to close the distance. I take a step closer as I lean my arm on the railing. I'm so close I could brush my fingers along hers.

"Tell me more about you. I want to get to know you, Poppy. But no boring how's the weather kind of shit."

Poppy chuckles. "Oh! I assure you my life has not been boring."

Poppy takes her arms off the railing and slowly turns to face me. Once her arms cross over her chest, I feel it again. The pins and needles in my chest. This indescribable tension in the air. It's like she wants to speak but is afraid of what she'll say.

Poppy bows her head for a moment, letting out a deep, strained breath. Then she begins to tell me her life story, or at least a quick, cliff notes version of it.

She talks fast and with her hands, giving me very little time to process or interject. And she's right. Her life is not boring.

She was adopted at the age of four after being left at a fire station. She has no biological siblings, no relationship with her biological parents, and no memories of them either. Her older sister's name is Nina. Her younger brother's name is Jet. He's two years younger than Poppy and he was born with cerebral palsy.

Her favorite things are animals, hiking, and staying up late with a good book or movie. She's only a sophomore in college but is convinced her life's purpose is to be of service to others. 'A voice for the voiceless' is how she said it. I wasn't sure what she meant by that, but I hope to come back to that comment later.

Poppy's dream is to retire rich on a white sand beach somewhere in the Bahamas. She wants twice as many dogs as children. And she wants to die surrounded by family while sipping on a Venti Mocha from Starbucks.

I'm intrigued by every word that comes out of her mouth and with how quickly she suddenly opened up about her life. Her authenticity and bluntness only make her more attractive. She may only be 21, but she sure doesn't act like it. She knows what she wants. I admire that about her. And her ambition only makes me more intrigued.

All I can do is smile at her as she finishes up her life story. "Let's see what else. Well, I still sleep with my childhood blankie. Yeah, I'm a weirdo. I know. And I don't care what anyone else says. I will never, and I mean *never, ever*, get tired of watching *The Notebook*."

"What's *The Notebook*?"

She lets out a mocking chuckle. "You're kidding, right?"

I pretend to play dumb. Judging by her scowl, I must be doing a good job. She seems extra annoyed the longer I stay silent. I never thought a girl could look this drop-dead gorgeous when she's legitimately pissed off.

"Is it a documentary?"

Her voice becomes shrill and testy. "Get the fuck out of here! It's a movie! Ryan Gosling! The guy from the *Barbie* movie! You know the greatest romance story ever written! Rachel McAdams! Nicholas Sparks! Does any of this ring a fucking bell?"

"There's a movie about a barbie? I don't think I've seen either of those movies," I continue my lie, feeling the muscles in my face on the brink of twitching into a full-on belly laugh.

Meanwhile, she's crestfallen—like I just ran over a puppy. I contemplate giving in, but this will be too funny to laugh about later.

"Look, it's not my fault, Poppy. I don't have time to watch movies. I train 11 months out of the year. Every day of my life is scheduled to a 'T.' Train all morning. Go to class. Ninety minutes of weight training. Twenty minutes with a physio. And twenty minutes of stretching. Then I food up to replenish all the calories I lost before it's back to class, followed by another session in the pool. I'm telling you, every minute is accounted for, from the time I take a shit at 6 o'—"

"Eeewww! I don't need to know when you shit! Jesus, Zane!"

"Why? You don't shit at the same—"

"Girls don't shit! Okay! And even if I did, mine would smell like roses."

"Touché, Poppy."

We share a laugh as she shakes her head with a flirty smirk.

"You really are sheltered, aren't you? Do you like swimming that much?"

I ponder her question while the tension in my chest shortens each breath. It's a loaded question for many reasons, and I don't know where to start.

"I like it...now. But it's had a complicated love-hate history. My dad put a lot of pressure on me early on. He also didn't like that I got in a fight and lost most of my swimming scholarships. But now that I don't talk to him much, it's been better."

"How come you don't talk to him?" Poppy asks. She bites down on her lip, waiting for my answer. Her eyes are glowing with empathy and concern.

It makes me uncomfortable to open up about these types of things. But it's a fair question given how I kind of led the conversation down this bumpy road.

"He and my mom got divorced right before I started high school. It was pretty shitty. Still is."

"That's hard."

"Yeah, but what're you going to do?"

"Well, you're clearly doing your best. Don't be so hard on yourself."

"How do you know I'm hard on myself?" I challenge.

Poppy angles her gaze. Her mouth opens, but she hesitates—probably choosing her words wisely.

"I can just tell. Maybe because I'm the same way. But we don't need to get all morbid. Tell me more about you. The good stuff. Things other than swimming. Do you have any brothers or sisters? Other hobbies? Bucket list items you want to check off?"

"Let's see." I stop to glance up at the stars. After a long exhale, a gust of wind whips across my face. It feels invigorating as I take another deep breath to chew over her question. Then I turn my gaze to Poppy. Our eyes lock and I'm awestruck once again by her beauty. Even in the dead of night, her eyes have this magnetic glow—like the stars are sending all of their light to only her eyes.

"I have one sibling, an older brother. I'm a coach for Special Olympics. I love barbequing with friends. I love traveling, taking road trips to new places. Every year I take one full month off from swimming around Thanksgiving and Christmas time. That's what I'm looking forward to right now. A nice long break."

"If you could go anyplace tomorrow, where would you go?"

"Wow! That's a hard question." I ponder it while running my hand through my hair. It feels impossible because there's so many places I want to see. Then a memory flashes through my mind.

"Well, I've always wanted to hike the Grand Canyon again. I did it with my brother and my dad when I was younger. But I don't think I truly appreciated it. How about you?"

"Ireland. That's my bucket list. I want to walk along the bluffs and beaches surrounded by endless greenery. Then I'll explore the local pubs and culture. Maybe even drink a warm Guinness just to say I did it."

Poppy laughs at herself. The shyness in her laugh is adorable.

"That would be amazing." I yawn. "Sorry."

"Am I boring you with my answer?"

"No! Quite the opposite, actually. This is as much fun as I've had in a long time. Conversations with girls usually don't have this much...this much uh—"

"Substance."

"Yeah," I quickly agree. "I'm not used to staying up this late either. I have training tomorrow morning at 4:30."

Poppy glances at her phone. "Oh shit! Maybe I should get going—"

"Oh! No, no, no. Please don't. Please stick around a little bit longer." I stop to look at my hand, realizing I just put it on the outside of her shoulder. I pull it off and awkwardly put it in my pocket.

Our eyes stay locked on each other. The swelling in my chest makes my heart feel like it's living in my ears. I'm about to say something when the screams from inside jolt our attention.

We rush inside. The first thing I see is a trail of shattered glass from where my glass coffee table used to be. And blood! Lots of it! Oh fuck!

Trey is pulling Lonny up to stand. He's half-naked with his shirt already being pressed into Lonny's forearm.

Poppy and I rush to her side. "Lonny! You okay?"

"What the fuck, Trey!" I'm blaming him even though he's helping her.

"Bro, she just tripped out of nowhere. I had just walked back in. I was outside helping Lisa."

"Get the first aid kit! I got her!" I order Trey. Then I slowly lift his bloodied shirt. The wound is just below her elbow and wide enough for stitches.

"All beeee f-fine guys," Lonny mutters, staring at the wound right as I push the shirt back over her cut. I meet her eyes as they roll back, and she falls into my arms.

Oh fuck!

CHAPTER 7

POPPY

My fingernails become my personal chew toy as I walk up to the counter. The nurse huffs out a frustrated breath the second our eyes meet.

"Any updates on Lonny Rumford?" I politely ask, even though I'll probably get the same answer.

The nurse adjusts her glasses and squares off her eyes with me. "Sweetheart, your friend has only been back there for fifteen minutes. I don't think she's even met with the doctor yet. I'll let you know when we have any updates. But it could be a while until the doctor stitches her back up."

"Okay, thanks."

I go back to sit down next to Zane. I make sure to leave a seat open between us because I'm pissed.

The longer we're both quiet, the guilt begins to gnaw at me. I know Lonny will be fine, but I'm disappointed that I left my best friend alone for so long. We both know better. And who the fuck is this Trey guy anyways?

I should've known he was trouble by the way he was undressing her with his eyes earlier. What's even more frustrating is Trey insisted he go back there with her. It leaves Zane and me alone in the back corner of this packed emergency room waiting area.

Zane takes another long, howling yawn.

"You know, you can go home. You don't have to stick around. It could be a while."

"No way. I feel terrible about this."

"You should."

"Poppy, Trey's a good guy. I know you don't know him, and I know given the circumstances it doesn't seem like it, but he's not what you think."

"Whatever you say," I mutter, rolling my eyes before looking away.

According to Trey, they had been hanging out for most of the night. Then he went out front with his sister who wasn't feeling like herself. He claims he was only outside for ten minutes with Lisa. When he came back in, he claimed Lonny looked disoriented. She was even a bit combative. When he tried to guide her out front for some fresh air, she pushed him away and tripped onto the glass coffee table.

Probably all bullshit!

The longer we sit here, the more I ruminate on how my anger may be misdirected. I mean, it makes sense to be a little mad at Zane. But he was also so quick to help her.

It's like Zane went from Clark Kent to Superman the very second he saw Lonny was hurt. For ten minutes he picked out each piece of glass with tweezers. Then he cleaned and dressed the wound. He was unsure if it'll need stitches or not. The main reason we came to the ER was due to Lonny's eyes. They were still dilated even after she woke from her fainting spell. She was also acting loopy and out of it.

On the drive here, Trey insisted she only had two or three beers. But something was off with her. I've seen her drunk before, but never like this.

"Poppy, I'm really sorry about your friend."

I turn to take in his drooping, puppy dog eyes. He's facing me now with one elbow propped against the back of his chair. His hair looks tattered and messier than earlier. It should make him look less attractive, but it somehow does the opposite.

Fuck! Why does he have to be so fucking hot!

"It's okay. Thanks for taking such good care of her. You'll make a good doctor one day."

His smile curls up, but only on one side. He seems oddly incredulous to my compliment.

"What is it?" I ask.

"Oh, it's just funny. You saying I'd be a good doctor."

"Why? I mean it," I insist. He gives me a disbelieving smirk.

"I'm sure I could be. It's just that applications for medical school are due in six months. But I'm not sure I want to go that route anymore."

"Why?"

"I don't know. I've had this realization lately that my life has too much going on. And I don't want to one day be married to my career like my parents. My dad was a doctor. I didn't see him much growing up. And with swimming being my life, I feel like I haven't had time to breathe it all in. You know, smell the roses, be in the moment, carpe diem kind of shit."

His gaze goes away from me—like he's lost in an alternate life or reality.

"What's the alternative?"

My question hangs stagnantly in the air. His eyes look up for a moment, like he's searching different parts of his brain for the right answer.

"Come on, I'm a good listener," I insist.

Then I watch his hand. The way it slowly glides down his razor-sharp jawline. He continues to look away from me while he speaks. "I don't want to go to school for another six years and then work a job that's going to take over my life. Swimming's done that to my life already. My dad was always very distant because his work became his life—kind of like my mom, too. That's why they're divorced. And I don't want to be anything like them. I want to be there for the people in my life. But more than anything, I want to be there for myself." His eyes come back to mine with a squinting intensity in them. "Does that make sense?"

I take a deep swallow, feeling his candor and vulnerability swell in my chest. It may be nothing I can relate to personally, but what he's saying makes perfect sense.

When my parents adopted me, they made a point to always be present in my life. To treat me as an equal to my sister and brother—make me feel like a daughter of their own blood. And it makes sense. I'm Hispanic and look nothing like them. They knew I would always get stares and questions to go along with plenty of judgment.

During my early teenage years, it was a bit suffocating at times. But it says a lot about them, given the around-the-clock attention Jet always needed. And even on days when my parents weren't there for me, I had my sister. It took me a while to really notice all of this. But the older I get, the more I appreciate how they always put the three of us first. And Zane doesn't seem to feel at all like that with his parents.

"You know, Zane, sometimes we keep ourselves so busy because we avoid the real things in our life."

"Real things?" he repeats my words with a questioning tone.

"Yeah. You know, the things we avoid. Maybe it's something we can't talk about. Or something we avoid doing. We all have them. I'm not immune to it."

My words begin to echo in my mind. I'm suddenly lost in my own cave of haunting thoughts. I push them away, further into the abyss of darkness. Partly because I'm being hypocritical of my own advice, and partly because this isn't the time or place to open the door to my demons.

An uncomfortable silence settles between us. Then I watch Zane's lips part the slightest bit. His eyes squint in my direction. But this time there's a fiery intensity in his glare. I feel it reverberating in my chest. Everything circulating behind those blue sapphires becomes so pro-found to get lost in. Maybe because it's more than just beauty—it's pain, too. And yet, like me, I feel like there's a distant world behind those eyes that I may not be ready to venture into.

"I think you're right, Poppy. It's a scary way to live by staying so busy and avoiding what's real. But...it's what I grew up with. It's what I know. It's a big part of who I am now."

"Maybe? But maybe not? I mean, we're young and al-ways changing. We've got our whole lives ahead of us to figure things out. Maybe it's okay to be a little lost. I think we just need support. You said you had a brother, right?"

"Yeah. An older brother."

"Do you guys not get along?"

Zane smiles. Then the corners of his lips slowly wilt. I watch as his tremendously large Adam's apple sinks in before he speaks.

"We get along. He's actually the most consistent thing in my life when it comes to family. Always dependable and there for me. But..." Zane stops, wincing in pain, searching for words. "I just, I just, I feel like I'm letting him down by not having a good relationship with my parents. He's been able to forgive them, whereas I'm just not ready to do that. It's just complicated."

"Well, I'm happy you at least have him in your life. Big brothers and big sisters are the best."

We share a long smile with one another. Then I watch as Zane abruptly gets up.

"One moment, please," he says, backing away before walking up to the receptionist.

I watch as Zane leans onto the counter with a smile as he speaks. I'm too far away to hear what he's saying. All I know is I can't take my eyes off his ass. The way it juts out of those jeans into the most perfectly sculpted bubble butt has me drooling.

The receptionist smiles at him as they share a laugh. Then I begin to wonder. How funny it is that I literally stumbled into this guy's life and ended up here tonight.

There's this mix of mystery and allure that draws me to Zane, but it's more than just his looks. It's his vulnerability and kindness.

He walks back looking much more at ease than he was moments ago. Then his hand extends out to me.

"Can I buy you dinner?"

I hesitate. "Don't you have practice in a couple hours? You should get going. Like I said, I can handle—"

"Nonsense," he cuts me off, pulling me up by my hand. "The receptionist said it'll be a while. Let's go."

He's dragging me in tow as he continues to speak. "I already texted my coach that I got food poisoning," he explains, looking over his shoulder to shoot me a wink. "Besides, I deserve a night to have fun for our first date."

"Date? In an emergency room? And you call this fun?" I quip, unable to hide my grin.

"True, it's been a bit of a disaster. But in other ways it hasn't." He pauses, smiling at me with all his pearly whites. "But the night is still young, Poppy. And now that we've aired out a bit of dirty laundry, I'd like to buy you dinner.

According to the receptionist, there's a romantic spot downstairs called the cafeteria. I don't know if they're still serving food, but they serve one hell of a honeybun out of their vending machine."

A giggle squeaks out of me. I can't help it. Then he gives my hand a tight, pulsating set of squeezes. I squeeze back because I can't contain my excitement.

Oh my!

CHAPTER 8

POPPY

TWO YEARS LATER

2024

The incessant knocking is fucking endless. The only silver lining is it snaps me out of my foreboding thoughts. When it doesn't stop, I huff out a loud grunt into my pillow. Then I will the strength into my limbs, peeling myself out of bed.

"Fire, Poppy. Fire, Poppy. Fire, Poppy. Fire, Poppy."

The muffled sound continues from outside my door. In any other house on earth there'd be panic. But not in our house. And to make matters worse, the monotone rhythm won't stop until I answer the door.

I swing the door open so fast a loose chunk of bangs falls over my eye. I blow it off to see Jet's bulging green eyes honing in on the very top of my forehead. It's as if my eyes are perched off the top of my head, like I'm some alien Martian.

"Come fire, Poppy. Come fire, Poppy. Come fire, Poppy."

Jet keeps repeating those words. He rocks his upper body back and forth while stimming his fingers along his chin. It's like he's playing the piano on his jawline.

Dad nicknamed it the mad scientist stim. The idea of Jet being a nefarious scientist conjuring up an evil plan makes me laugh. Jet is the antithesis of evil in every way humanly possible. He's more like an angel. *My angel of a brother*!

I take a deep breath in to find the willpower. On the exhale, I give myself a pep talk.

Find the patience, Poppy. You can do it!

"Okay, Jet. I'm coming."

I snag my phone off my desk and follow Jet as he hobbles his way into the living room on his forearm crutches. It's 6 p.m. on the dot. This is a routine I should be used to by now. But getting out of bed has gotten harder lately. Getting out of my dungeon of a room is even worse.

It's all understandable. The anniversary is getting really close. The closer it gets, the darker the cloud that hangs over all of us.

"There. Sit, Poppy. Sit now. Come on, Poppy. Ladies first!"

I take a seat. Jet's crutches hit the ground with a thud as he plops down next to me. He quickly snuggles into my side, resting his head on my shoulder. His hand clenches onto mine with the usual rhythm of pulsating squeezes. Then he un-pauses the movie at the *precise* spot.

It's one thing to obsess over a movie and watch it ad nauseam. I was that way after watching *The Notebook* for the first time. But *Rudy* is Jet's movie. And he'll only watch the scene at the end when the underdog main character takes the football field for the first time at Notre Dame stadium.

The scene starts with a teammate chanting his name to a slow clap. It's cringeworthy at best, even for an old 90's movie. But then the slow clap and chanting of his name catches fire throughout the fully packed stadium. Everyone rises for their hero in the movie, Rudy Ruettiger.

I look up at Jet because his eyes are fully dilated. There's even a hint of glossiness reflecting the deep-rooted emotions catching fire beneath his chest. This is the exhilaration that runs deep in his soul every single day at 6 o'clock. It's a different experience for Jet because it's real life. It's like he's there, in the stadium, ready to run onto the football field with 60,000 people chanting his name.

He starts chanting in sync with the movie. "Roo-dee! Roo-dee! Roo-dee! Roo-dee!" Then he stops suddenly because I'm not chanting with him. His furrowed glare guilts me into joining him. I fake a smile at him as I try to embrace his moment. That's when the darker thoughts begin to loom.

I can't be like her. Ever!

I'm not my sister. I'll *never* be able to fill Nina's void. Jet knows it, and it hurts him in a way he can't fully articulate. But I feel his pain—the pain he doesn't know how to show.

"Here's the part, Poppy. You watching! You watching!"

He's frantically pointing at the TV like a 10-year-old girl at her first Taylor Swift concert. All I can do is smile at all of Jet's stimming mannerisms. The way his hands flap in a disjointed rhythm. The way his shoulders bounce up and down as his neck gyrates. But mostly, it's seeing how he feels. The way he finds solace in the simple pleasures. I mean, it's just a movie, right? No. It's not. It's more than a movie. Rudy is his ingredient for joy.

I start to laugh because his face is turning pink. All the adrenaline is rushing to his head. "Poppy, look!"

"I know, poopie head! I'm staring at the screen!"

Jet squeaks out a giggle. He loves when I call him by his nickname. Then he swings his arm around my shoulders, pulling me into a headlock. He's being his usual, authentically crazy self. The kind that's impossible to not love unconditionally.

"Fire the water! Fire the water! Fire the water!" he hollers incessantly.

I join in unison with his chant. "*Fire the Water!*" He loves saying those three words more than any words on earth. Our family has just gotten used to it over the years and years of hearing it. It's his mantra for expressing his moments of elation and pure happiness.

Jet's never been able to articulate why he says those three words. We couldn't care less on the why. To us, it's just a part of his unique language. Others would label it a part of his disability that impairs his speech and limits his vocabulary. But we don't see it that way. There is absolutely *no dis*, with his abilities.

If anything, it's the opposite. Jet has special powers. His greatest special power being how he can piece the broken parts of me back together—flip my mood from depressing dark to glimmers of hopeful light. It's always a temporary fix, but it's something.

His other special abilities include his obsession with wanting to become a firefighter. It's been his dream since he was a kid and the reason why he collects replicas of all things related to firefighting. Fire Hoses. Fire jackets. Helmets. Plastic Axes. And even pictures of hunky firefighters, which I don't mind one bit.

The two of us keep hooting and hollering as the hero of the movie is carried off the football field by his teammates. It's the same inspiring end he's seen a million times. But it never gets old for Jet. His face is lit up like it's Christmas morning.

All I can do is look at Jet and marvel. It's amazing how my brother, whom I share no blood relation with, is still able to bring a bit of light and levity to my darkness. It's done with no conscious effort. This is just Jet being Jet. Others may always see him as different. The way he walks with a hunched over posture on his forearm crutches. The way he talks with slurred speech and a limited vocabulary. Or even the way he looks when he smiles, like he just bit into a lemon. But all those things are just the result of being born with cerebral palsy. It wasn't his choice. It was his destiny. And living with CP doesn't define anything about him. He's just my brother. My number one reason for living.

CHAPTER 9

POPPY

AFTER WATCHING RUDY, WE all have dinner at our dining room round table. I spend most of the time rearranging my food to different areas of my plate. I meticulously form it into different shapes and arrangements of color. It's a weird nervous tic I've had since I was a kid. I try shoveling in a few bites here and there, especially when Mom gives me looks. But like usual, I'm never hungry around Thanksgiving.

Other than the sound of Jet's lip smacking, the four of us sit silently at the round table. Our eyes are either on our food or zoning out into the nothingness of saddened thoughts. It's been like this every night since I graduated from college a few months ago and moved back home.

We are the way we are because of the fifth plate. It sits in its usual space between Mom and me. The plate and silverware still shine like they did a year ago. I wouldn't be surprised if Mom still shines it up every day.

"Are you going to watch the race with us tonight?" Mom asks, picking up the peas rolling onto the table from Jet's vibrating spoon.

"Of course."

"It'll start a little after 7," Dad chimes in, clearing his throat. Out of the corner of my eye, I can see my dad furrowing his brow at my mom.

"Fire the water! Fire the water! Fire the water!"

Mom's tender smile curls up at the corner as she gives my brother an endearing look. "Yes, Jet. Zane will fire that water like a fish." Mom's smile slowly widens as she wipes the residual pieces of mashed potatoes from Jet's chin.

Dad clears his throat. "So...your mom and I, well, we were thinking—"

"Don't worry, Dad," I harshly cut him off. "I'll be gone in a month. Lonny just texted me that our background checks got cleared. I'll be signing a 12-month lease tomorrow. I'll be out of your hair."

Mom squeezes my wrist. "Sweetheart, you are not in our hair—"

"Mom!" I cut her off, pulling my arm from her grip. "I'm a 23-year-old grown woman. I have no job. I live with my parents. Trust me, I'm in your hair."

Mom bites down on her bottom lip, taking in my bitchy tone that she didn't deserve. I watch her throat slowly retract inward. She slowly places her crumpled napkin on her plate before leaning back to speak.

"We just want you to get out more." She pauses to pan her eyes around the table. "We all need to get out more. Try and find our own sense of normal again. We all know that's how Nina would..."

Mom stops suddenly, her lips already quivering. She looks away, placing her hand over her mouth. The power of that name always gets her. *Every time!* It's why she rarely says it.

Dad quickly reaches across the table to hold her hand. I stare at their clenching hands, hanging on by a vibrating thread, knuckles as white as snow. But it's too late. The air is sucked out of the room. The knot collectively ties in each of our stomachs. Even Jet has a lifeless, blank stare on his face.

"I'm okay. I'm okay," she whispers with clenching eyes.

She says it to reassure Dad, but we all know she's not okay. Some days I feel like she's taking it harder than I am.

Mom excuses herself from dinner. It's a routine that happens most nights. She heads to the bathroom upstairs. It's the bathroom furthest from the dining room and on the opposite end of the house. But our house is so old. The thin walls aren't able to contain the agony in her muffled crying.

After dinner, the three of us pile onto the couch. Jet paces back and forth behind us on his forearm crutches. He keeps mumbling gibberish. The faster it comes out of his mouth, the more excited he's feeling. Right now, I'd say he's a mix between a machine gun and an auctioneer.

"There he is! There he is! Look, Jet! Look, Poppy!" Mom shouts, waving her mini-American flag.

"Fire the water! Fire the water! Fire the water!" Jet shouts faster. He can't contain his exuberance. It's like he's watching *Rudy* all over again. He even starts mimicking Zane's warm-up routine, making his right arm look like a windmill.

The camera zooms in on Zane. My heart rate spikes, like there's a jackhammer in my chest. I can't imagine how he feels in this moment. The expectations are unreal. Millions of people with their eyes on him. He's trained his whole life for *this* race. A moment that won't even last more than a couple of minutes.

All I want is to be there for him. Cheer him on to his Olympic dreams. Tell him I'm proud of him—that I believe in him, win or lose. But I can't.

The camera stays on Zane, zooming in closer on his body. My ears no longer hear anything the announcers are saying—let alone anything Jet is clamoring about.

Every detail of Zane Armstrong's body redefines beauty. Tree trunks for legs. Thick arms. It's ridges of muscles stacked on more muscles. Each of them look like they've been meticulously chiseled into his Zeus-like body.

My eyes slowly undress their way down his body. I love the way his stomach muscles form a perfectly carved "V." It has my eyes following down his happy trail to the thick bulge in his speedo.

An Olympic swimmer's body is a statuesque work of art. There's no denying that. However, Zane's is out of this world. Even his jawline has edges so sharp they could cut through diamonds. Every muscle group is purely defined with ripples and glowing sweat. It gets further defined by each movement he takes in his warmup routine.

Seeing all of him like this just overwhelms my senses, especially my hormones. But more than anything, it's the memories of how that body felt when it enveloped mine.

It's hard to still feel this level of attraction. Especially when Zane is the one person on earth I can never have. Yet, I can't forget how everything changed that day outside the Student Recreation Center. It was like my whole world stopped spinning when he eclipsed his way before me. There was his smile, so effortlessly gorgeous and sincere. His look of genuine intrigue. The way he wanted to know everything about me. Who I am? What am I about? What makes me laugh? It was sincere curiosity from the start. And the attraction between us has permanently altered my DNA.

The part I remember most is how he was so unlike any man I've ever met. He was so intent on listening to me and my story. To the point where everything I thought one man had stolen from me, could be fixed by him. He was supposed to be the cure.

Only him!

The camera eventually pans to a raucous section of American fans. Their faces are painted in red, white, and blue. They're all on their feet because the race is about to start. But the energy in the stadium is no match to the nervous energy in our house. We're all living it with Zane. We can't help it. We want this moment for him. *So badly!* He deserves to be on that podium—for himself, for Nina, and for his brother, Nick.

When the camera pans back to Zane, it's at the perfect time. He's stepping onto the starting block and giving his signal to Nick. It's a routine he now does in every race. It involves him using sign language to spell out Nick's name. Then he blows two kisses to the sky. One for Nick and one for Nina.

"Fire the water! Fire the Water!" Jet shouts louder and louder.

The swimmers ready themselves on the edge of the platform. Zane leans forward in unison with the seven other best swimmers on planet earth. The sound in the arena cuts out for a brief moment. Then the buzzing sounder goes off for the race to begin.

All eight swimmers hurl themselves into the pool in unison. Their underwater dolphin kick has a grace and flexibility that looks superhuman. Then they all rise out of the water and swim like hell.

It's the 200-meter freestyle swim—Zane's best event. It's also the race where he hopes to break the all-time Olympic record held by Michael Phelps. But more importantly, it's his opportunity to win his first gold medal at his first Olympics.

After the second turn, Zane pulls into the lead. The exhilaration and adrenaline coursing through my veins is like an out-of-body experience.

He's only leading by a hair. But that hair of a lead has all of us standing up, *screaming* for him to swim faster. *Begging! Pleading!* Then, by the third turn, he pulls ahead. He's almost a full body length in the lead and on pace to win. If he can just keep it up for another 50 meters, he's golden.

Then everything stops. His arms. His legs. His entire body. *Everything!*

He's no longer swimming. Zane Armstrong is nothing more than a floating buoy, stuck in the middle of the ocean. Every single racer has now finished ahead of him. The camera pans back to Zane. He's holding his shoulder, wincing in immense pain.

I look closer, noticing it's his right shoulder. Of course, it had to be the right shoulder. Let's pour some more salt in this guilt-infested wound. Let's shatter a heart that's already been pulverized over and over again.

We all sit in stunned silence. Even Jet has stopped pacing and stimming his body. Mom and Dad each have their faces buried in their hands. They can't watch the utter devastation of Zane getting injured right before the finish line.

As for me, I can't breathe. I can't think. I'm too distraught to even look away from the TV screen. Seeing the pain in his face has me paralyzed. All I want is to scream, but I can't even find my voice.

Not knowing what to do, I run upstairs in a panic. Once in my room, I scream into my pillow. The scream is so intense I'm suffocating myself. But not breathing is somehow better than visualizing the pain in his face.

Before the race I had begged God to give us a break. This was supposed to be his moment. The one glimmer of hope that Zane deserved. But more so, this was just as much a moment for Nina and Nick. He was doing this for them.

The worst, most dreadful thoughts then enter my psyche. His Olympic dream is over. Most swimmers don't come back from shoulder injuries. And to think, he was only 25 meters from a gold medal.

Time passes slowly. The tears pour out of me like I have a never-ending supply of pain. I'm left in the fetal position on the edge of my bed. All I want is one thing—to be there for him. But I'm stuck. In life. In my future.

Everything!

Besides, I'm the last person on earth he'd want to see. And could I blame him? The vile shit I spewed out of my mouth at the funeral is unforgivable.

I could blame it on the overwhelming emotions of grief. Or maybe the way funerals do shit for closure. They only open up the pain, putting it on full display for all to see. Then I'm supposed to pretend like I can move on. I'm supposed to pretend like their happily ever after wasn't stolen from them.

It's all bullshit. The funeral only did one thing for me. It brought out the worst in me. And now, I'll regret it for as long as I live.

CHAPTER 10

zane

THE FUNERAL

WHAT THE FUCK AM I doing? I mean, who comes to a funeral service without an invitation?

I've been standing outside the church doors for thirty minutes now. If there was a God, he'd put me on the first train to hell. I wouldn't blame him given all the expletives I've muttered under my breath and in my head.

It was a last-second decision to buy the plane tickets. But even when I landed an hour ago, I had my doubts that I'd make it this far. But here I am. I'm in San Diego. I've Ubered to the church. Then I made it up the stairs to the doors. But that's about as far as I could get.

The problem is I can barely breathe. It's like I'm living on the edge of a panic attack. The ground is splitting beneath my feet—like I'll crumble into a void of darkness.

The mere thought of even extending my hand to open that door makes the hurt unbearable. It would be like opening the doors to relive the worst nightmare all over again. It's guilt that knows no ending. It only knows how to gnaw on me. That's because it lives in my thoughts. It *is* my thoughts. Every. Second. Every. Single. Day.

The only saving grace is the transformation of smells in the air. The ominous dark clouds that were once in the distance are now hovering directly over me. All I can smell now is the scent of rain.

It was always Nick's favorite smell because he loved being outside. Maybe it's a good sign. Maybe it's the only glimmer of hope. And the more it infuses into my lungs the more I might be able to find a natural rhythm to my breathing.

I flinch when the first heavy drip hits my shoulder. Then a crash of thunder strikes right as I look up. It's a matter of seconds until the downpour is drenching me to the bone.

"Un-fucking-believable," I mutter, still looking up at the sky.

This whole situation is sickening. The chain of events that led me here feels like a bad dream I can't escape.

The bottom line is I'm not wanted here. I know this from trading texts with Poppy's best friend, Lonny. She confirmed that my parents were initially invited to the funeral. Then, they were uninvited. But I know it's not because Poppy's parents didn't want them here. It's because Poppy was worried that if my parents came, then so would I. And now, here I am, adding to her nightmare.

But I had no choice. I'm here because it's how Nick would want it. And if my brother wanted it this way, I had to be here.

In less than a minute, I'm sopping wet. It's as if I just fell into a pool. My black slacks and dress shirt cling to my skin like a wetsuit. Even my shoes are making sloshing noises as I pace back and forth next to the door.

Every morsel of my soul says to leave. *Do what the rain is telling you. Leave!* But I don't listen to it. I can't. I can't because I'm not only here for Nick, I'm here for both of them.

I finally slither my way through the double doors and take a seat in the first row of pews I see. It's the very back and there's two tall gentlemen in the row in front of me. Thank God! They're not as tall as me, but if I stay hunched like I am, I can be hidden from view.

The timing for my entrance is unbelievable. The reverend has just finished inviting Poppy up to speak. He steps away from the podium and waits patiently with his arms crossed over his waist.

I look around the church. I'm not able to see her. It's hard to recognize anyone amongst the sea of black and the backs of people's heads. All I hear is the murmuring slowly grow louder.

After a minute passes, I slide along the pew to look around the other tall gentlemen. This time I see her. The black headband with the white ribbon tied into it becomes my giveaway. Of course she's wearing a dipsey do. Of course, those light curls have that perfect shimmering tint of bronze and gold. It reminds me how it felt to inhale those tendrils of vanilla and lavender up close.

Her parents are huddled down next to her, trying to console her. Or maybe they're encouraging her to not go up there. Then I hear it. That familiar guttural cry. Those heaves of pain I've consoled once before. They're back. But this is different. It's different because her pain was caused by me.

The reverend begins walking back to the mic. Right as he leans in to say something, Poppy pops up. An audible gasp runs through the church as she quickly walks up to the stage.

She's wearing a black dress with long sleeves. The dress goes barely past her knees but is tight and form fitting. It has a conservative high neckline with white ruffles on the collar that match the white ruffles along the edge of her sleeves.

She leans her hunched-over body in to speak, but takes a long moment to clear the sniffles and blot under her eyes with her tissue. Then, she looks up. That's when I feel it. The stabbing in my chest. The panic of that night. The screeching sounds and screams of agony.

I may be on the opposite end of the church, but I know everything she's feeling. The desolate emptiness on the inside—like the most important parts of her are gone. The tension in her jaw. The feeling that your mouth has been wired shut. The hollowed-out cheek bones, sunken in because you can't eat when you grieve. Even the way she stares over our heads, refusing to look at the pain on people's faces feels so familiar—like I just lived through this exact moment a few days ago.

When she finally leans in to the mic, I wait on bated breath for her words.

"My name is Poppy Rodriguez. As you all know, Nina was my sister. Um, is...my sister. I have a speech written, but I don't want to read it. I don't, I uh..."

Poppy pauses, sniffling while she brings the tissue back to her eyes. Then she places both arms on the podium, puffing her chest out as she finally looks down at the crowd, panning her gaze to see what's easily a hundred people packed into this tiny church.

I watch as her eyes pan across a second time, until her line of sight reaches mine, and she freezes.

I'm instantly catatonic—unable to take my eyes off her. I briefly ponder the option of running out of here. It's either that or I hunch behind these people and pretend she never saw me. But that's hopeless. It's cowardice. She's found me, and like me, she can't believe I'm here.

Then, in a blur she rushes off the stage. Before I can blink, she's out the side-exit door. Lonny's the first one out to chase after her. Her mother and father are close behind until her brother, Jet, trips and falls to the ground.

I move on instinct, making my way out the back exit of the church and around to see Lonny already holding onto her. Poppy's back is to me. It's just the two of them, already drenched to the bone from the downpour. Lonny's hand rubs along her back as she keeps repeating the same words in her ear. Even through the thunder and rain I can somehow hear it.

"It's okay. Let it out," she keeps consoling. Over and over again, she keeps repeating those words to Poppy.

I give the two of them a moment as I lean against a large white pillar that's connected to an awning. I'm only a few yards away from them. Being this close makes it so hard to not run to her. But she needs Lonny just like she needs all of us to be there for her. And as her best friend, Lonny is like a sister to Poppy.

However, every thread of my being is telling me to go help her. Be with her. Hold her. Console her in the way I know. And most importantly, to tell her why I'm here.

Eventually, the two of them turn to walk back inside

"Wait! Please, wait!" I shout, jogging up to the two of them.

They stare at me like I'm a ghost. Lonny asks Poppy if she needs to stay, but Poppy tells her to head in.

When I reach Poppy, the wind begins to gust. The roaring whistle gets louder the longer I wait to speak. It's as if my presence is the storm.

"Poppy, I'm sorry I—"

"Why are you here?" she cuts me off, searing her eyes into mine with gritted teeth

"I know you don't want me here. And I'll leave. I promise. I just need to tell you something. And I had to do it in person."

"I know what you're going to say. I know, Zane. But I can't hear it. I can't hear it because it does nothing. Apologies don't bring people back from the dead. *You*...were behind the wheel. *You*...offered to drive. I didn't want to go. But *you*..." her voice trails off to whimpering cries and gasps for air. When she looks away it only compounds the pain that makes me want to shrivel up and die.

A part of me wants to run away. But I've come this far so I take a tentative step closer, my face now inches from her. Then, I gently place my hand on her shoulder. To my surprise, she doesn't flinch. She doesn't fight it.

"Just look at me, Poppy. I'll leave, but just look at me when I say this. One last time. Please," I beg, wiping away the mix of tears and rain in my eyes.

The rain pelts harder on us until it's coming down sideways. I should be frozen, but I can't feel a fucking thing. Pain and guilt have numbed me to my core.

I watch as her eyes slowly lift to mine. I lean in a hair closer, finding what feels lost. My voice.

"Poppy, I'm here because I had a dream about Nick last night. He was alive. We were floating in the middle of the ocean with one life preserver. We could both hang onto it to stay afloat. But he told me he had to go. I asked him why. He told me adventure awaits. Then he said two final words to me..." I stop, feeling out of breath. I lean in closer, absorbing the mix of emerald and honey in those emotive eyes. The same eyes that still take my breath away. Eyes that have altered who I am, and who I want to become. And eyes that from this day forward will forever be the reminder of all the heartache I've caused.

"What did he say?" she begs.

"Just two words...show up. He said it twice. With urgency. A desperate, dire, urgency. Then he smiled at me one last time, let go, and swam into the sunset."

"I can't," she cries, looking away again as a shudder ripples through her body. I follow her eyes to her parents and Jet. They're patiently watching from the side exit door of the church.

I think to myself, *what does 'I can't' mean?* Is it about forgiveness? Or is it about us? I don't know. But whatever it is, it's killing her. My mere presence in her world is killing her. And in spite of that realization, she still needs to hear it. She needs to hear me say it.

"I'm sorry. For everything. I'm so—"

"I can't!" Her scream is shrill and sudden as she slaps my hand off her shoulder. Her hands drive into my chest, pushing me away. "I don't care about what happened between us. Nina's gone. It's your fault. You can't bring her or Nick back. And I can't be near you because all I think about is her. And I can't forgive you. I'm sorry. I just can't."

Just like that, she's gone. The second she walks away, a crack of sunlight somehow breaks through the clouds, blinding me for a moment. I stand there in a stupor, watching her walk all the way to her mother's waiting arms. The second they embrace, I walk away knowing this is it.

I've never felt more hopeless than in this moment. But what could I have expected? Forgiveness? Reconciliation? A second chance? Heck, I still don't even know if coming here is what Nick meant by 'show up.' Maybe it was. Or, maybe he meant showing up for something else. But at least Poppy knows. At least I tried.

Chapter 11

zane

Present Day

January 18th, 2026

This is not how I imagined my second time at the Grand Canyon. The time before, I was just a petulant, ungrateful 14-year-old who didn't want to be here. It was just myself, my brother, Nick, and my dad. It was one of the few trips we did with just us boys because my dad spent most of his waking life as a workaholic, like most doctors.

At the time, my parents had just split up. We were still getting used to living under two roofs. There was so much anger inside me. I didn't just hate my dad for the divorce—I *despised him.*

Nick took it better than I did, in part because he was my older brother, albeit only two years older. But maybe he had no choice. He was already used to looking after me.

Mom and Dad were *always* too busy working. And when they weren't working, their minds were either obsessing over their work or their crumbling marriage.

Meanwhile, Nick attended every swim meet, rooting me on no matter the outcome. He helped me train. He taught me proper nutrition. And most importantly, he was the first to encourage me on the days I doubted myself. There were so many times I wanted to give up on my Olympic dreams. But he was always there to light a fire and give me hope.

Nick loved all things related to the outdoors. His dream in life was to become a park ranger. But I never fully understood his love for the outdoors until that day we visited the Grand Canyon. From the moment we parked, his mouth hung open for a good ten minutes straight. He couldn't even say a word. The beauty of every detail in the canyon had his eyes transfixed—so much so that with wide eyes and conviction, the first words out of his mouth to me were, 'be *present.*'

Teenagers aren't supposed to say things like that. I realize that now. But Nick was always a young person with an old soul trapped inside him. If he were here right now, he'd be saying the same thing.

Be present.

Nick would want me to breathe in every scent and morsel of this place. Every creosote bush. Every grain of Sedona red dirt. Every outcropping from each cliff. Every fissure in the canyon. Every blossom. *Every. Single. Thing.*

I'm trying to be present. I'm *really* trying. But it's incredibly hard to go on this adventure without him, especially with Poppy right next to me, feeling the same emotions for her sister. Every time I look at her, the guilt only grows heavier.

Poppy and I have been on the trail for almost an hour now. Neither of us has said anything since we met briefly at the top. I'm not sure who'll break first, but I don't mind the silence. Poppy doesn't seem to mind either. Aside from our occasional side glances, we're just stuck in our own worlds, taking in the majestic views all around us.

The further we descend the Bright Angel Trail, the more the landscape around us changes. It's like a never-ending staircase. The red rocks and cliff faces just keep growing around us until they're as tall as skyscrapers. But the biggest change has been the weather. It's gone from frigid cold at the top to both of us losing two layers of clothing from all the sweat.

We're getting closer to our first stop, Indian Gardens. We can now see it down below because it's an oasis of ash trees and greenery. It's like a mini-Garden of Eden that sticks out like a sore thumb because it's surrounded by nothing but red, brown, and beige.

The more the trail evens out, the more the residents of this place begin to also make appearances. We've seen elk, deer, mountain goats, squirrels, prairie dogs, lizards, and so many different species of birds.

The birds are my favorite. I envy their view from above. Every now and again I stop to watch the ravens and hawks quietly glide above me. Their wings are so still and sturdy as they cut through the wind with ease. I admire their speed and grace. But more than anything, I admire how effortless they look navigating through their never-ending world.

The sound of screeching tires and shattering glass hits me out of nowhere. My knees buckle. Eyes clench shut. I try to escape the visions by vigorously rubbing my eyes. But it's no use. The pit in my stomach enlarges—like a cancerous balloon that'll eventually pop.

The pressure quickly spreads up to my chest, suffocating me with crippling anxiety and panic. I fall to one knee. Everything inside me flickers off to an intense darkness—like a cave with no way out. I'm buried so far below the light. And all I feel is the panic of *that* moment. The moment of helplessness.

This is my daily reminder. One day they were both here. Living. Thriving. Loving one another unconditionally. Then, the next day, they were gone. *Forever.*

Life is unfair in that way. We have so many little moments and decisions we make in the blink of an eye. Most are done without foresight. And what I remember most in that moment was the insignificant sound it made when it fell through the crack. It was quickly followed by the moment I reached. The moment we all reached. Then, the moment I couldn't react fast enough.

I flinch when a gentle hand startles me. It's Poppy, lightly squeezing my shoulder to bring me back. I look up, noticing the reflective glossiness in her hazel eyes. It makes that hint of gold shine in those irises like I've never seen before. It's so enchanting. And the hold they have over me makes it hard to breathe.

I watch as the tears begin to slip down her cheeks, slow at first, then faster the longer I look at her. Her lips tremble as she bends down until our eyes meet. Then she leans in closer, her forehead almost resting on mine.

"I'm so, so, s-sorry," she stutters out a barely audible whisper.

Each of Poppy's achy syllables could not have carried more pain. It's like a thousand rusty syringes stabbing relentlessly in my chest, leaving me breathless. That's because it's an apology I most certainly *did not deserve.*

Her candor takes me deeper into the depth of those eyes. It's like I'm living in those hazel orbs, absorbing all of their emotion. It hurts to see them in such pain, but it's a conflicting emotion. It's conflicting because her eyes, and their warmth, feel like the only antidote to my pain.

I've never seen a woman look so utterly beautiful while crying. And there's so much I want to say. If only I could find my voice.

If I did, I'd tell her she's the bravest woman I've ever met. Then I'd tell her that it's all going to be okay. That I'll be okay—eventually. Maybe? Hopefully? But more than anything, I want to tell her what her beauty and kind spirit does to me, even on my darkest days. How it inspires me. Uplifts me. Gives me hope.

Then I'd tell her how the sun is hitting her teary eyes just perfectly in this moment. It gives them an angelic sparkle that washes right through me. Cleansing my spirit until I'm full of warmth and goodness. Then I'd tell her how this feeling of hope makes me want to hold onto her. Never let her go.

But I can't do that. I can't hold onto her because of what I *did*, no matter how much I need it. Not unless she wants it.

Eventually, after what feels like an endless number of shaky breaths, I find the bits of oxygen that give my voice back to me.

"Why? Why are you sorry, Poppy?"

Poppy tucks a few loose, golden-brown locks behind each ear. Her eyes never break from mine. And after a long exhale, she speaks with a certainty like I've never heard in her voice.

"What I said at the funeral was so cruel. And I'm sorry. I didn't mean it. It's not your fault. None of it...was ever your fault." She pauses to clench her eyes shut. But it's like the clenching of a wet sponge as the tears pour out faster. The pain in her suddenly becomes too much to bear. I close my eyes, feeling empty and aching all over. But then it's gone, in an instant, to her touch.

Her forehead leans into mine with intense pressure. I feel her hair drape onto my skin. Then the warmth of her breath awakens all my senses. The closeness makes me remember things. The taste of her lips. The sweet scent of lavender and vanilla in her hair. It's all so familiar, these feelings. But at the same time, it still feels so distant.

"I'm so sorry, Zane." She finally gasps.

Our arms wrap around each other. Then the floodgates open. We cry together through heaving, shaky breaths. And the longer we hold our emotional embrace, the more

I realize how our pain is the same. No one is hurting more than the other. The only cure is this hug. The tightest hug I've ever given and received all at once. The most important hug of not just my life, but maybe hers, too.

I hope.

CHAPTER 12

POPPY

I DON'T KNOW HOW long we stayed in each other's arms. All I know is that it was the longest hug I've ever shared with anyone. Not even at the funeral did I hold a hug for that long.

Now, my mind can't stop fixating on how good he smelled. There was this manly, musky, clean-shaven kind of scent. It was invigorating, like that first whiff of wet pavement when rain hits the street.

Then there's his touch. The safety I felt in his arms. The way his body melded into mine, spiritually, emotionally, and physically—it meant everything and *more*.

Leaving the serenity of his arms was hard. But now I feel this tremendous release of pressure in my chest. I can finally breathe again.

Indian Gardens is just a few more minutes down the trail. What happens when we get there will be more than just our first stop for the pouring of ashes. It'll also be the time I give him the deeper explanation for why we're here.

"How's Jet?"

His question comes out of nowhere. Probably because it's been a few minutes since the hug and neither of us has spoken a word.

"He's still his jolly old self. Still watching *Rudy* every day at six. Still eating the same meal every day for breakfast, lunch, and dinner. And still my favorite person on earth."

I watch the corner of Zane's lips curl up into a smirk. But it doesn't last long. All I notice next is how his Adam's apple falls inward for a deep swallow.

"But, how's he dealing with everything? You know..."

His voice trails off. We both stop walking. I let out a long exhale as I take in the tenderness in his eyes before speaking.

"Well, he can't always articulate how he's feeling. And when we talk about Nina, he gets this glazed look in his eyes. But to be fair, we all probably have that look. He's just better at masking how much he misses her. But every now and again, I see it in his face."

I picture Jet's smile in my head. The way it looks now compared to how it looked before our sister died. It's just never been as full as it used to be. He also goes mute whenever Nina's name is mentioned or even alluded to in conversation.

"Sorry. I just...I don't know why I asked that. It's a stupid question. I'm sorry, Poppy."

"It's not a stupid question. He's just hurting in a way that's different from the rest of us. But thanks for asking about him. People don't do that enough. They always ask how I'm doing or how my mom or dad are doing. It's really kind of you to ask about him."

As I finish my words, I notice the sign. We finally made it to Indian Gardens. It has both of our heads on a swivel as we take in the lush green oasis. The cacti are greener. The leaves have a rich emerald hue to them as they dance in the breeze. And the further we get down the trail, the larger the ash trees are as they canopy over our heads.

"It's so beautiful, Zane."

"I know. And look up there," he says, pointing to a tiny little log cabin up on a hill. "There's a restroom up there and a place to refill your water if you need to. Then we can do what we came here for...if you'd like."

"Of course." I nod as we turn in that direction because I've had to pee for the last hour, and my bladder feels like it's about to burst.

"Look at that, Zane." I point to the top of the canyon where we first started down the trail. "I can't believe we made it this far. And look at how dark those clouds are."

"Yeah, they said the rim could get two to four inches of snow tonight. But it may already be snowing or raining up there."

The clouds are dark and ominous. It feels like they came out of nowhere, given how the sky was a sea of blue when we got here this morning.

After we use the restroom and top off our waters, we make our way back down to Indian Gardens. We decide to veer off the trail for a short bit until we find a collection of large trees surrounding a thin little creek bed.

"Should we do it here?" I ask, gazing all around us to get a panoramic view.

It seems perfect. It's secluded from any other hikers passing through, so it gives us privacy. There's lush greenery all around us. It's also got a bunch of massive 70-foot ash trees that trail their way down the creek. I can even admire the breeze. The way it makes the branches dance in the wind to their own natural melody is so calming.

I notice Zane's eyes tilting up to the sky. My gaze follows his right as a strong gust of wind has the branches swishing and the birds chattering louder. I can barely see the sun's light crack its way through all the foliage. But all I feel is a profound sense of something I'm not used to feeling. A smile. But not just *a* smile. A smile that's becoming more content as it spreads its way across my cheeks.

"Can we do it here?" I ask, keeping my eyes on the beauty above me.

"Yes. It's perfect...absolutely perfect."

We make our way down a small rocky incline to get on level ground. Then I slowly pull my urn out of my backpack. I only have half of Nina's ashes. The rest of her sits on a mantel above our fireplace. It's right where Mom and Dad wanted it as a focal point in our living room.

"Why here?" Zane asks, pulling out a silver urn with a copper rim at the top. "I mean, I get the Grand Canyon.

They both loved the outdoors. But why this spot? Why Indian Gardens?"

I hesitate for a moment, but this is my opening to tell him. "She, uh…" I stop to clear the tension in my throat. "Well…Nina said something to me before she died."

Zane's face turns to chalk at my words. "Excuse me?"

"I, uh, I didn't know how to tell you this through text. So, I figured I'd tell you when we got here."

"Tell me what," he presses, stepping closer to me.

"Before Nina got wheeled away for surgery, she said something about us being here. It didn't make sense until recently. It's hard to explain."

"Wait, so this has nothing to do with Nick wanting to propose here?"

My mouth drops to the floor. "Pro…pose?" I ask, barely sputtering out each syllable.

"Yeah! I think he mentioned to me once about wanting to do it here. Maybe not here at Indian Gardens. Probably somewhere up on the rim. I don't know, he didn't specify."

"Really?"

Zane nods. He's acting like this was common knowledge. But I'm still in shock. Nina had alluded to the possibility of Nick asking once they finished up graduate school. But I don't think it ever feels real to girls until it actually happens.

"But let's back up for a second. I don't understand. What do you mean she said something about…*us*…being here?"

Goosebumps prickle their way along my skin as Zane takes a step closer. He's looking down on me like I'm hiding something.

My mind ponders how to answer his question—especially when I don't have a perfect answer. Heck, I don't even know the real answer. All I have are the breadcrumbs she gave me. The clues that led both of us to being at the Grand Canyon together.

But before I can tell Zane anything, he needs context. He needs to know what happened to me when I was 13. He needs to know how Nina saved my life.

CHAPTER 13

NINA

TEN YEARS EARLIER

I LOVE THAT EARTHY smell of wet concrete. It's like a shot of adrenaline to the senses. There's nothing like it after a heavy rain shower. The way it opens my lungs. The way the soft breeze coats my skin with that perfect chill—the kind that tingles up the back of my neck.

The cold makes me feel alive—like I can breathe again. But not the forced kind. It's pain-free and natural after a rainstorm. Everything just looks and feels clearer in my world. Things make sense.

It's helpful to have things make a little more sense. Especially because I don't know what's been happening to me lately. All I know is I don't like it. The bad dreams. The way those vivid images stick with me, popping into my consciousness out of nowhere. It happens to me very rarely, but when it does, it can get stuck in my head for days.

I don't feel comfortable yet with telling Mom and Dad. If anything, I think I'll talk to Poppy. I need to tell someone. Even if she thinks I'm crazy at first, I know she'll at least listen and be there for me.

I take another deep breath to slow down my racing brain. Then another deeper breath, focusing on my diaphragm as I let out a long exhale. I try to let all my senses truly take in this perfect San Diego weather. And it's working. It slowly becomes cathartic to watch the fluffy marine layer of clouds make their way inland.

Enjoying the outdoors is my antidote. It's my cure for all ills. Especially when I get these weird feelings and premonitions. But I can't decide what I like most. Is it the scent of wet pavement? The plant life no longer parched by thirst? The dew dripping off the birds of paradise. Or the way everything about being outside makes my mind feel lighter—like the rain has this special power to wash away all the morbid thoughts. It may just be weather. I know that. But today, it feels like a magic wand that can wash away the bad, cleansing my mind into a clean slate.

I take a seat in our tree swing as I wait for Tara. It was only an hour ago that I told my best friend to "fuck off." I was joking, of course. She's my bestie, and it's just how we talk to each other. I just didn't believe it when she told me my crush, Ethan Pomeroy, would be playing beach volleyball at precisely 5:00 today. Seeing the sweat glow on his half-dressed body is reason enough to head down there. That and the way the sun makes the whites of his teeth sparkle when he gives that effortless smile.

The plan is to *accidentally* run into him while walking along the boardwalk of Mission Beach. If it goes to plan and he's not inept like most of the 16-year-old boys—the hope is he'll ask me out.

Using my phone as a mirror, I primp away at my blond hair. I'm trying to keep the volume and layers flowing like they did when I left the salon a few hours ago. It looks good with my cropped long-sleeve white top and black skirt. The way the top hangs lower on one shoulder to show off a little extra cleavage is what I'm going for. But the real question is, will he even notice?

"Nina! Where's my...Oh! Never mind!"

The shouting from my younger sister is the reminder of my potential buzzkill with seeing Ethan. But bringing Poppy with me wasn't an option up for debate. It never is because she's always at my side. I just hope she doesn't embarrass me because she rarely thinks before she speaks. Things just come out without a filter.

Apparently, she's meeting up with her best friend and her crush. I tried explaining that 13-year-old girls shouldn't have real crushes or boyfriends yet. However, that got nowhere quick because Poppy is naturally stubborn and hard-headed.

Mom thinks she's already boy crazy because she's started to see how I'm dating and obsessing over boys. I want to tell Poppy to not obsess over any one boy, but with the way I've been obsessing over Ethan my entire junior year, I'd be the biggest hypocrite.

"Paulina! Poppy! Rodriguez!" I shout towards her bedroom window. "You better be ready when Tara gets here! You got less than five minutes, or else we're leaving without you!"

I hear my mom shout something back. It resembled something along the lines of "No, you're not!"

Poppy says nothing because she knows I'm kidding. Mom should know by now, too. I rarely go anywhere without my baby sister stuck at my hip like a conjoined twin.

Poppy may have been adopted into our family. And with her Latina heritage, it's obvious. She looks nothing like the rest of us. But it doesn't matter because she is every bit *my* sister. We're so close that some days I feel like a mother to her. Every day I look out for her. I help her with her homework. I'm even the one that just walked her through her first menstrual cycle. And on days she's an emotional wreck, I'm *always* the first one she goes to.

My role as a 16-year-old pseudo parent comes more out of necessity. Mom and Dad just don't have as much time for both of us. Their priorities are their full-time jobs and our younger brother, Jet. We always come in third place to those two things. Some days that reality sours me. But I know my parents are doing their best, and when it matters most, they're always there for us.

Regardless, I've gotten used to being a 16-year-old with extra responsibilities. I can handle it because it's become routine—having a brother with cerebral palsy to take care of. Braving a full schedule of honors classes. Then working 20 hours a week on top of it all. It's all made me grow up quickly.

The sound of Tara's hatchback pulling into the driveway has me running inside to round up Poppy. The second I walk in, she's right there, using the hallway mirror to make final adjustments with her makeup.

She's at the age where she's using too much concealer and slopping it all over her face when she should be using foundation. I could bring it up now or I can give her another tutorial later tonight.

Later tonight.

"You look fine. Now let's go," I tell her, nodding my head to the door.

I kept my voice calm because nagging only makes her move like a sloth. When she ignores me, I walk up to her side, putting my hand on her shoulder to see both of our reflections in the mirror. She doesn't say a thing as she brushes in the last bits of eyeliner.

"You look nice," I say, rubbing my hand along her shoulder. Then I run my hand through a few loose tendrils of curls. "I love your curly hair, Poppy."

She closes the cap on her eyeliner while puckering her lips. "I put on too much makeup again, didn't I?"

I take a deep swallow. I'm the worst poker player when it comes to facial expressions. "Well, uh—"

"I did! Fuck me! I look like a vampire from those *Twilight* movies. Don't I?"

"No. Stop it. You look beautiful. I'll teach you some tricks later tonight so the caramel complexion of your skin can look more natural."

Poppy takes an unsteady breath. Her body is changing, and she's just insecure about everything. It's no different than any other teenage girl—including myself.

We file out of the house and through the courtyard with my arm around her shoulder. I squeeze her tight into my side for reassurance because I know she needs it. The life of being a girl in middle school is a beast of confusion. It'll only get harder when she goes into high school next year.

"What up girls!" Tara playfully shouts, lowering her sunglasses as she whistles. "You look stunning, Poppy!"

"Told ya!" I say, pinching her cheek. She slaps my hand away as her cheeks pinken.

I giggle to myself as Tara turns up the music. My hand grabs the door handle right as a blinding flash of light steals my vision.

All I feel is a piercing, intense pain on the back of my head. It's like knives stabbing one by one into my skull. Then a suffocating feeling in my chest, like an elephant's paw slowly bearing it's weight to steal my breaths.

The blinding white light gives way to squealing brakes. Sharp, stabbing sensations begin to ping their way through my body. I hear glass shattering. I smell burned rubber. Then there's screams of agony. I hear Poppy screaming. Tara is crying hysterically. It's a cacophony of panic all around me. And it's all weighing on my chest—this overwhelming sense of suffering. This loss of hope, like two hands clinging for dear life—only to disconnect and fall into the void.

The light keeps getting brighter. My labored breathing morphs into a gasp for air. Then all the panicked sounds go away in an instant. I'm left to the sound of myself, wheezing through my last breaths. Then the air from my lungs, the only sound living in my ears, cuts out to a deafening silence. Everything in my world goes black.

I try screaming, but nothing comes out. I need to be heard. I need to stay. I'm not ready to die. But no matter how hard I try to scream, to make my voice heard, it's hopeless. I'm already dead.

The second I think I'm dead, the light suddenly comes back. I open my eyes, seeing only water fall from the sky. But it's not coming down from the clouds. It feels more like a fountain of water shooting up all around me. It cascades down on my face as a lightness settles over my body. Then a distant voice faintly whispers two words in my ear. The sound of the voice has me covered in goosebumps. Then the two words echo in my head with perfect clarity.

"Stay home!"

Chapter 14

zane

Present Day

We stand staring at one another in pin-drop silence. It's eerie to not hear anything because Mother Nature is always talking. But the breeze has stopped. The birds are no longer singing at Indian Gardens. I can't even hear the trickle of water as it flows down the creek by my feet.

I'm still shocked by Poppy's story about Nina. How at the age of sixteen, she felt the death of three people in a car accident. Then Nina begged Poppy to *not* get in the vehicle. She even begged for her friend not to leave. Poppy described it as the kind of begging where you get on your hands and knees. And Nina was right. Her friend, Tara, died in a car accident 10 minutes later. Nina somehow, some way, saw it right before it happened. She saved Poppy's life.

Now we stand intimately close, facing one another in the most beautiful place on earth. But neither of us knows what to say next. All we have are our heavy urns cradled in our arms like newborn babies. And a lingering thought that I know is front and center on both of our minds.

If Nina had this intuition about death that Poppy believes she had, why didn't she stop the four of us from getting in the car that night? Why couldn't she at least save Nick and herself—spare us the burdens we live with every single day.

"Say something?" Poppy begs.

"I, uh, I don't know what to say. Do you really believe it?"

"Yes. I do."

Poppy takes a deep breath, looking confident in what she's telling me. But she also seems scared. She knows there's still a question of mine that's gone unanswered.

"Okay. But you still haven't told me what Nina said at the hospital before she died."

I let out a long exhale, waiting for her to speak. Her eyes go up to the sky—like she's asking for permission. Then her gaze burns into mine as she speaks.

"She saw part of what she saw ten years ago right before Tara died. But only part of it. Nothing about a car accident. Nothing about anyone dying. But she saw water shooting up through the sky then flowing down on so many people. But the way she described it, it was...beautiful."

"What do you mean, Poppy? I don't understand."

"I don't either. It's hard to remember it all." I squint my eyes shut, trying to will the bits and pieces of that horrid memory back into my brain. "She said be brave. It's a celebration to change the world. I know that doesn't make sense. But I definitely remember that part. A 'celebration to change the world.' She said it was beautiful to see the water shoot up and come down on so many people. Then she said the four of us will follow the bright angel to the gardens and have an adventure. She said that part twice, and I never thought anything of it until recently because at the time she was high on drugs and in a lot of pain. I never thought it meant anything. But it did mean something because here we are. All four of us. On an adventure."

Poppy bows her head down, shaking it in a way that looks frustrated and emotionally spent. She starts rubbing her eyes with such vigor it turns her eyes pink. Meanwhile, I don't know what to think. I'm less frustrated and more confused.

It's a lot to process all at once. And I don't want her to be fearful or reticent of my reaction. But how can I process it all when I still haven't even processed how to forgive myself?

The more I ponder in silence, the more it just doesn't make sense. None of it.

"What do you mean the water shot up? Do you mean like a fountain? Is that what she saw?"

"I don't know. Maybe. I'm sorry."

"Poppy, don't be sorry. Even if none of it makes sense, I'm glad you're telling me. You know, when you texted me about hiking here, I just…I couldn't believe it. You wanting me to come. With you. To pour out their ashes. Do this together. I still can't even believe I'm here."

I take in a long sigh, closing my eyes to try and quiet my anxious thoughts. But all I hear next is the pinging noise of her urn being laid on the ground. Then I open my eyes right as her hand reaches for mine. Her grasp is forceful, to the point where her hand is shaking. Then she encases her other hand around it so she can squeeze it from both sides. I watch her hazel eyes widen as she speaks.

"I'm glad you're here. This is about more than just saying goodbye to them. You need to know that I don't blame you for any of it. None of it. I was wrong at the funeral. So…*Fucking*…*Wrong*! It was all an accident. It wasn't your fault. And you may not be ready to believe it, but it's the truth. I. *Don't. Blame. You.*"

Poppy steps even closer, tilting her chin up to find my eyes. I watch as her eyes slowly become glossy. The moisture builds until a single tear rolls down her cheek as she speaks.

"I'm done hating you. I'm done blaming you. Because even if we can never be together, I want you to know…I need you to know… I *like* YOU! And I will never regret that first night we shared together. You hear me?" Poppy leans closer until her lips are all the way up to my ear. "Don't ever forget it."

I can't wait a second longer. My arms lasso around her body, refusing to let go. Our embrace is with every bit of strength we both have left in our bodies. And I feel it in my bones. This carnal, dire need for closeness.

The desperate nature of this hug is rooted in so many things I've needed to hear. Now the weight on my shoulders has lifted. Every burden I've ever carried drifts away like grains of sand in the wind.

The breeze slowly picks up until it's a powerful gust. It sends Poppy's hair across my face. The rich smell of vanilla infuses its way into my lungs, freeing my breaths. It gives me a sense of calm I haven't felt in forever. A feeling of hope. A feeling of believing that maybe, just maybe, I can *truly* forgive myself.

I hope.

Eventually, we pull out of our hug. But our arms don't leave one another. Hers stays around my waist. My arm stays around her shoulders. She glances up at me with a smile full of illumination and a profound sense of relief.

"I'm ready," she says. "But I don't have anything to say—at least not right now. Maybe later."

I give her a gentle nod and smile back at her.

We watch the ashes flow out of our urns simultaneously. There's a beauty in seeing the wind guide them away, exploring parts of this canyon that we'll never touch. But it's how Nick and Nina would want it. They are one with the outdoors in perfect solitude. And they have us together on an adventure—just as Nina and Nick foresaw it.

CHAPTER 15

POPPY

WE MUTUALLY DECIDE TO save some of our ashes for the hike up to the rim. Then we load our urns into our backpacks and begin our five-mile trek out of the canyon.

Those five miles up feel like a trip to another world. It's so high up and so far away I have to squint to see the precise spot where we started on the Bright Angel Trail. It's astonishing how small this place makes you feel. I'm nothing more than a single grain of sand in this vast desert crater.

It's hard to imagine an end to this trip. It has my mind wondering about so many things. But mainly, it's the man walking at my side. The one I can't stop looking at. The one that held me in ways I thought could never be replicated to our first night together. But these last couple of hugs took intimacy to an unfathomable level. And once again, I'm addicted—addicted to everything, that *is*, Zane Armstrong.

"How are you doing?" he asks with a feathery lightness to his tone. It breaks me from my reverie that already has us married with a third kid on the way while he rubs my pregnant feet on our wraparound porch. Did I mention it was my dream home, too?

I'm barely able to stifle my giggle. But I can't hide my ear-to-ear grin. "I'm good. Real good. How about you?"

"Yeah. Me too. I feel like I can finally breathe. But it doesn't hurt in my chest. I don't know..." Zane sighs softly, taking his gaze to everything around us as he speaks. "Maybe it's this place. Maybe it's having you here with me," he says, curling the corner of those luscious lips in my direction. He holds that breathtaking and heart-stopping smile on me, and I'm magnetized by the ocean in those eyes.

Then, quicker than the blink of an eye, I'm flat on my ass! I'm writhing in pain after eating shit. I should be morbidly embarrassed, but I'm in too much agony to care. All I can see now is a thick blanket of clouds in the sky and Zane, kneeling at my side with so much concern in those eyes.

"Oh, fuck! You okay?"

"Aaaahhhh, fuck me! My ankle!"

"Let me look at it."

Zane slowly unlaces my shoe. He pulls it off slowly as I scream out. Then he slides down my sock as the sweat makes it cling to my skin.

"Ow, be careful!" I bark, biting my lip to fight off the pain.

"Sorry. Shit! This thing is already puffing up. What happened?"

I look back down the trail. Other than a few loose rocks, I don't know how to explain my twisted ankle. I mean, do I tell him that he has the most gorgeous smile I've ever seen on a human being—and that's what twisted my ankle? It's either that or I tell him I was eye fucking him like crazy.

"I must have twisted it on one of those loose rocks," I tell him with a head nod. "I don't know. Can you help me up?"

He slowly pulls me up. I try bearing a little bit of weight, but the pain is already a ten.

"Ahhh no, no, no. I can't! I can't! Fuck! Fffuuuck!" I scream with gritting teeth.

I stand on one foot with both hands clinging to his shoulder for balance. We both look ahead to the high canyon walls. It's how I'd imagine an explorer feels before hiking up Mount Everest.

I'm terrified, unsure of what to do. And judging by the lines etched around his eyes, he's just as lost as I am.

"I'm so sorry. I'm bad luck. That's what this is. I'm fucking bad luck."

"Don't say that, Poppy. This isn't your fault. These things happen."

Then I remember something from when I first started doing research for this trip. There's multiple ways to go down and up the trail. Specifically, I remember reading how over half a million visitors have made their way in and out of the canyon on mules.

That's it!

"What about the mules? Won't we see them? Maybe I can get a ride out on them?" I ask, feeling a glimmer of hope.

Zane's listening to me but busy moving his phone around in the air for reception. "Fuck! Not a single fucking bar," he mumbles under his breath as he puts his phone back in his pocket. His brow furrows right as his eyes meet mine. "I doubt it, Poppy. Just look at that. And it's coming our way," he says, pointing towards the rim.

Even from far away we can see nothing but darkened clouds. The flashes of light inside them are foreboding. And to make matters worse, the Bright Angel Trail is taking us right into the eye of the storm.

"But I, uh, I saw it online. They have mules taking riders down every half hour. We should've seen..." My voice trails off as it dawns on me. We haven't seen one group of mule riders yet. No one heading down with us, and no one heading out of the canyon. Not a single fucking one!

"Trust me, there's no mules. They don't use them in the snow or torrential rain. But there is another option."

"What?"

"Phantom Ranch," he says, like I should know what the fuck that means.

I throw my hands in the air. "Okay? What's that?"

"It's a lodge at the bottom. There are cabins that people rent out along with a ranger station and, well...hopefully a place to stay."

"Hopefully?" I spit the word back at him in a bitchy tone. It's unintentional, but I need reassurance because I'm fucking scared. I need Zane to tell me everything's going to be okay. Because despite all the good that's happened on this trip, I feel like I'm letting him down. All because I was too busy eye fucking his adorable face.

Fuck!

"I need to sit down."

I slowly go down on one knee. He hangs onto me the whole way down and helps me get comfortable. Then he reassesses my foot while I'm busy moping and wiping away my never-ending supply of tears.

"It's getting puffier. You didn't break it, but it's definitely a high ankle sprain. I can tell by the bruising coming in and how high up it is on the shin."

The next thing I know, Zane is pulling out what looks like a bag of peas.

"Instant cold compress," I say, reading the words on the bag aloud.

He's busy squeezing and patting the bag. It's like he's a cook patting around a fresh batch of dough in a pizza joint.

"I'm just getting it cold for you. This'll help with the swelling," he says, pressing it into my skin.

I look away, sucking in air to fight the mix of cold pressure and sharp pain. Then he begins to wrap the cold compress to keep the ice pack in place.

"What're we going to do?" I whine, sniffling away the tears.

"I'm getting us out of here," he says with nonchalance. "That storm will probably be on us in an hour or so. So we need to get moving."

"Uhhhh, how?"

"I'll carry you out," he says without lifting his eyes from my ankle. He's so enthralled in wrapping my foot that he didn't hear himself. He just said the dumbest thing I've ever heard.

"Um, no, you're not," I shoot back with a bossy tone.

Zane lightly presses onto the ice pack to make sure it's securely attached to my foot. Then his eyes meet mine as he speaks with confidence in his tone. "I'm getting you somewhere safe. But we're not going back up the trail. I could maybe do it, but probably not in the snow or icy rain. Plus, it's the same distance heading back up to the rim as it would be going down further into the canyon to Phantom Ranch. I say we go there to get a roof over our heads tonight. They have a ranger station, food, water, restrooms, phone reception, and hopefully a bed we can sleep in for the night."

I just look at him, still feeling dumbfounded by a plan that takes us further away from home—further into the depths of the Grand Canyon. It's also lower in elevation, which will only make it harder for me to get out of here on one foot.

I sigh, digging my nails through my hair with frustration. "But Zane...I can't walk. All I'm good for is hopping on one foot. I mean, how many miles away is Phantom Ranch? And even if we go that way, you can't carry me for that long. I may be short, but I'm not..." I sigh, unsure of how to say it. "I'm not lightweight. Do you even know how much I weigh?"

Did I really just pose that question? *To a man!* A man I have feelings for. In the middle of a fucking hole in the earth. Of all the motherfucking places to ask *that question.*

"Why are you laughing?" he asks.

The realization that I'm laughing at myself for this reason only makes me laugh harder. But I also feel the tears trickling down. It's an odd, strangely cathartic reaction to cry and laugh at this whole fucked-up situation.

Zane scoots closer to me, wrapping his arm around me to pull me into his side. His eyes go out in the distance as he speaks.

"First off, I would never be dumb enough to guess how much you weigh. That doesn't even matter anyways. All you need to know is I can squat over 400 pounds on a surgically repaired shoulder. So yes, I can get you to the bottom on my shoulders. And it's only about 4 miles away."

"But Zane, you..." My voice trails off as I huff out a frustrated breath.

"Hey! Stop that! Look at me!" Zane demands, pulling my chin up until his eyes and lips are just a few inches from mine. "This is the best option. It keeps us both safe. You just have to trust me. Come on, let me take care of you. You'll just sit up on these shoulders, hang on tightly, and we'll make our way to somewhere safe. And tomorrow we'll probably head out on mules to get you home. We can figure out a plan B if we need it. But let me do this. Let me help you. Let me protect you."

His fingers stay on my chin, leaving me speechless. Then he takes his thumb to lightly mop up the wetness under my eyes.

"I really love your eyes," he whispers in awe.

"Thanks."

Everything about this moment has me transported to *that* night. The way his eyes felt up close—like I was staring into a sea of aqua blue that glowed in the night. There's also the warmth of his skin on mine. The electricity his touch still ignites my body. And the incredible feeling of seeing a man obsessed over my beauty.

It was a special night we shared four years ago. It should feel like forever ago. But in this moment, it feels like yesterday. Probably because I've yet to go a day without thinking about that night. All the things he not only said, but did for me. All of it redefined what it means to show true compassion and understanding.

When he leans back and pulls his hand from my face, I feel like a puppy ready to yelp for more attention. But instead, I just smile back at him. I'm smiling because I trust him. Not just his words, but his track record of keeping me safe.

"Okay, Zane. On your shoulders it is."

After we hydrate and get packed up, Zane helps me maneuver my legs around his neck. Once I'm up in the air sitting on his shoulders, I feel unsteady at first. I'm not used to being this high up in the air. But the view is exquisite.

We descend further into the canyon to a place I never knew existed, Phantom Ranch. The view from ten feet up in the air has me contemplating the irony of our situation. Moments ago we were heading out of the canyon, and all I wanted was more time with Zane. Well, now I have it.

We may be heading in the wrong direction—to a path that takes us further from home. But with the tragedies we've endured in our lives, who's to say what direction will ever be the right path. The only thing I know about this path, is how I feel safe with Zane. I also know the two of us are by no means alone on this journey. We're with Nick, his kind-hearted, loving brother. And we're with my sister, just as Nina foresaw it.

CHAPTER 16

zane

FOUR YEARS EARLIER

THE HOSPITAL CAFETERIA

2022

I haven't even known the girl for 24 hours, and I'm already obsessed. There are so many things about her that leave me in awe. The way she tells stories with her hands, like she's conducting an orchestra. The way her belly laugh explodes out of nowhere and has me laughing so hard my ribs are starting to ache. Or how her smile looks so effortless. How it has the ability to melt my insides into a butterfly infused mush.

However, what stands out most are the random acts of kindness. To most it would just be little things. But those are the things that draw me into Poppy Rodriguez. It was on display when we first walked into the cafeteria. She acknowledged a mom and her wheelchair bound, non-verbal son. It was more than just a smile, wave, or simple hello. She kneeled down to his level, looked deep into his eyes, and complimented the young boy's smile. It made his day, and his mom's day, too.

Then we sat down, and she started up a conversation with the janitor mopping by our table. Again, she did more than a simple smile and hello. She asked how his night was going and if he had any plans for the weekend. But she didn't just say these things to say it. She meant every word and question she asked. Then, when the cordial conversation came to an end, she thanked him for his service after seeing the Semper Fidelis tattoo on his wrist.

It was three complete strangers. All three left with smiles because of her kindness. The recipe was simple. She showed people that she cares by treating them with dignity.

Given how this night has gone with her best friend being in the ER, I'm completely surprised at how the mood has shifted between us. It's much more relaxed and flirty. The only part that sucks is that it's getting late. The need to extend this night and maximize every second I get with her until she leaves suddenly means everything.

"So, remind me again, when are you headed back to San Diego?" I ask, taking a bite into my third honeybun.

"This is it. Tomorrow, or I guess later today. My flight leaves at three. But I'll be back. I visit my sister and Lonny at least a couple of times a year."

I glance at the clock on the wall directly behind her. It's 2:30 in the morning. I have basically half a day left with her. It's all the motivation I need to keep our flirty and fun conversation going.

"So..." I lean in from across the table, propping my elbows to get closer to her hazel eyes. "You're telling me I only get 12 more hours with you?"

Poppy flashes her best pouty lips. Then giggles to herself as her grin stretches wide. "I guess so."

"Well, we'll just have to make the most of our time when we hang out later today."

Poppy leans back in her chair, cocking a mischievous grin. "Hhhmm, so presumptive, Mr. World Class Swimmer."

There it is again, those pearly whites accentuating that flirtatious grin. Then her tongue quickly glides along her top lip as she giggles quietly.

"Come on, please. Hang out with me again before you leave. What's another few hours?"

"Hhhmmm." Poppy furrows her brows, angling her gaze with a questioning stare. "One condition." She leans in closer across the table, propping her hands under her chin like me. Her tongue takes another tantalizing glide along that top lip before she bites down on part of her bottom lip. It's so sexy I can feel my pulse thrumming everywhere inside of me.

"Zane, we can hang out..." Her pause is overly dramatic, and she knows it. "But under one condition...only if you bring Kitty with us."

I laugh right away at her demands. "Ha! Did you just say her name?"

"I did. As much as I think Kitty is the most abhorrent name for a...*dog!* She's still my favorite out of you both. But hey, at least you're in the top two, right?"

"Oh! Now that hurts. Using me for Kitty." I lean back, pressing a hand dramatically to my chest as if I've just been shot. "Now, I'm a modest guy...usually. But I'm also a soon to be Olympian who's won two national championships, set two world records, and is about to break Michael Phelps world record in the 200-meter Individual Medley. So, to quote my favorite movie, *Anchorman*, I'm kind of a big deal."

I cross my arms over my chest, flexing a little extra for effect. Her face speaks of boredom to my soliloquy and my accomplishments. Then a flirty half-smile cracks its way through those bubble gum lips.

"Well, I don't know what any of that means. A medley is a bunch of different frozen veggies. And I don't know this Michael Phelps guy from John Doe. What I do know," she leans closer, flashing a full smile, "you may be a national champion—"

"Two time!" I cut her off.

"Whatever," she says, swatting my accomplishment away like she's shooing a bug. "But I, *Poppy...fucking...Rodriguez*...have many...and I mean *many*... participation ribbons from my elementary school."

The sarcasm in her shit-eating grin has my mouth aching to laugh. Luckily, I'm just barely able to keep it together. "Oh wow. Participation ribbons, you are a big fucking deal, aren't you?"

Poppy brushes off her shoulder. "Yes, sir."

We both share a laugh. Once again, my ribs are aching and my cheeks are sore from smiling.

"Well, in that case, how about breakfast with me at 9?" I propose.

"Let's do it." Poppy smiles at me as she checks her phone. "Oh, wait! Fuck! Fuck! She's already home!"

"What? Who?"

"Lonny! She just texted me that Trey drove her home twenty minutes ago."

"Seriously? We've only been down here for like..." Oh, shit! I do the math in my head, realizing how long we've now been down here. "It's been over two hours."

Poppy becomes hyper-focused on typing a message back to her friend. Then my phone alerts me to multiple missed text messages from Trey.

Trey

> We're checking out. She's all sewed up and clear to go home. Where you guys at?

Trey

> We'll just order an Uber. I'm guessing you already went home.

Trey

> Where you at bro? I just got home. BTW, we need to talk tomorrow. It's about Lonny and Lisa.

I look up from my phone to see Poppy still busy typing away. It gives me a window of time to respond.

Zane

> Cool, man! Sorry I missed your texts. I skipped practice to stay out with Poppy. I'll

> be back in a bit. Not sure when. Is her friend
> okay?

I look up at Poppy, who's still frantically typing at her phone. Then Trey's message pops up.

Trey

> She's okay. I'll tell you more tomorrow. En-
> joy your time with Mrs. Pussy Cat!

"Well, I'm officially the worst friend on earth," Poppy mutters, slamming her phone down. She blows out another hefty exhale.

"What's going on?"

"She got released like 30 minutes ago. I guess her phone had died. But her roommate said she got home safely."

"Yeah, I just realized I missed a couple texts from Trey. I'm really sorry. What did she say?"

"They put three stitches in her arm. Then they prescribed her some drugs, and she has a follow up appointment in two days. She's already in bed. I have a key to get into her dorm, so if you want to just drop me off."

I contemplate another way to extend our time tonight. But Poppy looks visibly shaken—like there's more going on than not being there for her friend.

The drive to the dorm is full of silence with some small talk. The flirty aura of our conversation earlier has become the antithesis of that. I'm having a hard time reading where her head is right now.

When I put the car in park, I'm the first to speak. "Can I walk you to the door?"

"Sure."

Lonny's dorm is close to ten stories high. The closer we get to the front entrance of the building, the more anxiety builds in my chest. I feel like there's something else going on. Maybe something Lonny texted her. I'm not sure.

"Everything okay, Poppy?"

She ignores my question, digging into her purse when we stop in front of the door.

"Poppy?"

"Fuck," she mutters under her breath. Her eyes tilt up to mine. "I'm fine. It's just...I thought I put her keycard in my purse. But it's not here."

"Oh. Well, you want to call her?"

Poppy spends the next couple of minutes calling Lonny's roommate. When that doesn't work, she tries her sister and then a couple other friends of Lonny. After each failed call, she gets increasingly flustered because no one is picking up. She keeps re-calling people, but its clear people are asleep with their phones on silent.

"You can stay at my place—"

"Oh! No!" she quickly interrupts me. "I can't do that, Zane. It—"

"Poppy, come on!" I cut her off. "You can sleep on my bed or the pull-out mattress underneath my bed. Either one is really..." I stop talking. Her eyes are suddenly bulging out. She looks visibly shaken, so I come up with an alternative. "Or...I can take the couch in our living room, and you can have the room to yourself. What do you think?"

Poppy is still a deer in headlights. She turns her back to me. I watch her head bow into her hands. Then I hear the first sniffle.

"Hey, what's going on?" I put my hand on her shoulder. She slowly turns around, wiping the tears away. "Was it something I said? Or did? I'm sorry, I just..." My voice trails off when her lips start to quiver. Then she becomes undone, crying profusely.

Without a second thought, I wrap my arms around her. I shush and rub my hand along her back. But she only cries harder.

"I'm so s-s-sorry," she cries.

We spend the next five minutes like this, holding each other in front of the dorm. There's clearly something else going on. What that something is, I may never know. All I know is what's going on in her mind is much bigger than Lonny getting hurt and being stuck with no place to go.

Eventually, her wailing cry slows to an intermittent sniffle. She steps back, tilting her glossy eyes up to mine.

"Okay. Okay," she whispers, trying to catch her breath. "I'll stay at your place. Just promise me one thing."

"Of course. What is it?"

"Tell me it's safe."

I hesitate, noticing the fear in her eyes. There was too much pain resonating in the tone of her question.

I slowly clear my throat before speaking. "Poppy, I promise you...if you're with me. You're safe. Always."

CHAPTER 17

POPPY

HOSPITALITY WAS A BIG deal growing up. The treatment of others, even strangers, was always paramount to my mom and dad. If we had guests in our home, we treated them like kings and queens. "True character is giving. Do the right thing, even when no one's looking," Dad would always say.

It's why I'll never forget the vividness of that day 16 years ago. Our neighbor came over to complain about our overgrown trees and how they were shedding into her backyard. We had just moved in, so it was our first time meeting her. I'll never forget how my dad just listened to Ms. Penny. She was loud, obnoxious, and a straight-up rude 75-year-old African American woman.

Even as a five-year-old, I knew Ms. Penny was being a terrible person to my dad. I mean, we had just moved in a couple of days earlier. It wasn't our fault the prior owner had overgrown trees.

My dad could have easily given that excuse to Ms. Penny. But instead of doing that, he patiently listened to a tirade that easily lasted ten minutes. Then, when she was finally done, he apologized. He never once raised his voice to her or got upset. Instead, my father offered her a drink, then grabbed his rake, and went into her backyard to clean up the mess.

At the time I was 5-years-old. I had only been with my adopted family for about a year. I wasn't even calling them Mom and Dad yet. But I spied on my adopted father and Ms. Penny through that quarter-sized hole in our backyard fence. Every second of their conversation while my dad raked up those leaves was something I'll never forget.

You see, growing up, my parents taught me how every person has their own story. Some people just don't care to learn about it or tell it. But not my dad. He took the time to learn Ms. Penny's story.

It turned out she was coming up on the anniversary of losing her husband. Her children hadn't spoken to her in over a week, which only made her feel alone and abandoned. That's the reason she was so angry. The leaves shedding into her yard were a mere cherry on top to her grief and her need for human connection.

After that day, Ms. Penny would become one of our closest friends—and now she's like family to us. Every Sunday night we'd have her over for dinner. And every Thursday my parents would go have a glass of wine with

Ms. Penny on her front porch. As for me, Nina and I saw Ms. Penny almost every day after school. She'd always have snacks, fresh-squeezed lemonade, and the time to lend her ear and learn about our day. She was an important part of my life since I grew up with no grandparents. And she still is, even at the ripe age of 91, I still talk to her once a week on her landline telephone.

It's fun to reminisce while I'm in Zane's house. I can't help it. The hospitality he's shown me just brings me back to being an impressionable five-year-old who witnessed those first interactions between Ms. Penny and my father. She was just a lonely old lady starving for human connection. Oh, how I miss it in the most intimate of ways. *Human. Connection.*

Zane doesn't know my *full* backstory. Nor does he know why I became suddenly emotional at his invitation to come over. He doesn't know why I completely went off the grid with social media recently. And Zane doesn't know about post-traumatic stress. How it haunts you every day like a never-ending bad dream.

Zane's just a beautiful person. But it's more than physical beauty. He's emotionally aware. He's hypersensitive to my needs. It's unlike most boys my age. In fact, unlike any boy I've ever met. There's this heightened emotional sensitivity and aura of kindness that has drawn me to him.

It further resonates in his actions and the little things he's done. Since setting foot in his house to spend the night, he has done nothing but make me feel at home. There was the cup of chamomile tea he made me. The brand-new toothbrush he let me have. A fresh towel in case I wanted a shower. He even offered me a late-night snack that I politely declined.

Then, there was my favorite part. He lent me his black Led Zeppelin shirt to sleep in. It hangs down to my knees, and I look ridiculous in it. But the way this shirt is laced in his scent makes me want to never take it off and never wash it. Every time I take a big whiff, it brings me back to our hugs. I've never smelled a more perfect mix of Aqua Di Gio Cologne and musky man.

His hospitality didn't stop there. When I told him I'd happily sleep on the couch or the pull-out mattress in his room, he wouldn't allow it. He thought I deserved a comfy bed to sleep on. He even called me his guest of honor.

Now, here I am, brushing my teeth in his bathroom as we both get ready for bed. It's hard to not let my eyes snoop around. Everything is very neat and organized. Almost to the point where it's anal-retentive. It's hard to believe there was a party going on here a few hours ago. Every toiletry is arranged in a single file line like a perfectly aligned marching band. Even the labels are all facing the same direction. The dual sinks look like they've just been polished into shimmering silver. There's even enough lotions and face washes to open a Bath and Body Works.

It's nothing like I'd ever imagine for a group of bachelor college boys living off campus. It even has me wondering if there's a woman who lives here.

When I spit out the water, I feel him walk in behind me. He's still brushing his teeth. It's been almost ten minutes, and I'm about ready to make a quip. But I can't be funny when he looks the way he does.

While drying my face with a washcloth, I let my eyes do another undressing of his body through the mirror. I try to make it quick and discreet. But it's really hard. The way his grey sweatpants hug the bulge in his groin area is my kind of eye candy. It has me fantasizing about pulling that white drawstring and salivating at what's underneath.

It's been way too long since I've had sex. Lonny thinks I need to wait as long as it takes before I feel comfortable again. She also thinks I've never been with a man who truly knew what they were doing. I don't want to admit it because I'm 21 years old, but I know she's right.

When Zane turns around for a brief moment, I take in the way his bubble butt practically defies gravity. It's quite literally floating upwards in those sweatpants, like there's not an ounce of fat in those glutes. I could probably bounce a wrench off it, and he wouldn't even blink.

I stifle a giggle as he turns around. But I don't stop admiring him. My eyes do another pass over his arms and chest. *Oh fuck!* His white tank top is skintight. It accentuates his mountainous pecs and biceps. Even his forearms and hands have such definition, girth, and veiny strength.

Fuck! Fuck! Fuck! It's been too long!

His eyes suddenly lock on mine through the mirror.

Stop ogling, Poppy!

"What?" he asks after spitting out the toothpaste. His eyes stay on me as his hand scoops water into his mouth to swish around.

I typically have no filter about the words that pop out of my mouth—let alone the thoughts that swim through my mind from the middle of nowhere. So, why not let the first dumbass thought fly out of my mouth?

"Do you read romance novels?"

His eyes scrunch, like I've asked the dumbest question on planet earth.

"Does Clive Cussler or Lee Child count?"

"Nope," I say, popping the p. "You know what...never mind."

"Why do you ask?"

"Just..." I shake my head. "Never mind. It was a dumb question."

An awkward silence settles between us. I watch him closely as a playful smirk slowly dances across his lips. He takes two steps back, his eyes not leaving mine. Then he puts a hand on the doorframe that's only six inches from the top of his head. He winks, then clears his throat.

"Is this the pose you're looking for," he says with an exaggerated, deeply sexy, husky voice.

My throat locks up. He puts his other hand on top of the doorframe. Then he hones his gaze right through me, leaving me ovulating and pooling in my own wetness.

This motherfucker knows exactly what he's doing.

Before I can call him out, he busts out a loud, boisterous laugh. Right away I'm laughing with him. I can't help it.

"Oh my god! You lying sack of shit! You have!"

"One of my first girlfriends got me reading them. But I read everything. Fiction, non-fiction, and all types of genres."

He lets go of the doorframe, breaking his pose. My heart instantly sinks, wanting more of this playfully hot Zane. But before I can say anything, he nods towards his bedroom.

"It's late. Let's get to bed."

I follow him into his room. But from a technicality standpoint, I'd say my eyes are a tractor beam following his bubble butt.

Zane lies down on the pull-out mattress. It's right below his bed frame and only a couple of feet from where I sleep above him. It makes me feel like a dick because the mattress looks paper thin while I sprawl out on his queen size bed.

The second my body hits his mattress, it feels like I'm sleeping on a cloud. Even the sheets feel like they have an inexplicably high thread count. Not to mention how his scent permeates from his bed.

I should be exhausted from the day, but instead I'm wide awake. The silence of the night feels too quiet and too sudden. The habit of my mind racing at bedtime is now in full overthink mode. Especially because I feel like there's so much I have to explain to Zane. Well, *have to*, is not entirely accurate.

My therapist, Dr. Mason, always said that when I'm ready and feel safe, I'll tell my story to the next guy I want to be intimate with. The problem is I've known Zane for barely 12 hours. We barely know each other. But if I were to tell Zane what happened to me, where would I even start? And do I really want to go there right now? A time when the nightmares in my head feel right around the corner.

"Sweet dreams, Poppy."

"Good night, Zane."

When my eyes close, the paradigm shift in thoughts is instant. I'm picturing him in all those perfect moments of beauty. Like when he kneeled down to tend to my wound. The way he hugged me when I desperately needed to be held. Or the way he listened to me, because he genuinely wanted to learn more about me and my story.

There's also the way he laughs. His body will gyrate in every which direction. It's guttural, deep, and insanely sexy. Then there's the way he just looks at me. The way his eyes make me feel so desirable and attractive.

My mind slowly transitions to what he'd look like naked, sprawled out next to me. I imagine Zane propping his elbow on the bed. His eyes are salivating over my naked body. Then he gives his body up to me. He lets me explore, touch, smell, and taste every inch of him.

The what ifs begin to play out in my mind. What if I could erase all of my past trauma and just share an intimate moment with Zane? One where I don't have to worry about nightmares or horrid visions popping into my mind. It would just be an endless night to fuck around and give in to our desires. To live in the moment and do what feels natural to each other's bodies. That's the happy place my mind has fallen into. But it's also the happy place that was stolen from me.

CHAPTER 18

POPPY

Just a fantasy?

I keep telling myself this, but do I believe it when it feels so tangible? So possible?

My only instinct is to roll off this bed and onto him. Given his proximity, it could so easily happen. If only I could climb into his head—see he's thinking the exact same thing—in this very moment. If he was, *oh my*!

The possibilities have everything inside me running molten hot. There's the pulsating and pooling warmth between my thighs. The need to taste his body—every single inch of him, from the warmth of his throbbing cock to the taste of his mouth.

I imagine him taking control when he fucks me. But he'd do it at an agonizingly slow pace, hitting all my special spots. Then when I'm on the brink, I'd beg for it. He'd fuck me hard and reckless. Then I'd let him cum inside of me. While coming down from my "O," I'd ask him to then taste his seed as it drips from my opening. He'd do as he's told, looking me in the eyes as he licks up every drop of his cum from my pussy. Then he'd eat me out again because he wants more. And when I beg for even more, he'll finger me until I'm seeing stars.

Afterwards, I'd lie in the nook of his chest. The only sounds would be his beating heart and our shared gasps of post-orgasmic bliss. Then we'd drift into a slumber together while holding each other until the sun comes up.

Just a fantasy? Or a real possibility?

My breathing begins to shudder into mini gasps for air. My moans are suppressed, but barely. That's when I realize my hand has already trailed its way downward. I've never felt this type of wetness in my life, like it's ready to pour out of me, lubricate over his shaft, and pulsate into an endless number of mind-altering orgasms.

My mind begins imagining his long, girthy fingers inside me. I imagine them gliding light circles around my clit, which I begin to *emulate* on myself. When the intensity overwhelms me, I imagine his middle finger *slowly* sinking into my insides, feeling a newfound level of wetness and heat.

All the ways I want to be touched would be the way he'd do it. He'd follow my commands because *I would be in control.* He'd listen to find all the right spots and read my mind when I myself didn't even know the new ways I could be touched. But most importantly, he'd make me feel safe. He'd ask how I'm doing. If it hurt or felt too good, he'd let up. He'd give me the reassurance that I'll constantly need. Head kisses whenever I wanted them. And each time he did something different, he would ask for permission, making me feel safe and prepared to bask in the moment. His patience would teach me how to let go until my body is set free to explore the highest levels of intimacy.

The overwhelming euphoria begins to blanket through me. I feel like I'm ready to completely let go to this feeling. To this need. This fantasy that feels so within reach. So real because it is. And now I'm getting close. So close!

Holy shit! Holy Shit! Don't moan! Don't moan!

"Poppy? You okay?"

Fuck! Fuck! Fuck! My breathing! I can't stop it!

It's too late. My fingers can't be stopped, even as I clench my thighs together and bury my face in his pillow. I'm shaking uncontrollably and biting down so hard I almost gag on the taste of fabric and cotton. Then my whole body goes into periodic spasms, while I hopelessly try to quiet my breathing and marinate in these final moments of orgasm.

The orgasm came so quickly, and so unexpectedly, but now I need it to end. The problem is I don't want it to end. It feels so euphoric I want to scream louder than I ever have in my life. It feels wrong to have to fight away and resist every carnal sound that wants to escape me.

"Poppy?"

Fuck! Fuck! Fuck!

The orgasm slowly tails off, even though my legs are still vibrating and pulsing on their own accord. Every last bit of willpower has me fighting to get it together until I finally pull my hand out from inside my panties. The quickest way to dry it is on his blanket. It leaves me in an unfathomable situation with so many impossible explanations playing back in my head.

"Oops! Sorry for masturbating when you're six feet from me."

Or, *"Oh, I'm okay, Zane! I just o'd my brains out. Yep, these sheets will need a good washing. By the way, while you're down there, may I please straddle over your cock?"*

Or, *"Sorry about that. My fingers accidentally slipped inside my panties and found my engorged clit."*

"Poppy? You okay?"

I slowly turn over, praying he's not sitting up staring at me with a dumbfounded expression. Luckily, I don't see him. He must still be lying down at the foot of my bed.

"I'm...o-kay," I finally murmur, feeling out of breath

I slowly army crawl until my head is barely peering over the edge of his bed. As I peer downward, he's perching himself on his elbow and locking eyes with me. I'm taken aback by how close our faces suddenly are from one another— maybe a few inches at the most. But I'm more shocked by how well the moonlight is shining through the window. It gives me just enough light to drink in all of my favorite features on that face—especially those eyes. There's an emotive energy in them right now that's palpable in my chest.

"S-sorry," I mutter, trying to swallow each manic, racing breath.

"For what? Are you okay? You sounded like you couldn't catch your breath. But it sounded kind of, um..."

His voice trails off. But I swear his face just inched upwards, a hair closer to mine. I reciprocate by moving a hair closer to him—my heart now thudding incessantly in my ears.

Everything that happens next is like a force of nature. A reflex driven by something bigger than want or need. It's as if everything I've starved myself of, gives way to him. *All of him!*

My lips engulf his mouth. He's like a warm tide washing over my skin. Every ounce of desire that's been locked inside of me releases at once—like a tsunami, I swallow him as he pulls me into his arms.

The supple, sweet taste of his lips mixed with his pheromones satisfies all of my senses. It's everything! Our bodies consume each other. It feels so ungodly per-fect, I wonder if it's real. But it is. I'm quickly straddling his hips with my breasts pinned into his chest. His cock already rubbing hard along my panties.

We can barely catch our breath between kisses, letting out gasps and moans. But then, he slows things down by cradling his hands around my cheeks. He paces my lips with slower, more sensual kisses. The kind where his tongue slides over the tip of mine, with a sweetness that's addicting and teasing me for more. Then he adds a light nibble along my bottom lip, and my mind is spinning out of control.

The kissing makes me grind harder into him. He's matching my strength with his own, grinding tighter into my clit. His girth glides perfectly over my already drenched panties, electrifying every perfect nerve ending of pleasure.

It's all unreal, like I'm still living in this dream-like, pain-free world. It makes me want to *tear* off my panties and let him fuck me into a thousand orgasms.

Tear! Tear! Terror! Terror!

"Stop! Stop! Stop!" I keep screaming, slamming down on his chest in a sudden panic. Before I know it, I'm pummeling him with my fists—scratching and clawing for a way out.

Quicker than a bolt of lightning, every morsel of my soul, and who I am in this moment, changes. It's like my body is still here in the physical sense, but my mind is two years ago.

Tear! Tear! Terror! Terror!

All it took was one thought. One word. Or technically it's two words that just sound the same. However, they both elicit the same horrific, helpless feeling.

My mind is in a daze. The room is spinning. He keeps saying words to me, but nothing makes sense. All I feel is the desperate need to punch and escape. It's why I trampoline off his body. But there's nowhere to go and nowhere to run. All I'm left with is the feeling of cowering in a corner in the fetal position.

My vision gives way to flashes of blinding white light. Each time they flash they get brighter. And they won't stop. These lightning bolts keep blinding me with screams and sounds of begging. They come one after another, relentless. Each time they hit, every instinct in me jolts awake, every emotion surges in panic, as if I'm reliving it all over again with no escape.

The sound of fabric tearing.

The feeling of arms and legs that no longer work.

Feeling voiceless.

Unable to scream for help.

Unable to fight.

Unable to remember.

But somehow, unable to forget, too.

Eventually, the lightning bolts dim and slowly fade away. All that's left is the residual thunder rolling inside me, stealing each gasp in the darkness as I plead for my lungs to work again. I feel trapped on the inside, needing an escape from this nightmare but not knowing how.

Then, through the moonlit darkness, I open my eyes to the silhouette of him. He's patiently waiting at my side while not too close and not too far. The sense of safety I felt earlier slowly comes back. It allows my mind to slowly sludge its way back to being self-aware. That's when I realize where I really am and what just happened. The reality that I'm not in danger truly sets in. I never was with Zane.

The sweat beads on my forehead as I slowly look deeper into his eyes. It really is Zane! Not *him*! I may barely know Zane, but this man does not want to hurt me or do things against my consent.

Not him!

Zane remains crouched at my side while we're both still stunned into silence. My silence is my recurring demons. His silence must be confusion and fear—not knowing what to do or say. And I have this feeling like he wants to reach out to touch me—to provide comfort and assurance. He wants to help me.

When he extends his hand towards my shoulder, I flinch right away. I can't find my voice, but he knows.

Not yet!

The residual panic is still an electrified current buzzing through every nerve ending in my body. And while the panic is slowly dying down, it's *never* leaving. It's just going back to its hiding place. The place where horrid memories and flashbacks live on in immortality.

We sit next to one another for a long time. The more time goes by, the less I feel numb. Then I feel it. It's cold and wet. It's a single, solitary tear, rolling down each of my cheeks.

"I'm suh-sorry," I stutter, still feeling out of breath.

My vision fights through the blurriness, trying to absorb the tenderness in his eyes. The blue is hidden by the moonlit darkness, but somehow, I feel the wave of emotions in those eyes.

Then his body slowly leans closer. "It's okay, Poppy. You're safe. You're safe. And I'm sorry. I'm so...so...so sorry."

I am safe.

Zane leans his forehead into mine as he whispers those same words again.

"Do you hear me? I'm sorry. But you're safe, Poppy. I promise."

His arms slowly wrap around me. The warmth and scent of his skin envelops the darkest parts of my soul, allowing my body to slowly absorb into his light.

"You're safe, Poppy."

He keeps telling me I'm safe. He doesn't have to keep repeating it and telling me how sorry he is either. But he does just that. It doesn't stop. And even though a part of me feels like I don't need those words said incessantly, the reality is, I *do!*

Eventually, Zane helps me up and leads me back into his bed. I climb in as he pulls the blanket snug over my body. His hands begin caressing my face, from my temple down to my cheeks; he takes care of me. Then the back of his hand goes across my forehead and down the path of my tears. He's wiping them away, trying to absorb or lessen my pain. And he does it without uttering a single word. He only speaks to me with his eyes, hovering above me like an angel, not wanting to leave—only wanting to protect me.

His spot on the ground is only a few feet away. But if he slept down there, it would feel like he's on the other side of the world. It's the last thing I need. So, I lift up my blanket, inviting him in as two words barely sputter out of me.

"H-hold me."

There's no hesitation. Zane slithers his way under the covers, spooning me in his arms all night long. I'd say the best part of the night was being held while I drifted into a peaceful slumber, but he did more. His lips were like a pillow over my ear—constantly whispering reassurances and words of kindness. He even gave an endless number of light kisses in my hair. Each one melted my insides, allowing me to feel and be present in the moment.

I wonder if one day I'll look back on this night, remembering how terrifying and beautiful it truly was. It's because Zane truly changed something inside of me. It was bigger than safety and allowing touch. It was much, much more than that. Zane made me believe again in the one thing I need most.

Trust.

CHAPTER 19

POPPY

ONE MONTH LATER

THANKSGIVING 2022

I'm so fucking ready for this break. This semester has been more than rough. It's been like an endless number of gut punches. One after the other they keep knocking the air out of me.

A week of relaxing with my family and doing nothing is exactly what I need. I've been on edge since spending the night at Zane's house. It's affecting my schoolwork, my personal life, and my mental health.

I told my counselor the other day how it's the conflicting thoughts and feelings that hurt the most. After all, I fell head over heels for Zane only to have my heart broken the next morning.

The next morning at Zane's house is when I woke up to the *real* story of what happened to Lonny. It's why I slapped Zane in the face and called him a pathetic piece of garbage.

I walk into the house expecting Jet to be bobbing up and down like an Easter bunny on crack cocaine. But he's nowhere to be seen. Not even Mom and Dad are here to greet me. It's as quiet as a library.

All I know is that Nina is already here. She's introducing everyone to her new boyfriend. I only know him as Thor. Apparently, that was the Halloween costume that she met him in.

"I'm here!"

Still nothing.

"Anybody!"

That's weird. Their cars are here. Plus, my voice is naturally loud. I take it up a few octaves. "Anybody! Hello!"

"Hey! Be down in a second!" Nina's voice echoes from the bathroom upstairs.

I lay my stuff down and make my way to the fridge as I hear the bathroom door open. I grab an apple because I'm starved. As I bite into it, she tackles me from behind with a bear hug.

"Eeeekk!"

Her screech has me excited.

"What! What!"

Nina grabs me by my cheeks and plants a long smooch on the top of my head. "I'm just so happy to see you!"

She starts giggling and gyrating her body. I join in with her, because why not.

Why the hell is she so giddy?

"Well, you're...acting weird. But in a good way...I guess. Where's Jet?"

"He's out back in the pool."

"Why are you so happy? Did you just have sex with Thor? Your cheeks are pink, and you're glowing like you just had an orgasm."

"Shhhut up!" she hisses with clenched teeth. Then she's giggling again, but this time her cheeks are like strawberries.

I take a step back to eye my sister from head to toe. Having just got laid or not, there's something different about her. I can't put my finger on it, just to say I've never seen her so happy.

"Is this all because of a boy?"

"Mmmaybe." She playfully giggles.

Seeing Nina happy like this only makes her look more stunning. I want to tell her how gorgeous she looks, but she knows it. She's wearing a black two-piece bikini. It contrasts so well with her naturally toned body, runner's legs, and naturally tanned olive complexion.

"But seriously, where's Jet?"

I ask the question again because Jet typically has zero interest in going swimming. His version of swimming is dipping his toes in the pool.

Nina points at her ear. Then I hear it. The sound of Jet hooting and hollering like it's Christmas morning.

"He's having fun with the boys," she says.

"Boys?"

I turn to head to the backyard right as Nina grabs my wrist. "Wait! I have to show you something first. Then you can meet him. It'll only take a second."

"But! Ahhh, fine!" I huff out a frustrated sigh. I was ready to go meet the infamous Thor that has transformed my sister into this smitten version of Nina.

Once I get up to her room, she pulls a large brown envelope from her suitcase. As I reach for it, she pulls it from my grasp. The demeanor in her face morphs into discomfort and tension.

"I know you said don't bother. But I'm telling you, I had to trust this feeling. It's not going away, Poppy. I'm sorry if you're not ready. But I figure if I give you this now..." She pauses, looking down at the envelope one more time before extending it to me. "Maybe you can try to look into it...when you're ready."

I grab the envelope, reluctance seething through every cell in my body. Then I notice the return address on the corner. Those four words at the top make the back of my throat taste like bile.

Department of Health Services.

All I want to do is give it back or tear it into a thousand pieces. But I know I must listen to my sister. She's been right before with feelings and intuition. I just don't know if that's what's going on here or if it's something else.

My eyes bow down to my feet. There's too much kindness and good intention radiating from behind those amber colored eyes. And I get it. She's just trying to help me. She can't help it. It's who she is.

Her arm comes around me as she lays her head on my shoulder. "It'll be okay, Poppy."

The envelope is a sign that Nina's been having some vivid dreams lately. She's been telling me for years to research and search for my biological mother. But as I've told her many times before, I'm content with the parents I have, even if they don't have my Latina heritage in them. They're enough for me. They always have been.

Before I can tell her I'll do it, I need some reassurance. I need to know if this was just her idea.

"Did Mom and Dad—"

"No," she quickly cuts me off.

"Then why?" I beg.

"I'm just worried something will happen if you don't try. Like it'll be too late if you wait too long."

"What do you mean?" I hold my hand on my chest, pleading for more.

"I don't know. Like I said, it's just a feeling I have inside me. And I can't shake it."

I scoff, swatting at the air in frustration.

"What do you mean? What'll happen, Nina?"

"Guys get down here!" Mom shouts.

I watch Nina rub her hands down her temples to her cheeks. Her mouth opens. But there are no words, only a strained breath.

"The food will get cold, girls!" Mom hollers again.

"We'll talk about this later," I insist.

Nina nods, putting her arm around my shoulder as we head downstairs to see everyone.

Nina knows I don't want to talk about this. Not now. Not in front of Mom and Dad. And not when she's going to be this level of cryptic about what she's feeling. Besides, for now they're just feelings.

I follow Nina downstairs. When I walk through the back door, my mouth falls to the floor.

"Holy fuck!" I shout, taking a step back with my hand over my stomach.

No! No! No!

All I see are *two* hulk-ish men staring back at me from the grill. One is the only man I've ever slapped across the face. His arm is in a sling. His tan skin quickly becomes pale white, like he's just seen a ghost. But I'm the ghost. I'm the reason his eyes are bugging out of his pretty, model-esque face.

"Poppy, what's wrong?"

I ignore Nina as I take in the guy next to Zane. He looks more like a Zane clone. Or maybe, just maybe…his brother?

They're like carbon copies. The dirty blond messy curls flow wildly on their head. Their biceps and pecs bulge out underneath their clothing like marble statues of impenetrable strength. There is no doubting their beauty on the outside, but on the inside, where it counts, I know to my core that one of these men is a piece of garbage.

The worst!

A sharp tingle runs down my arms as I ball up my fists. The electricity courses through my hands, all the way to the tips of my fingers. The gratification of slapping him a month earlier plays back in my mind—like I can still feel the residual tingle of hurting him. Yet, it's clouded by the memory following that moment—when my insides felt hollow. And how the feeling of burning attraction and infatuation disintegrated into a pile of heartbroken, hate-filled ash.

"Poppy?"

I ignore Nina again. Instead, I grab a drink from the closest table and march right up to Zane. His hand goes up a second late as I douse him in a full glass of orange juice.

"You're a worthless piece of garbage! Allowing innocent girls to get roofied in your home by your friends! Go to hell! Go to fucking hell!"

I quickly turn away from him, marching inside and slamming the door behind me. I wish I could've watched the pulpy orange juice drip down his face while he stewed in embarrassment. But I knew I couldn't look into those blue eyes a second longer. Those were the same eyes that had my chest swelling with affection, until he pummeled my heart into nothing, reinforcing how I can never trust a man's intentions.

Never again! Fuck him!

CHAPTER 20

POPPY

I LOCK THE DOOR, sliding down until I'm sitting on the icy cold tile floor of our bathroom. My arms hug tightly around my legs as I pull them into my chest.

There's still commotion going on. Most of it's Nina shouting at the top of her lungs. Then I hear my mom and dad pipe in with voices equally shrill.

"Get the fuck out of here! Both of you!" Mom yells.

After the front door closes, I wait a couple of minutes to calm my nerves. Deep breaths help slow my heart rate. Then I get up to splash some cold water on my face. But the relief is temporary. It can't distinguish the anxious thoughts still running full bore in my head.

All I keep picturing is his face. The bits of pulp stuck on his eyebrows and hair. The way his curls dripped with sticky orange juice. It felt so satisfying at the time. But now, all I can picture is the look of remorse on his face. The way he begged to give me an explanation.

I still don't know the full story. All I know is the people Zane associates with—his so-called friends—drugged my best friend at his house on the same night I slept over. They probably would've drugged me if they had the chance. If Lonny hadn't hurt herself, who knows what they would've done to her.

When I spoke to Lonny a couple of days ago, she mentioned that Zane and Trey had tried to reach out to her on multiple occasions. She ignored all their outreach. She also made it clear to the investigator that she's not pressing charges on anyone. Her decision is based on the idea that it likely won't go anywhere since she doesn't remember much. I tried to talk her out of it—make her do something, but at the same time, I get it. Men get away with this shit all the time. It's despicable.

After a long sigh, I pull out my phone. I need to tell Lonny what just happened. She needs to know I'll always have her back, just as she'd do the same for me. It's a brief message, but I'm sure to highlight the best part—giving Mr. Olympic a swim in my orange juice. And once it's sent, I feel a huge wave of relief.

The relief gives me time to reflect on things. Neither Lonny or I know if Trey and Zane had anything to do with her getting roofied. They both claimed their innocence and naivety, but I honestly don't fucking care. If he's friends with people this heinous, or if the two of them had anything to do with drugging girls, or even the slightest inclination, I hope they both go to fucking hell.

The knock on the door jolts me out of my musing.

"They're gone." Nina doesn't say anything else. But I hear a deep sigh through the door. Perhaps she doesn't need to say anything else, because I know exactly what she's thinking. Her empathy, her worry for my well-being—it's all permeating through the door. And the bigger problem is I don't know what to say to her. She's with a man whose brother may have been a part of something that's unforgivable.

I wipe away the tears and summon up the courage to open the door. Before I utter a word, Nina's hugging me. It's so tight and desperate—like she's giving me her last hug on earth.

"O-kay. Can-not breathe," I barely sputter.

Nina squeezes tighter, whispering in my ear. "I didn't know anything. I swear."

"I know. I know," I try to console her.

By the time she pulls away, my ribs are sore. We take a long moment to just stare at each other. Then Nina takes her thumb along my cheeks, wiping away the fresh stream of tears. My gaze goes away from her. She's too empathetic with those weeping eyes. And seeing the pain in Nina only reminds me of the day I told her what happened to me two years ago.

"Hey! Look at me!" She raises her voice, palming my shoulders in her hands. I slowly bring my eyes to her, zooming in on the pinkened circles around her eyes. "Look, Nick doesn't talk much about Zane. All I know is he's kind of estranged from his family. That, and he recently got hurt and in big trouble for getting in a fight.

Nick wanted to bring him to Thanksgiving because he's in kind of a bad headspace. He thought it would cheer him up. He also didn't have anyone to spend Thanksgiving with. I didn't know that you knew him. Or that something happened between you guys. I swear."

My mind chews over everything Nina just said. I realize that Thor is actually Nick. And Nick must be Zane's older brother. I have so many follow up questions, but my mind is swirling in morbid thoughts—*only* the morbid thoughts.

"Poppy, talk to me. How do you guys know each other?"

The sound of my phone vibrating along the sink draws both of our eyes to it. It continues to vibrate erratically with text message after text message. I turn to reach for it until Nina's outstretched hand stops me.

"It can wait! Talk to me!"

I take a deep breath, not knowing where to start. After all, Nina knows nothing about Zane. I haven't mentioned a word about him to anyone other than Lonny since that night. All Nina knows of that night is we went to a boy's house and Lonny got drugged. She doesn't know about my time with him in the ER. How I disclosed very personal things that I would never think about telling others, especially a boy. Nor does she know about my evening cuddle time with Zane.

Keeping secrets like this from Nina is something I never do. I was just too embarrassed to tell her. I mean, how do I explain that night? Everything went to shit with Lonny and on that same night I slept over in a boy's bed. And it's the same boy who threw the party at his house with friends that tried to drug an innocent girl. Then the cherry on top would be me trying to explain to her how I was wildly intimate with Zane for the first time since my assault.

The guilt does me in. I tell her the full story of my time with Zane. When I'm done recounting every single detail—from sleeping in his bed to what happened the following day when I slapped him—I feel mentally exhausted and deeply confused.

"Ooohhh, fuck!" Her hand slaps over her mouth.

"What? What?"

"Just hold on," she demands harshly, putting her hand on my chest. "I need to call Nick real quick. I, uh…just give me a few minutes. I think there's some things you may have gotten wrong about his brother."

Nina puts her phone to her ear and rushes out of the bathroom. I'm confused by her brevity. I also feel like I've fucked up this whole Thanksgiving for everyone.

When my phone starts vibrating again, I finally take a moment to look at it. It's eight messages from Lonny. The first one is a link to a news article. I tap the link and start skimming through it.

"Holy fuck!" I gasp.

There's so much to comprehend. Each sentence is like a puzzle piece connecting in place. Except, the puzzle pieces are the opposite of everything I thought I knew about Zane and Trey.

After reading the article, I take a moment to read the rest of Lonny's messages.

Lonny

Holy fuck!

Did you read what they did!

We were wrong!

They beat the shit out of those guys!

Felonies!

We were so wrong about them!

Please call me!

CHAPTER 21

POPPY

"Is this the house?"

"6, 7, 6, 7, yes!" Nina exclaims.

Nina's ready to fly out of the car, but I latch onto her wrist the second I put the car in park.

"Wait! We need a plan."

Nina's eyebrows shoot up to her scalp. "A plan? Poppy, you just need to talk to him. Maybe even say, um, I don't know, *thank you!*"

"But what else do I say?"

"Just, uh..." Nina huffs out a loud breath that morphs into a growly sigh.

"Exactly! And you don't understand, Nina. I fuckin' like that boy. Like...*really* like him."

My chin falls into my chest. I'm sinking into the void of worrisome thoughts like an anchor falling into a dark, oceanic abyss. The harder I pinch down on my eyelids, the more I realize how weird this whole fucked up situation is. And to think, the one boy my sister brings home just happens to be Zane's brother.

What are the fucking chances!

The article stated that Zane and Trey beat up two guys at a fraternity house. Lonny believes they beat up the same guys that tried to drug her and Lisa.

The article also stated how Trey and Zane beat them up so badly that both of them are being charged with aggravated assault. As a result, they've already lost their athletic scholarships and have been suspended indefinitely from the school pending an investigation.

The article went on to mention how Zane was set to compete in the Olympic trials. However, he won't be able to if the felony charges are held up in court. To make matters even worse, Trey was set to be a draft pick and go into Major League Baseball. But that's in jeopardy as well. This means both of their athletic and academic careers are at stake over this incident.

I let out another loud exhale while observing my sister. Her eyes begin to soften on mine. Then the corners of her lips curl up just enough to tell me she has faith in us being here.

"Come on, Poppy. Let's go. It's all going to work out. Trust me."

I follow her to the door, trailing behind her like a leashed dog going to the vet. Then Nina glances back, flashing a smile that gives me another dose of much needed reassurance.

"We got this," Nina says while pounding on the door. Each echoing thud reverberates in my chest until Nick opens the door.

"Hey, sweetie," he mutters with droopy eyes.

"Hey."

They dive into each other's arms, whispering apologies to one another.

"It's okay, baby. None of us could have known," Nick tells her, running his hands along her back.

I see Zane inside down a hallway. It looks like he's loading up a duffel bag. When he sees me over his brother's shoulder, he stops what he's doing and walks the opposite direction.

"Can we come in?" Nina politely asks.

"Of course." Nick nods, opening the door fully with his arm, welcoming us inside. I hear a door shut towards the back of the house as I take the first step into their Airbnb.

When the door shuts behind me, I take another step further inside, and Nick extends his hand to me with a warm smile.

"I'm Nick. Zane's older brother. It's nice to meet you, Poppy."

It suddenly dawns on me. He and my sister have been dating for two months, and this is my first time meeting him.

"Hi."

One syllable is all I can muster. We shake hands. When he lets go, I notice him wiping his hand on his jeans. He gives me an apologetic look.

"Sorry about that. When you gave my brother a bath earlier, I got some of the orange juice on my hand."

I clear my throat before speaking. "About that…I am so sorry. I, uh, I don't know how to explain—"

"Poppy, stop," Nick interrupts, holding his hand up. "You don't need to apologize. You didn't know. And I fully defend what my brother did to those pricks. I would have done the same thing Zane did. Full stop—without a fucking second thought."

His harsh words catch me a little off guard. But Nina doesn't seem to blink. She hooks her arm around Nick's waist and gives him a prideful look.

"This is *my* Nick. And Nick, this is my sister. Don't you love her already?"

They both share a nervous laugh that makes me feel even more awkward. Then a door opens, drawing my attention as Zane rounds the corner with his duffel bag in hand. He slows when he sees me blocking his path out the front door.

"Hey, Poppy."

"Hi, Zane. I, uh…" My mouth stays open. I don't know what to say. It's more than being tongue tied. I literally don't know where to start.

"My Uber will be here in five minutes."

"You're leaving?" I whimper. It's a stupid question since his one good arm is holding a duffel bag.

One good arm?

Nina clears her throat, *really* awkwardly. Then she nods. "Um, how about we give you two some privacy? What do you say, Nick?"

"Yeah. Of course. We'll be out back."

The second the back door closes, I'm able to finally find my words.

"I just read about what happened to you and Trey. I mean...I read it after I threw orange juice in your face."

He lets out a nervous chuckle, flashing a crooked smile that pierces my chest. "Oh, well, that's good. I mean, the timing was shit."

"Yeah, I know. And your arm?" I point to it being immobilized in a sling. "Are you...o-kay?"

"Not really...um—"

"It's from the fight, isn't it?"

Zane nods, bowing his head down as he looks away. He doesn't need to say anything more. The article already told me. His Olympic dreams are in jeopardy. Everything he's worked for in his life could be over because of a fight. But it wasn't just any fight. He was fighting to protect us.

"I'm sorry."

I don't know what else to say to him, because I'm genuinely sorry. His eyes slowly tilt back down to mine, and I realize it. There's nothing I can do to right the situation or fix that glazed, dejected look in his eyes. But in spite of feeling stuck, I still need to know.

"What happened?"

Zane purses his lips, releasing a shaky breath before he speaks.

"We, uh, we found out who the two guys were and where they lived—the ones that roofied drinks that night. You see, Lonny wasn't the only girl. Trey's sister, Lisa, also had her drink spiked. Luckily, nothing bad happened to her. But you know, that could've been you that night. It could've been someone else's sister, or niece, or daughter. And, uh, we just did what was right. What *needed* to be done. So, we found those fucking cowards and taught them a lesson."

"You didn't call the police?"

"We did. But it was just our word against theirs. Plus, your friend didn't want to press charges, and neither did Trey's sister."

"And your arm?"

"Well, uh, apparently if you hit a guy enough times, and hard enough, you can dislocate your own shoulder." He stops, grimly looking at the sling that holds his arm in place. "I'd be fine with broken bones, but, uh...this is bad. *Really* bad. It may require another surgery. But we'll see."

"I'm sorry, Zane. I'm so sorry, I just—"

"This isn't your fault, Poppy!" He cuts me off with a demanding harshness in his tone. "I don't regret hitting those fuckers! And neither does Trey! I just wish you would've believed me. But I know you barely knew me, and I could see why you'd want to blame me. I just, I don't know I—"

His phone dings twice, causing us both to flinch at the same time. The tension in the air builds. My heart is beating so loud I feel each ramming thud in my ears.

He looks at his phone. "That's my ride. I guess it's just always bad timing when we meet, eh? I'm going to say goodbye to Nick."

"O-kay." I pensively nod.

He heads out to the backyard. The second the sliding glass door closes, I'm left to muse in silence. The converging thoughts in my mind mixed with ebbing and flowing emotions have me overwhelmed. However, one thing is crystal clear. *This is so fucked up!*

It's utterly unfair for Zane and Trey. But aside from being fucked up, a part of me feels nothing but gratification. A gratification that lives and breathes in my bones, knowing those fucking men—check that, *boys*—got their asses kicked. It means everything to me—to the point where my heart is soaring. It soars for every woman that was assaulted like me. Every woman who wasn't believed, or heard, or taken seriously. And like many women, including myself, they were too afraid to report their abuser. But not today.

Fuck them all!

When the back door opens back up, I quickly wipe the wetness from my eyes while eavesdropping on their conversation.

"I'm good, bro, really," Zane persists over Nick's pleading. Nick wants him to stay, but it looks like Zane has already made up his mind.

He shuts the door in his brother's face while he's still pleading. He walks past me with a polite nod and a strained smile, moving so quickly that a rush of air carries his scent to me. I breathe it in, greedy for a reminder of how it once drove me delirious with lust. And before I can tell him to stop or come back, the door slams shut behind him, the bang so jolting it makes me flinch.

Fuck! Fuck! Fuck!

I run after him. "Wait!" I yell as he's just about to open the car door. He waits as I jog up to his side.

"Where are you going?" I beg, feeling out of breath.

"Home. Phoenix. Why?"

"With your parents?"

"No, I'm not spending Thanksgiving with them. We're not really talking right now. Dad's pretty upset with me about the fight and all the fallout from that," he explains, then he takes a deep sigh.

"Please stay! You can't spend Thanksgiving by your-self!"

"I'm not. I'll be with Trey's family. They're kind of like my family right now."

There was too much nonchalance in his tone. He may be telling the truth, but he's clearly in pain. I can see it in his droopy eyes. There's even a tenseness in his jaw, like he's been grinding his teeth nonstop for days. I don't know what to do or say. All I know is I want to help him.

"Can I just say something before you go?"

He sighs, nodding his head the slightest bit. "Sure."

I take a deep breath, knowing what I'm about to say is something very few people know. But given what he's done, I owe it to him, and to myself.

"I'm sorry about today. I'm sorry you hurt your shoul-der. But I need you to know why I freaked out the next morning after spending the night at your house. It's, uh....it's because I had something similar happen to me when I was 19. Someone, well, not just someone. Some-one I knew well, someone I trusted, slipped something into my drink. And they, uh...they, uh..." I feel my voice crumbling. Then I barely whisper out the words. "They hurt me. *Really bad.*"

Time freezes as Zane steps towards me. I look down because I'm already crying. I wipe the tears away, but it feels pointless. One after the other, the tears just keep falling out of me. My vision clouds up right as a soothing hand runs up and down my back. Zane tilts my chin up. That's when I see a single tear flowing down his cheek as he speaks in the most caring tone I've ever heard from a man.

"You don't owe me an apology. For anything. And I'm so sorry that happened to you. So. *Incredibly. Sorry.*" He pauses. Then the heat in his breath barely brushes over my ear, igniting my body with electricity as he whispers. "You are courageous. You are brave. And in spite of what happened, you have so much to offer this world. So much, Poppy. Don't you ever, *ever*, forget it."

Everything after his words is a blur, partly because I'm now blind to my own tears. The only thing that makes perfect sense is the feel of Zane's body wrapped around mine. His hug, even with one arm, envelops me with so much power, pulling me flush into every ridge and crevice of hardened muscle. He's not just holding me or hugging me. It's more. It's so much more because he's trying to empathize with my pain and extract it out of me.

It reminds me of our first night together in his bed. My flashback showed him the heavy scars of trauma I carry. But he didn't try to fix it. He didn't make me explain it. All he did was hold me. It was all I needed then, and it's all I need now. The feeling of knowing I'm safe.

After a long hug, neither of us can muster a simple goodbye. We just go our separate ways. When he gets to the door, he looks over his shoulder one more time. The yearning in his eyes hits me like ice picks in the chest—leaving me breathless and drowning in my own yearning.

All I want is for him to stay. I want him to not be hurt by my pain or his own. I want his shoulder to heal and his parents to love him and be proud of him. But that's not our reality. It's only a fiction world. And maybe, that's all it ever can be.

The car drives off. I'm left alone until Nina comes out to give me a bear hug. She whispers reassurances in my ear, but I can't hear them. I feel her love, but I can't make sense of anything she's saying.

My mind is too busy planning my next move. I'm going to help Zane. Not because I owe him. Not because it's the right thing to do. I'm helping Zane because he needs me. And I need him.

CHAPTER 22

zane

ONE YEAR LATER

THANKSGIVING 2023

"How close are we?"

"This is it. You ready?" Nick asks, turning onto a street I haven't been on in a year.

The last time I was at my brother's girlfriend's house, I took a shower in orange juice. It happened right in front of her mom and dad. It wasn't my finest hour, being screamed out of their house and treated like a sexual predator. Hence my surprise to be invited back here one year later.

It's been quite a year since I was last here on Thanksgiving. For one, my shoulder has healed, and I'm almost back to feeling a hundred percent in the pool. I'm back in school after a semester long academic suspension. My felony charges have been reduced to misdemeanors. I still got suspended and will not be able to compete in swim meets for my senior year. However, next year when I'm a fifth year senior, I'll be fully reinstated with the team and able to compete in my final year of athletic eligibility.

On the family front, I'm still not talking to my parents. After my arrest, they cut me off financially. We rarely speak. Dad was not only upset with the fight, but the last straw was my decision to not become a doctor. In a way, that lack of communication and finances has been a blessing. I've enjoyed managing my own path.

I haven't spoken much with Poppy since I saw her at my court hearing about six months ago. Trey and I both had our assault crimes reduced to misdemeanors that day. It was largely because of the testimonies submitted by Poppy, Lonny, and Lisa.

Those three women defended our retaliatory actions. But they weren't the only ones. All of my teammates from swim and all of my coaches showed up. Even Trey's baseball team came along with his family. The only family member I had was my brother, who spoke on my behalf as well. Every single testimony meant a lot. But the fact that Poppy flew out to Phoenix and spoke on my behalf meant the most.

My biggest regret was not being able to thank her in person afterwards. I tried, but she went straight to the airport after her testimony.

When Nick knocks on the door, I feel my heart shoot up to my throat. Nina squeals as she swings the door open and rushes into his arms.

Since they both go to ASU, it's only been two days since they last saw each other. But you'd think it's been two years with the way they're hugging and kissing.

Sheesh! Get a room!

To say these two are serious is the understatement of the century. Nina is all Nick talks about. It's also who he spends most of his time with. Every time they see each other, it's like a newborn puppy meeting its adoring owner. It seems a bit fast since they're both only 23, but my brother thinks the world of her. And if he's happy, that's all that matters.

"Is Poppy here?" Nick whispers, barely moving his lips to try and be sly.

"She's just in the shower. She'll be in there all day." Nina then leans into Nick's ear, whispering something that causes a playful smirk to dance across his face. Then she playfully pushes Nick away and spears me with a tight hug.

"Welcome back, Zane! Thank you so much for coming."

"Of course. Thanks for having me."

Nina leans back, grabbing my shoulders, and squaring off her amber eyes with a peculiar look.

"You look thirsty. How about a fresh cup of...*orange juice*?" she asks.

"Umm—"

The floodgates open. Nick and Nina are laughing hysterically. Even though it's a laugh shared at my expense, I can't help but to smirk a little.

"Oh, come on! It's funny!" Nick exclaims, playfully punching my good shoulder.

Then I see Jet, sliding up in his forearm crutches with his mouth fully open and his neck contorted.

"Fire the water! Fire the water! Fire the water!"

"Hey, bud! How are you?! I'm Zane. It's so nice to see you again."

I reach out to pat his shoulder. I make sure to give it a firm squeeze. Then I lean down to look him dead in the eye with a smile. He starts laughing as he angles his gaze.

"Fire the water! Fire the water!" he shouts, shaking all over.

I look at Nina and Nick, not knowing what those words mean. They just smile back at me as if that's his way of greeting me. I take my gaze back to Jet, feeling the exuberance in his infectious smile and the way he's lightly bobbing his head.

"That's right, my friend. Fire the water. Nice to meet you, too."

I suddenly notice Poppy's mom, Nadine, coming down the entryway as she sneaks around Jet. The smile on her face could ignite a thousand suns. But right as I think she's going to tackle Nick, she slams her body into mine with an airtight hug.

"Welcome, Zane! I'm so happy you made it. Welcome to our home, son."

Son?

I stand there flabbergasted by her welcome and her high energy. She hugs Nick just as hard. The two of them share a laugh as Jet starts talking to me. I nod even though I can't articulate everything that he's saying. But judging by the way his body is gyrating, he seems super excited.

"He's a fan of swimming. He's watched a lot of your races on TV," Nina chimes in, rubbing her hand over Jet's shoulder. "Yes, Jet! It's him! It's him!" Nina exclaims, smiling at him with genuine admiration.

Jet continues to chant, "Fire the water." His energy is that of a person meeting a celebrity, which is funny. I've accomplished a lot in my swimming career but never felt famous. Even in my biggest races, in jam packed stadiums, it never felt like fame. It was just something I've worked hard to get good at.

The next thing I know, her mom is hugging me a second time. But this time she leans back, placing her hands on my shoulders as she angles her face with an intense stare.

"I am so sorry about what happened last year. Please forgive us. A man that stands up for women is *always*, and I mean *always*, welcome here." She pauses, panning her bright smile from me to Nick. "You both are always welcome. No matter the holiday or the time of day. You hear me?"

"Thank you. We appreciate you having us, Mrs.—"

"Oh, Nick!" Nadine cuts off my brother, raising her hand in contempt. "You boys don't need to call me 'misses' or 'ma'am.' There's no need to be formal. Just call me Nadine. And Zane, honey, your bed is made, so feel free to unpack and make yourself at home."

"Thank you, misses—I mean Nadine," I quickly correct myself. "We really appreciate you welcoming us into your home."

"Of course."

Nadine greets Nick with another big hug. Then Charles, Nina and Poppy's dad, greets me with a firm headshake. He also apologizes to me for last year.

It feels odd to have everyone roll out the red carpet for us when last year they were screaming to 'get the fuck out.' But I hold no ill will towards the way I was treated that day. Poppy's parents believed her and stood by her, as parents should. That kind of unwavering support is exactly what every child deserves.

It's odd seeing Nick get along so well with the parents and Jet. He may not be estranged like I am from our parents, but I know he's not happy with how Mom and Dad are treating me.

"Zane!" Nina calls me into the living room. "Your guest bed is just down the hall—to the very end."

I follow her directions and turn the corner down a long hallway. Halfway down, the bathroom door opens to my left. I freeze for a moment, seeing the thick flow of steam permeate out. When no one walks out, I make a mad dash to my bedroom. But right as I walk past the bathroom, Poppy comes out, wearing *only* a towel.

"Fuck!" She jumps back with her hand over her mouth.

I'm in shock, trying not to stare at her body and the fact she's practically naked.

"You guys are early," she huffs out, trying to catch her breath. She holds her hand over the thin towel that's draped over her breasts, while her other hand is held over her mouth.

The hallway suddenly feels shrunken, like I'd have to rub past her barely covered body to get to the guest room. I'm so embarrassed that all I can manage is a stammering of words.

"I, uh, um...yeah, our flight landed 30 minutes early. And we got an Uber right away."

"Oh, well, that's good. It's nice to see you...again"

I clear my throat. "You, too, Poppy. I, uh, I never got to truly thank you for all you did at the courthouse."

"Oh, that," she murmurs, swiping her hand in the air like it was nothing.

"No, I'm serious. Trey and I could never repay you guys."

The corner of Poppy's lip perks up into a smile as she looks away for a moment. When her eyes come back to mine, I'm lost in the gold shine in those hazel eyes.

"Well, believe it or not, you both have done more than enough for me...and Lonny...and Lisa."

She holds her gaze on me, to the point where I feel frozen again by her beauty. She's giving me this shy smile, like she's undeserving of my praise but also grateful. Whatever it is about this smile, I'm here for it—happily lost in it and right where I want to be.

Nina edges between us, making her way down the hallway. I notice her biting back a grin. It snaps both of us out of our trance.

Poppy clears her throat. "I'm going to, um, go get, uh—"

"Oh, sorry. Of course," I tell her, maneuvering out of her way as we awkwardly step around one another. When

I get to my room, I shut the door. I'm finally able to breathe.

The last time I saw her was at the courthouse about six months ago. I texted her after that day. It was a long message of gratitude that never got a read receipt or a reply. I took it as a sign that she's no longer interested, which sucks. But after seeing her just now, I feel different, like maybe that ship hasn't sailed yet between us.

The other thing weighing heavy on my mind is what Nick told me twenty minutes ago. He said it was Poppy's idea to invite me back for Thanksgiving. It surprised me at first, but after seeing the way she looked at me by the bathroom, I can't help but think about the night we spent together.

It's been almost 14 months, and I still think about that night every single day. It's why being here feels much more important than just connecting with people over a Thanksgiving meal. For me, it's my second chance to reconnect with Poppy. That's what makes me thankful.

CHAPTER 23

POPPY

ALL HE'S DOING IS forking a slice of pie into his mouth. Fucking harmless, right? I mean, we're all doing it because it's dessert time as a family. But why, *oh why*, does he have to make it look so seductive.

Then he completely does me in. My lady bits literally become an inferno as I watch his tongue trace along that plump upper lip. He's getting that last bit of whipped cream, but all I can dream about is being the one to lick it off myself.

My eyes move from his lips to his biceps. The way they hug his black tee and have tree roots for veins that bulge down his forearm makes him look superhuman.

Even those eyelashes are gorgeous. They're so long. The way they naturally curl up to showcase those blue gems is unreal. And each time those gems lock with mine, I feel my insides begging for his touch.

The other thing about him is the way he's smiling tonight. It's so full and genuine. It's the perfect match to his infectious laughter. It's the kind of laugh that has me joining with him every time. The muscles in my mouth are even starting to ache again. It reminds me of our first date in the hospital cafeteria.

The foreplay leading up to my dinner time eye fucking was equally as good. Once Zane was settled in his bedroom, he came out and went straight into the kitchen with Nick. The two of them grabbed an apron and helped. Nick helped my dad with the turkey. Zane helped my mom mash the potatoes and prep all the side dishes.

The gesture to help on Thanksgiving Day meant a lot to both of my parents. But it was also fun to observe how Zane talks to my mom with such genuine respect and kindness. He even told her on multiple occasions how thankful he was to just be invited over.

However, nothing, and I *mean nothing*, compares to the way he treats my brother. He doesn't treat Jet like a person with a disability. He treats him like his peer. His friend. And more than anything, he treats him with dignity. It's the way every single person with special abilities like Jet deserves to be treated.

There's no pity. No sympathy. There's no, "Oh, can I do that for you?" He just talks to him and listens to him. They share laughs. They share long smiles for no reason. And even when Zane can't fully articulate what Jet is trying to tell him, he maintains eye contact and patiently waits for Jet to finish talking.

Nick's no different in how he treats Jet. But right now, Zane is the shiny new toy. Nick's just happy to have Nina back in his arms. They haven't had their wandering hands off each other for more than a few seconds since they got here.

"Hand check!" I shout across the table. Nina pulls her face out of the crook of Nick's neck to stick her tongue out at me and flip the bird.

"Stop it you two," Mom says, getting up at the head of the table.

Nick and Zane quickly stand up with her, like she's the Queen of England.

"Can I help with the dishes?" Zane pipes in.

"No, no, no. Me and Nick already called it earlier. But don't we need a fire?" Nina says, scrunching her eyes at Mom. "Uhhh, right, Mom?"

Nina's eyeballs keep pinging between my mom and Zane and me. It's incredibly awkward and as smooth as sandpaper. It's obvious that Nina is trying to fix me and Zane up.

"Right! Right! Zane, go help Poppy start a fire in the back. We're going to make s'mores tonight."

"Mom, I can start a fire on my own. I don't need a man—"

"Nonsense!" Mom interrupts. "Poppy, don't make me tell Nick and Zane about the time—"

"Mom!" I shoot her a glare, feeling my cheeks catch fire. Nina's already giggling while Nick and Zane look confused.

"Yeah, Poppy's singed her bangs off...a time or two, or four."

"Three times! I was 8! What kid doesn't experi—"

"You were a pyromaniac, Poppy!" Nina cuts me off. "Remember the time you used our hair spray bottle as a blowtorch to try and—"

"La! La! La! La!" I chant obnoxiously with a finger in each ear while everyone's already laughing.

"Fine! Let's go, Zane." I motion for him to follow me. He's smirking at me all the way into the backyard. I should be annoyed, but there's something about the way he's looking at me tonight. The long glances and smiles in my direction felt fun and flirtatious—just like when we first met.

Once I show him the pile of logs, he steps in front of me. I scoff as he begins to pile all ten of our logs into his arms. Then he begins stacking them on the firepit. I try helping, but he shoos me away.

After a minute of watching him fumble around, I take a step back. I'm trying to understand his fire building logic. But there is no logic. The logs keep tumbling on top of themselves. It feels like I'm watching a toddler with his first block set.

I let out an exasperated sigh. "Here, let me do it." I kneel down next to him and give him a playful nudge into his brick wall of a shoulder.

He giggles under his breath and steps back to give me room to build a real fire. I construct it in the shape of a teepee so it'll have better airflow from the bottom and start more easily. It only takes ten seconds and looks pretty damn good. It turns out Girl Scouts taught me more than just the capitalism of spreading diabetes.

"There! What do you think, Zane?"

He takes a step back, placing his hand under his chin as if he were the supervisor of this project. "I think I need to learn more about your pyromaniac days. Because this is actually impressive. You know, for a—"

"Excuse me, sir!" I playfully raise my voice. "A girl can start a goddam fire just as good as a man," I cut him off, spraying lighter fluid onto the wood pile. His eyes begin to linger on the bottle of lighter fluid as I keep spraying it on. I ignore his worried stare and coat a little bit extra since we don't have a Firestarter log or any kindling. The second I strike the match, he freaks out.

"Poppy! Poppy! Are you sure you want to be that—"

The fire plumes up like a mini mushroom cloud. Zane flinches like a scared little boy even though he's basically two of me in size. I discreetly rub my fingers along both eyebrows. *All there!* Did the fire almost singe off my eyebrows? *Maybe.* But did I look like a badass Girl Scout? *Fuck yeah!*

My arms cross over my chest as we share a flirty smile. I can tell he's a little impressed. It's either that or he really thinks I'm obsessed with fire.

"Poppy the Pyro. I like it," he says with a shit-eating grin. "You know, Poppy, I'm talented at a lot of things. And very competitive. But today, with building a campfire, you win."

He gives me the sexiest smirk I've seen all night. His beauty is also magnified by the way the fire dances off those eyes. The fire even gives his lips this sexy glow. All I can think about is how delicious it would be to taste those lips one more time. Or how those lips would feel buried between my thighs.

A chill runs up the back of my neck as a gust of wind blows into my back. We both inch closer to the fire at the same time. Our shoulders are now only a couple of inches from touching. It takes willpower to not lean into him and let him hold me like he has before.

I shiver again, putting my hands out to the fire to warm them up. The fire is raging but only able to keep half of me warm. The back of my body feels like a block of ice from the unseasonably cold weather. I contemplate running in to grab my hoodie. However, that would mean 30 less seconds with the man who's been on my mind for the last 400 plus days.

"You, okay?" he asks, glancing down at me.

My teeth are chattering as I stammer out the words. "Y-yeah. I, uh, I'm good."

My eyes stay lost in the fire. But I can feel Zane's eyes peering down on me. Then it happens so quickly. His sweater comes right off.

"Here, put it on. My mom got it for me a couple Christmases ago. It's 100% wool. It'll keep you nice and cozy."

Before I can protest, he's practically putting the sweater on me. The second my arms go through the sleeves; I feel his natural scent and warmth overtake me. The mix of Aqua Di Gio and his natural pheromones brings me back to how it felt to be in his arms—the one time I felt *truly safe* to be in another man's arms.

"Thanks. Are you sure you won't get cold?"

"I'm good. If I need to, I can always run inside and grab my blue hoodie. In fact, I can run in and get it if you think that sweater isn't enough."

His eyes have lost me once again. I can't answer his question because the natural glow of the fire on his blue eyes is unreal. I'm once again hypnotized by how gorgeous this man truly is—inside and out.

Say something, you drooling dumbass!

"No, no, I'm good. I'm, uh, warming up now. Thank you."

Well, I'm mainly warm in my baby maker, I think to myself, fighting back a grin.

He smiles back at me with a gentle nod. Then he crosses his arms over his broad chest. Time passes as we both get lost in the trance of the fire. The sound of the embers popping and the light breeze is all that needs to be said. Occasionally I'll feel the need to start a conversation. But for now, his presence at my side is perfect enough.

Life just feels different when Zane Armstrong is close by. It's like my world becomes smaller. There are fewer distractions. It's just him. He's the only distraction, and a perfect one at that. And my mind has less worries. He makes me feel like I can be happy without any conscious effort.

It's funny to think how this all started. A dog named Kitty found me, scared the shit out of me, and then Zane helped me—in more ways than he'll ever understand.

Since that day, I haven't been able to deny his magnetic pull. The way my thoughts always pull to wondering about him. What he's doing. Where he is. How he's feeling.

But more than anything, it's the way he made my body feel for one night. It didn't matter that we never had sex. What mattered most is how I felt cared for in his arms. I felt safe.

"How's Lonny?" he asks, breaking the long silence between us.

It takes me a second to process his question.

"Oh, Lonny."

"Yeah, your friend."

"Sorry, um, Lonny's really good. She's on pace to graduate a semester early. She also just landed an internship with a marketing firm. She's going to work in their social media department next semester."

Zane smiles. "That's great. Please tell her I said congratulations."

"Yeah, of course. How's Trey doing?"

"He's great. Well, actually not great, but better. He tore a ligament in his elbow a few months back. It's healed now. But since he's a pitcher, it's going to unfortunately end his baseball career. But he's a lot better now. He graduated recently. In fact, he's already working for a local fire department."

"So what? He's a fireman?"

"Sure is. He's now every woman's fantasy."

I start to giggle because Zane's right. What girl wouldn't be attracted to a hot fireman like Trey. I can already picture Lonny's face lighting up when I tell her this news.

"That's great. I mean, the injury sucks. But please tell him I say congratulations on the job."

Zane nods. His eyes stay on mine. Then his tongue quickly traces along his upper lip, sending another warm shiver between my thighs.

"Can I ask you something, Poppy?"

"Sure."

"After your testimony. You know, at the courthouse a few months back. Did you get my text?"

"Text?" I furrow my brow at him.

"You know, the one where I told you how much I appreciated your testimony. And that we should hang out the next time you're in town."

"Text? I didn't get a text from you. I swear." I pause, looking away to think, when it hits me. "Oh, fuck!"

"What?"

"Oh, shit! I think I still had you blocked."

I pull out my phone, realizing right away that he's been blocked this whole time. I had Lonny do it for me the day I thought his friends drugged her. After unblocking Zane I start scrolling for old messages. I can't find anything. It's probably not retrievable if he messaged me while I had him blocked.

"I thought you were ignoring me," he says, nervously running his hand through his hair.

"I, uh, I thought you didn't want to see me either."

He turns to face me, eyes now glaring into my soul. "Why would you think that?"

"I don't know. Probably because I'm a girl with plenty of emotional baggage who slapped you in the face and called you a worthless piece of garbage."

Zane lets out a nervous chuckle that barely reaches up to his eyes. "I have plenty of emotional baggage, Poppy. I don't care about that."

"You don't?"

Zane reaches for my hand. His fingers interlace with mine and it feels like I've forgotten how to breathe.

"Poppy, I don't think differently of you just because a guy hurt you." Zane pauses, inching his body closer to mine. "It doesn't change how I feel when I'm around you. You see, I like you. Just as you are. And I know, well, I think, you like me too."

All I want is to scream out how much I like him. How much I need him. But when the back of his hand glides along my cheek, my voice is rendered useless. All I feel is his sensual touch. His eyes undressing me. His closeness as he leans in a hair closer. And how his lips would be mine if I just lifted up on my tippy toes and leaned into this moment.

The glass door suddenly slides open. Our heads are on a swivel as we see Jet.

"Fire the water!"

Really?!

CHAPTER 24

zane

"Netflix is calling. Goodnight, y'all. Happy Thanksgiving." Nina waves, still giggling over something Nick just whispered in her ear.

"Goodnight, bro. Goodnight, Poppy. Sweet dreams," Nick says. He gives me and Poppy a hug.

"Enjoy your Netflix. And your *chill*." Poppy winks with a mischievous smirk.

It had been just the four of us by the fire for the last couple of hours. Nadine, Charles, and Jet have been asleep for a while now. The four of us had been shmoozing about everything—from high school days to favorite movies, to plans after college. It's been nice connecting with my brother and Nina. But I'm ready to pick up where I left off with Poppy.

We huddle closer to the fire, standing shoulder to shoulder. It's mostly hot coals dusted in grey and white flakes. It's so easy to get lost in the tranquility of the fire. The bluish-white flames fluttering in the breeze. The occasional pop of embers add to the tranquility. It's so relaxing and meaningful because I have Poppy right next to me.

"You want to go for a walk?" she asks.

I tilt my head to look down at her. My eyes are drawn again to the golden flecks in those irises. The way the moon and fire work together, making her eyes come to life. It's like a mosaic masterpiece. And it has me so tongue-tied, I can barely stammer out a response

"Um, yeah. Let's do it."

"Do you mind if I borrow your hoodie? You know, the one you offered me earlier."

I hesitate for a moment, wondering why she wants to wear my hoodie when she probably has her own jackets in her room. But who gives a shit. "Of course, let me grab it."

"Okay. I'll meet you out front. I just have to use the restroom."

After I grab a hoodie, I meet her out front. "Here you go."

Poppy turns around as I hand over my hoodie. But before grabbing it, she flinches her hand back and takes a step back.

"Oh! Um, I can't wear that. It's, um, it's red. I don't wear red...*ever*."

"Oh, sorry." I notice her chest bouncing up and down. Her eyes are still wide like I just scared the shit out of her. "I must've grabbed the wrong one."

"It's no big deal, Zane. I'll be fine, I just thought you were grabbing the blue one."

"The blue one...rrrright. I forgot. That's my bad. Let me go get it."

I sprint back in while the fear in her face flashes in my mind. Her words play back in my head, making me wonder about the color red. Why it scared her. Why she couldn't even touch it. It was weird.

When I meet her back out front, I see genuine relief in her face that I brought the right colored hoodie. She slides it on quickly, looking like a completely different person when her head turtle pops its way out. It's a size bigger than the red one, which is the reason I didn't bring it out before. I want to ask her why she got freaked out, but I figure since she looks so relieved, I could do it another time.

The hoodie is also a reminder of how tiny she is. It's hanging down just past her knees. Even the sleeves have to be rolled up so her hands can hang out.

"You ready?" she asks, tying a white headband into her hair. My insides begin to sing at the memory of her wearing the green headband with the bow on top the first night we met up on my back porch. Once it's tied in place, she looks at me with an elongated smile. Before I can respond, she's hooked her arm around my elbow, leaning into me for warmth as we start our walk.

Her ability to send shivers throughout my entire body is how I'd imagine the most addictive drug on earth. And it's her. She's the addiction in my life. I may only be 22, and a bit of a lost soul, but she always finds a way to brighten my path. And there's something about the way she's smiling as I look down at her. It's like every perfect, euphoric feeling in my bones is a mirror to that smile.

"So, does your brother want to marry my sister?"

Wow! Cutting right to the chase.

"Marry?" I scoff, trying to play dumb.

A giddy smile dances across her face. Then her tongue glides along those luscious pillows for lips as she bites back a giggle.

"Come on, I can keep a secret. And to be fair, she never said I couldn't ask you. So...what do you think?"

I pull her in closer to me, slowing my stride to match her tiny legs. Her eyes widen up to mine, so full of wonderment. For a second, I almost forget what we're talking about.

Right! Marriage!

"Let's see, Nick marrying Nina? Hhhmm...I'd say there's a good chance."

"Really?!" Poppy shrieks, bobbing up and down.

"Well, he's not in any rush. I imagine Nina isn't either. But I wouldn't be surprised if he rings her up some time after he gets his master's degree. At least, that's my guess."

Poppy is like a champagne bottle ready to burst, screeching and howling with excitement.

"That's so exciting!" she shouts, letting out a dreamy sigh. "Oh! I love your brother. Can I tell you something he did for me?"

"Of course."

"Well, I went to visit Nina for a 3-day weekend. She and Nick hadn't been dating that long, so I was still getting to know him. But I'll never forget crossing security at the airport. Nina was still at work, so he picked me up and was going to take me out to lunch. But he had a dozen white roses and an array of balloons waiting for me when I got off the plane. He even wrote a long note on the card saying how excited he was to get to know me. But how sweet is that? I mean, what kind of guy does that?"

"Only my brother. He's the best, right?" I nod with a smile. It all sounds exactly like something Nick would do.

"I still have the note."

"Really?

"Yeah. I have every note that's ever been given to me. Every birthday card, Christmas card, you name it, I kept it. It's just my thing. I'd rather get a sweet note over jewelry or any other bullshit gift like clothes or gift cards. Yuck!"

Her comment brings a giggle out of me. "Hhhmm, that's good to know. You're a simple creature, aren't you, Poppy?"

"I'd call it sentimental. You can call it whatever you want, though. I just feel like a good love note can never be forgotten. It's permanent. It's a forever reminder of how someone feels in that moment of time. And once it's written, it can't be taken back. It's permanently etched on that card. I don't know, maybe it's a weird thing to obsess over."

"I don't think it's weird at all."

"Well..." She hesitates, taking a deep breath. "Was it weird for me to ask to borrow your jacket?"

"Um, no." I hesitate for a moment, contemplating a question about the color red, but decide to keep things general. "But since you asked, why did you want to wear my hoodie?"

Poppy starts to giggle. "Oh, man," she mutters.

"What, Poppy? Now I have to know."

"Oh my god! You're going to think I'm a weirdo," she says, stopping suddenly. Her eyes go down to her feet. I can't tell if she's embarrassed or maybe a little bit flattered.

I lightly grab her hip, pulling her just enough so she can face me. It may have been too forward, but I couldn't resist. She also didn't seem to mind it. And I couldn't help myself, I'm desperate to get lost in those eyes again. But when her eyes don't meet mine, I lightly tilt her chin up.

"Come on, tell me?" I beg.

"O-kay...fine." She pauses to take a deep breath in and out before speaking. "I love how you smell. I can't explain it. It's intoxicating. Your pheromones after that night haven't gone away." She pauses again, letting out a nervous giggle. Her adoring smile feels like something more to me. Maybe it's the way my chest tingles with warmth and goodness—to the point where my heart feels like it's fusing to hers, fitting perfectly.

"Tell me more?" I ask, taking a small step closer to her. My hands grip tighter to her hips.

"Well, after our first night together, it didn't matter how angry I was at you. I knew I'd never, *ever*, be able to forget that night. And I kept your Zeppelin T-shirt. You know, the black one you let me borrow when I slept over. I still have it, but it only has a little of your scent. I may have slept in it a time or two. Or a hundred."

Her hand goes to her mouth. She's trying to stifle a giggle. Then a strong gust kicks a few loose strands along her face. When the wind settles, I move a few locks behind her ear. She then does the same thing to me, moving a few loose hairs out of my eye.

I can feel her loosening up. I inch my body closer while wrapping my arms around her waist. My hands interlock as her breasts graze along the top of my stomach. I can feel the tingle from her hardened nipples as they barely perforate through the hoodie.

Poppy interlocks her hands behind my neck as a smile stretches across her face. The need to unleash my lips on hers is overwhelming. I want every part of her. Mind, body, and spirit. But more than anything, I want her to trust me. She needs to know she'll be safe with me.

Always.

I reach into my back pocket while still keeping one of my hands on the very bottom of her back.

"Give me your hand," I tell her.

She opens her hand against my stomach. I place what's hers back in her palm.

"What is this?" she asks, gasping when she realizes what it is. "Oh! Oh! This was mine."

"It's your little..." I pause, remembering the silly nickname I gave her headband. "It's that dipsey doo thing you wore the night you came over to my house.

"Dipsey-what?" She laughs.

"I don't know what it's called. But I loved how it looked on you. Green's a good color on you. Anyhow, you left it at my house that night. So I kept it. This way I would never forget the smell of your hair." I stop to take a long sigh, feeling my cheeks flush with heat as I take another deep breath. "Who's weird now? You keep cards. My oversized t-shirts. I keep...dipsey doos."

Poppy lets out a sniffle. All I see next is a single tear roll down her cheek. The way it reflects off the full moon and sky full of stars, enhancing her beauty, is a core memory I don't want to ever forget.

She wipes her eyes, then takes a small step back. I watch in awe as she removes her white headband and gracefully puts the green one into her hair. Then she gives me a ta-da pose with her hands.

"It's just called a headband, Zane. But I like what you call it more. From this day forward, it will forever be a dipsey doo. So, what do you think?"

She does a couple of runway poses, angling her face at me with sexy smirks.

"Perfect." It's only one word, but it has me out of breath.

I pull her back in by her hourglass hips, letting my fingers barely glide along the top of her jeans. My hardness presses back into her belly button. Then I slowly lean my lips down to her, resting my forehead on hers as I close my eyes. I want nothing more than to ravage those lips. But not until she knows.

"You're safe, Poppy."

"I know," she whispers back, sounding out of breath.

"I mean it, Poppy. You're safe."

"I...I know, Zane," she whispers again, leaning her lips the slightest bit closer to mine.

I want her so badly. But I feel the need to tease her a bit. My lips glide down the side of her face, brushing through her hair until they rest over her ear.

"Can I kiss you?" I whisper softly into her ear, awaiting her consent as I hear her breath hitch.

"Yes. *Please!*" she begs, window washing her hands along my back, digging her nails in like talons.

I tilt my head back. Then my lips fall into hers. My mind begins to swirl in so many euphoric feelings. It's hard to believe this is real. All I know is the taste of her lips and tongue is my addiction—my oxygen. The sweetness of her mouth is the nectar of everything I've been starving for in my life. And it's here—living and breathing in a kiss that feels timeless.

Eventually, our lips slowly pull apart. I open my eyes and get greedy for a couple more light, teasing kisses. Then I pull my mouth up to her forehead, planting head kiss after head kiss as our arms coil around each other in an embrace that feels permanent.

❦

We walk up the carport, hand in hand, with smiles that feel permanently etched along our faces. I'm giddy with nervous excitement but trying to contain it. It may be late, but I don't get the feeling I'll be sleeping alone tonight.

"Hey guys!" Nina calls out. The front door closes as she and Nick walk out.

"You guys are still up?" I ask, surprised to see them both.

"Yeah, Nina here has a midnight craving," Nick says with a lingering smile on Nina.

"For sausage," Poppy quips, already laughing. "I would've thought that craving's been satis—"

"Poppy!" Nina interrupts, clearing her throat. "It's pancakes I'm craving. And you're one to talk about night cravings. Where've you guys been anyways? We've been texting you."

"Oh, you know, we just got a little lost," I murmur, looking down at Poppy's blushing smile. "With the time, I guess."

"Well, whatever you lovebirds were doing, we need a ride since Nick and I have been drinking. The delivery rates are surging like crazy," Nina says, tossing the keys to Poppy.

"Really?" Poppy scoffs.

"Yeah, it's a 60-minute wait for Door Dash orders. And I'd much rather eat in a restaurant. Let's go. Come with us. It'll be fun."

"Really? I'm tired, and I don't like driving your car," Poppy complains

"It's okay, I'll drive," I tell her, placing a hand on her shoulder. "I'm more than happy to drive."

Poppy huffs out a frustrated breath. I get it, we both want to continue our red-hot kiss. Luckily, the night is still young. It's also the first day of a four-day trip.

We all load up into Nina's Subaru as Poppy keeps on needling her sister. Nina needles her right back. They have this playful banter always running, and it's always full of sexual innuendos that have me and Nick cracking up.

I back out of the driveway while everyone is still giggling. The second I put the car in drive, I glance into the rearview mirror. I notice the smile on Nick's face. How full it is. How happy he truly is as he gives Nina an adoring look. It swells my heart to see him so happy.

If only I knew how fleeting this moment would be. Or how everything in our lives would change in the next couple of minutes. And most regrettably, how the Thanksgiving evening of 2023 would be the last time I ever see my brother smiling.

zane

GRAND CANYON: PRESENT DAY

JANUARY 18TH, 2026

I've never heard a girl laugh like this in my life. Poppy is quite literally hyperventilating with laughter as she sits up on my shoulders. All I'm waiting for next is a damp shirt and warm neck for when she pees herself.

Every part of her laugh is infectious. But my favorite part is when her voice starts to squeak and squeal. Sometimes she'll even snort a little. It has me laughing right along with her—to the point where the smile in my cheeks is starting to ache.

"Oh my." She gasps, trying to catch her breath while still giggling sporadically.

"Who would have thought you farting on my shoulders would send us over the edge—pun not intended."

"For the millionth time...*sir*! I did not fart. And for the record, we ladies do not pass gas. EV—ER!" she shouts, playfully curling her eyes down on me with a smirk.

Her legs dangle at my side as we continue down the trail. We are now about an hour further into the canyon from Indian Gardens, with about another 90 minutes left until we reach Phantom Ranch. We've descended a good thousand feet, and this place just continues to blow my mind.

I've been hanging onto her ankles this whole time. There have been a few hikers walking by us. Each time they either give us a funny look or they just ask us if everything is okay. Three of them have even asked for pictures with us. Poppy thinks it's because I'm carrying her on my shoulders. She doesn't realize that there's much more to why these random strangers want a photo with *her*.

I've thought about spilling the beans, but I think it would be cooler if she figured it out on her own. Eventually, she'll put it all together.

As for me, I couldn't be happier—even if my neck and shoulder muscles are on fire. It's worth every moment of pain and soreness I know I'll be feeling for the next couple of days.

The more I think about it, the more I realize how badly I needed this closeness—*her closeness*. It's not putting my arms around her shoulders or her hips. It's not holding her hand and guiding her down the trail. But having her sit on my shoulders is a wildly intimate way to hold a woman.

My mind is now imagining how amazing it would be to bury my face in between these legs. Tease her clit. Taste her center. Finger fuck her. I'd do it all, and I'd take my time, edging her into so many orgasms she'll be screaming my name.

"She would always fart around Jet and blame him for it," she blurts out.

My mind snaps right out of my sex dream. I try to process what she's telling me, but I'm completely lost.

"Excuse me?"

Poppy giggles. "Nina would do that all the time. She'd literally seek Jet out in the house and stand or sit by him and fart."

"What? Wu-why?" I fumble my words, unable to hold in my laugh.

I look up, barely able to see her face. But even if I couldn't, I can feel her aura open up. I can even feel the smile on her face deep in my chest as she recounts a memory.

"Yeah, Nina did that all the time. And it always drove Jet up a wall. But I know why she did it. Jet only knows certain emotions. You know, being crazy, fun, loud, and just his authentic self. But the one emotion, the one emotion he always had trouble showing, was disgust or anger. But farting, yep, farting was the one and only way to bring that emotion out of him. He'd grimace, scowl, and just react with such annoyance. It was comical to witness. And as weird as it sounds, I get it. Nina wanted him to feel *all* the things normal people feel. She wanted him to be disgusted."

I look up at Poppy right as she curls her eyes back down to mine. Her smile looks serene as she runs her hands through my hair. It's as if there's no more tension in her face. She's simply content in a perfect memory with her sister.

It's beautiful and sad to see because all it can ever be is a memory. That part still gets to me like icepicks slowly stabbing deeper and deeper into my chest.

My breaths begin to go shallow. I can't bring her back. Nick and Nina are gone forever. And it's my burden to carry to the grave.

"You okay?" Poppy asks, concern dripping in her tone.

I give her a gentle nod, forcing a smile that feels faker than a car salesman. Then I clear my throat because I don't want to kill her joy. She shared a story of her sister that was absolutely beautiful.

"You know, Nick loved your brother. And even though I've only met Jet a couple of times, I really felt connected to him as well. But I still remember the way Nick talked about meeting Jet. Then I met him, and I got it. He's just got this energy about him that's infectious. It's hard to not smile or laugh in his presence. He's just—"

"Himself. He's unapologetically, always, *himself*," Poppy interjects, finishing my thoughts perfectly.

"Yeah. That's Jet. Hey, next time you see him, tell him I'm going to give it one more go and fire the water for him."

Poppy wraps her hands around my jawline, yanking me by my chin until our eyes meet. Her eyes widen as she speaks.

"Really?!"

"Yeah, I started training again recently. The LA Olympics will be my last shot in 2028. That is, assuming this guy holds up," I say, patting my surgically repaired right shoulder."

"Oh my God! Am I hurting your shoulder right now?"

I hesitate for a brief moment. "No, no, no. I'm uh—"

Poppy bops me on the top of my head. "Let me down. You need a break."

"I'm fine, Poppy. Really—"

"Ah, ah! Stop it! Let me down!"

I concede to Poppy. The second she's off my shoulders, it feels like all of my neck muscles can finally breathe. We decide to take a break under a shaded tree, sitting shoulder to shoulder against the trunk.

"Does it still hurt?" she asks, keeping her gaze to the sky.

I follow her line of vision as a raven begins to squawk and soar in circles above us.

"Does what still hurt?"

"Your shoulder. You know, from the fight. Or your last race."

"No. At least not in the last few months since I got back to training. But they told me it'll never be 100 percent. But I feel like if I believe that for a second, I'm done. So, no, it hasn't been hurting. Training has been really good, too. My times are right on track for the 2028 Olympics."

Poppy and I lock eyes as she takes a huge bite into her apple. Her chewing slows. Then her brow furrows. The lines in her forehead have her deep in thought. Then she starts shaking her head as she looks down.

"What is it?"

"Oh, nothing. It's just that we watched your last race. Me. Jet. My parents. We felt bad for you. And I just wish I could've been there for you in some way."

The weight of her words, while caring, has my chest collapsing into shallow breaths. The memory of being so close to the finish line flashes back. I can still see it, like the wall of my final lap is right there at my fingertips—until my right shoulder stopped working.

"If you never got in that fight for us, your shoulder would've been fine. You'd probably be a gold med—"

"Don't say that! You don't know that," I interrupt, probably a little too harshly.

Poppy sighs. "Maybe. I just, I just, wish it could've been me. You know, beating the shit out of those guys—to get that feeling of pummeling someone's skull in. I bet it felt good."

"It did," I quickly agree. "And Poppy, my shoulder went out on me because I've swam over a million miles in the pool. A single fight may have just aggravated something that would've eventually happened anyways. But I don't think it's the reason I lost."

"So, you still don't regret the fight?" she asks, tilting those curious, hazel eyes up to me. Her gaze becomes more contemplative as I chew over her question.

"I have plenty of regrets in my life. The biggest being getting behind the wheel *that night*. But beating the shit out of those guys...that will *never, ever,* be one of them.

In fact, I'd call it a highlight of my life—not a regret. I promise. No bullshit, Poppy."

The corner of her lips perks up into a smile. That smile, albeit only half a smile, is all I need to relieve the tension in my chest. I can't read her thoughts, but that smile tells me she feels protected by me—and that means everything.

"What about your parents?" she asks, leaning her shoulder into mine.

"What about them?"

"I just know the last time you spoke about them, you guys weren't really talking. I mean, do they even know you're here with me?"

"Oh yeah. They know I'm here. And we're doing better..." I pause, thinking long and hard about the last time I saw my parents. It's amazing how well we've been doing for the past couple months. How I talk to them regularly. How picking up the phone to call them no longer feels like a chore."

"Really?"

"Yeah. In fact, when I told them why I was coming here and that I'd be going down here with you, they were really happy."

I feel my smile widening. Poppy angles her gaze with curiosity in her eyes.

"I'm really glad you guys are doing better. That makes me happy," she says, placing her hand on top of mine. She starts caressing the top of my hand.

The electricity from her touch has my heart rate spiking out of control. I want to kiss her so badly—just one more taste of those sweet, succulent, pillowy lips.

"Hi there!"

We both turn our heads at the same time. It's a young woman, close to our age, with jet black hair fluttering in the wind. Her smile is vibrant and welcoming.

She takes a long drink from the tube of her CamelBak before speaking. "Sorry, I didn't mean to startle you guys," she explains, walking right up to us.

We both start to get up. "Oh, hi there. Can we help you?" Poppy asks, slowly pulling herself up by my shoulder to stand on one foot.

"Well, I feel like I should be asking you the same. I saw you two from a ways back. It's not every day you see two adults giving a piggyback ride down this trail."

The woman lets out a nervous laugh. The awkward silence has me rushing to say something.

"Yeah, um, she sprained her ankle pretty badly a couple miles back. We thought about hiking back out, but she's not able to—especially with the snow and rain in the forecast for the rim. We were hoping to get down to Phantom Ranch and get a roof over our heads for the night—hopefully figure it out from there."

"How funny? My sister is the park ranger down there. Her name is Lettie. Lettie Ortega. I was heading down there to visit her for the weekend."

"Do you think we'll be able to find a place to stay down there—at least for the night?" I ask

"Of course. In fact, once I get a little further down, I can reach her on my walkie," she explains, pulling the walkie out of her back pocket. "I'm a trail runner. I do ultramarathons so I can get down there pretty quick. You know, give her a heads up that we have an injured hiker. She may even be able to send up a mule to help you the rest of the way down. That is, if they have any down there. I can usually get reception about a mile further down the trail—just before the Colorado River bridge."

"Oh my!" Poppy exclaims, squeezing my shoulder with exuberance. "That would be great. Thank you so much, uh—"

"Sorry, I didn't introduce myself. I was a little starstruck when I recognized you. I'm Christina, but everyone calls me Chrissie," she explains, shaking my hand.

I introduce myself, but the whole time her eyes are starstruck on Poppy. Then Chrissie extends both hands to Poppy, bowing her head down in respect as she speaks.

"It's such an honor to meet you, Poppy. Such an honor."

Their handshake lingers while Poppy's mouth falls to the floor. Poppy's in shock. I don't blame her. After all, she never introduced herself to Chrissie. Yet, this random woman hiking into the Grand Canyon knows exactly who Poppy is.

Chrissie puts her hand over her heart and continues. "I'll get going to beat the storm, but I just have one baby request before I go. Can I get a quick picture with you?"

Poppy nods at her. Then she gives me a confused look before awkwardly smiling her way through a couple quick pictures that I take of the two of them.

"Do we know each other?" Poppy finally asks.

"No, of course not. But, uh, I just think you're a brave person. And what you did was beautiful. Anyhow, I'll get going to get you guys help. It's the least I can do for my hero."

Before Poppy and I can say another word, she gives a quick wave goodbye and starts jogging down the trail.

"What was that all about?" she asks.

"I don't know. But let's get going, these clouds look pretty nasty."

I'm playing dumb, and Poppy probably knows it. Luckily, she seems a bit distracted by the bad weather moving in on us.

Once she's back on my shoulders, we make our way down the trail. But my mind is not worried about the bad weather or the fact that we have no definitive plan on getting Poppy out of the canyon. Instead, I'm thinking about Chrissie's choice of words.

"*My hero!*"

It tells me that there's so much change on the horizon—so much happening outside the walls of the Grand Canyon. Poppy is a hero—in more ways than one. She just doesn't know it yet. But soon enough, she will.

CHAPTER 26

POPPY

THE RAIN HAS BEEN coming down in thick sheets for the last thirty minutes. The gusts are so strong it's making it hard to see and hear. I know Zane's sore and tired, but he refuses to complain. He also keeps shooting down my requests to take a break so he can get a short rest.

The piggyback ride down to Phantom Ranch may have been our best option, or maybe our only option, but I don't like feeling helpless. The damsel in distress was not the woman I was raised to be. But my ankle is useless and still aching like hell. I've also been shivering on his shoulders for the past 20 minutes, and I know it's just as concerning to him as it is to me.

The one saving grace is Zane brought ponchos that are keeping us dry.

"How much further?" I raise my voice through a deafening gust of wind.

"We should get to a tunnel soon. It'll lead us onto a black suspension bridge. That'll put us only a mile out from Phantom Ranch. The bridge will take us across the Colorado River. We can take a break in the tunnel if you want."

I nod down at him. Then I take my panoramic gaze, noticing the changes in color from the rain. The red rocks have taken on a deeper, more vibrant red. Even the trees and bushes feel like they're sucking up the water and turning green before our very eyes. There are low lying clouds in every which direction, which give the canyon an eerie, foggy feel.

Once we make our way around another cliff face, we can see the Colorado River again. We've seen it multiple times from a distance, but it's amazing how it gets grander in size with each new view through the endless valleys and chasms. It's got this brownish color that's a mix between Sedona red and chocolate milk. The white-caps in the water are also more pronounced, reminding us that the river is quickly moving through the rapids.

I remember in my research of the Grand Canyon I learned how people pay to go white water rafting down this river. It looks like it would be quite the adrenaline rush. However, my research also told me that there have been numerous drownings and accidents over the years because it's so dangerous. The closer we get to the river, the more I can see why.

"That's it!" Zane points.

I look ahead to a dark tunnel around the corner. It's like a black hole that's the size of a door sitting at the bottom of a canyon wall. It looks so tiny because the cliff wall is at least 50 feet tall. If not for the torrential downpour pegging down on us, it would probably look scary. But I'm more than ready to get out of this rain and wind.

Once inside the tunnel it feels like two worlds. One is quiet, calm, and pitch dark the further you go in. And outside is the raging thunderstorm pattering down on the canyon. We take a seat at the entrance, sitting far enough inside to shield us from both the rain and the wind. The first thing we do is load up on water and snacks. After eating the last bits of beef jerky, I give Zane my last protein bar. He doesn't take it at first, so I lie to him, telling him I have another.

"You doing okay?" I ask after he inhales the protein bar in two bites.

"Yeah." He yawns, tenderly stretching his ear down to each shoulder. Then he rotates his head around in light circles to relieve what has to be major tension in his upper back and neck from lugging me around.

Poor guy!

"You're not okay," I tell him, shaking my head. I slide my back into the tunnel wall and spread my legs. "Here, sit in between my legs. Let me rub your neck and upper back."

Zane's smirk catches my eye for a fleeting moment as he slides over to sit in between my legs. Once he's pressed his butt all the way in between my thighs, I feel my heart racing, trying to catch up with the manic fluttering sensation in my tummy and chest.

"How's that?" I ask, trying to knead my fingers into his neck.

"Aaahhh, thanks, Poppy. That feels great."

I'm surprised he likes it. It feels like I'm pressing into concrete. His muscles are so wound up. He's also so fucking tall I can't get any leverage to really dig in there.

"Fuck! This isn't working for me. Lie down and let me get on top."

He slowly arches his head around to lock those iridescent irises on mine. But this time he's happily wearing a playful smirk across his lips. "You want to get on top of me?"

The deep tone in his voice has me ovulating. And the smirk he's wearing has all the blood in my body flowing to my cheeks. I can only imagine how pink they already are.

"Yes, I'm going to get on top of you…to massage your neck. I need the leverage. Is that okay with you?"

"Well, twist my arm." His eyes linger a couple seconds longer before he lies face down, using his backpack as a pillow.

I straddle my way over his lower back, sitting on the mound that is the perkiest looking ass I've ever seen on a man. It would make Kim Kardashian jealous. But I'm thankful for the extra leverage it gives me. It allows me to really lean into the massage with all my body weight.

The harder I dig into his thick muscles, the more I can feel him slowly letting go. Then he lets out these subtle moans that warm my heart. I feel so lucky that I can give this reprieve from pain, even if it's temporary.

The thought of pain and taking it away sends my mind wandering. I think back to the start of the hike, pleading with Zane that none of this was his fault. And I meant what I said. It truly was just a horrible accident. He seemed to believe me, but at some point, believing me won't matter. He needs to forgive himself. Or maybe just find a way to accept the pain for what it is. I feel like I'm somewhere on that path with my own demons, and I'm making something of my life.

"You know, you don't have to massage me for this long. I can—"

"Shut up and enjoy this!" I playfully reprimand him. "It's the least I can do given how you're basically saving my life."

He giggles a little, then goes back to moaning softly. It's a sound he lets out intermittently when I get to the tight spots in his neck. It's not meant to be erotic, but there's just something about a large, masculine man making this sound. It makes me warm and fuzzy all over, fantasizing about all the places I can be putting my hands.

I try my best to rein in my dirty thoughts so I can focus on the massage. I look outside the tunnel, admiring the sound. The rain is slowing to a pitter-patter. The relaxing rhythm of the rain has my mind wondering about other things that have happened on this trip.

"So, what's up with that Chrissie lady? Why weren't you weirded out by all of that?"

Zane slowly turns his head around to look at me. Then he props himself on one arm, fidgeting his fingers as he speaks. "Do you really not know what that was about?"

"What do you mean? I've never seen that woman in my life. I swear."

"Well, she clearly knows you," he says as the corner of his lips tighten into a smirk.

"What's going on, Zane?"

Zane sits up. His grin gets wider—until it breaks into a soft giggle.

"Poppy, when was the last time you talked to Lonny?"

"A couple days ago, why?"

"Well, she may have shared out the video you posted on Insta. But she wasn't the only one. A lot of people reshared that reel. So many that I'm sure Chrissie—"

"What! No!" I raise my voice. It feels like the tunnel is caving in all around me. Then he quickly grabs my hand.

"Hey, hey, hey. It's okay," he tries to reassure me, leaning closer while his other hand glides up and down my back.

"Zane, I posted that video for like a couple of minutes. Then I deleted it. Or, at least I thought I did. I don't know, it's all a blur. But are you saying people saw it?"

Zane gives me a tentative nod back, speaking slowly. "Yyyeah. A lot. Of people."

My stomach is doing somersaults. I feel like I might vomit.

"What's a lot?" I ask.

"Well, let's just say it went viral. *Very*...viral."

I bury my face in my hands. It's not that I regret posting the video. I only deleted it because I showed the picture of Jonathan. *That*, is the only part I regret doing because I feared retribution.

Zane's hand continues to glide up and down my back. I wish I could truly feel it, but everything inside me feels suddenly numb. And my thoughts are racing to every worst-case scenario imaginable.

"Poppy, honestly, I'd think you'd be proud to see—"

"I don't want to know!" I harshly cut him off with my hand in the air. "Please, Zane! Can you just keep it to yourself? I don't feel like talking about this. Not right now. Please."

"Okay. Of course."

The sound of heavy clacking brings both of our eyes peering down the tunnel. It's nothing but a pitch-dark abyss until the clacking gets louder. Then we see it, the silhouette of two people on mules riding towards us.

"Howdy, y'all!" the voice echoes through the tunnel. "Sorry it took a while!"

I realize it's Chrissie coming up the rear. The other woman must be her sister. She has a Park Ranger emblem on her shoulder and top hat. She shimmies off her mule first, like she's done it a thousand times. Zane helps me up as they walk up to us.

"Hi there! I'm Chrissie's sister." She puts her hand on her chest. "My name is Lettie. Lettie Ortega. I'm the acting park ranger down at Phantom Ranch. You must be Poppy and Zane."

I nod, feeling a flush of relief in my lungs. Lettie's handshake is firm, like her sister's. It even lingers for a good 10 seconds like Chrissie's did. I can't help but drink in this woman as she removes her hat, letting her silky, jet-black hair hang down to the base of her back.

"It's so nice to meet you, Poppy," she tells me, shaking my hand a second time.

"You as well. I love your hair."

"Thank you."

It's obvious they're sisters. The resemblance lives most in their smiles that form the deepest, most attractive dimples I've ever seen. And their faces just have this happy glow about them. It makes me feel instantly warm and welcome. But I also get the sense that they're a bit nervous too.

When no one says another word, I clear my throat, trying to think of something to say. But I'm tongue tied by these two women and their starstruck expressions focused solely on me. It's like this model-esque world class swimmer by my side doesn't exist.

"Thank you for helping us. We were hoping there was a place to stay down at Phantom Ranch since I sprained my ankle. Poor Zane here has been towing me along on his shoulders since Indian Gardens."

I look up at Zane right as he wraps his arm around my shoulders. He warms me with a smile that sets off fireworks in my chest. It's more than just a smile. It's so natural and real—authentically my Zane—*my protector.*

"It's all handled. We're having a cabin prepared for you guys as we speak. And it's no trouble at all. In fact, it would be our honor to have you spend the night down there. A real honor," Lettie says again with a slight bow of her head.

My body begins to tingle all over. It's more than being touched by their generosity. It's how these two women are looking at me like I'm some messiah. It makes me a little uncomfortable because they're the ones doing me the favor.

We continue to exchange pleasantries, and the more we talk, the more we all begin to warm up to each other. They tell us that the Bright Angel and Kaibab Trail are officially closed at the top. Apparently, the rim of the canyon has already received about 6 inches of snow. They're even advising hikers leaving the canyon to wait at least a day or two to hike out.

Eventually, we decide to get going. Chrissie joins Lettie on her mule. Zane helps me onto the other mule by easily picking me up by my hips. He sets me on the saddle with the amount of effort it takes to put a canned good in a cupboard. Then he climbs on in front of me. I feel him slide his ass in between my legs while I wrap my arms around his waist. The second my hands interlock, I feel at home.

Holding onto him the rest of the way down is all that matters now. Inhaling his scent and basking in his touch means everything. It's everything because I'm exactly where I need to be. I'm home. Zane is my home.

zane

AFTER CROSSING THE BRIDGE over the Colorado River, we find ourselves snaking our way down the shoreline, following the river's path. We're linked up by rope to the mule carrying Chrissie and Lettie as they lead us further into the canyon.

The high canyon walls on both sides are at least a hundred feet high. It's amazing how it holds this tremendous flow of water from the river. The rushing rapids are moving so fast it creates a deafening sound that's further amplified by the way it echoes off the walls. It's so loud we can't even carry on a conversation. But we're fine with that. It's especially fine because Poppy's arms have been snuggly wrapped around my waist for the last hour.

It's hard to believe we're at the bottom of the Grand Canyon, *together*. This was never the plan. I woke up this morning reminiscing about my last trip with my brother and my dad. It felt so odd to be back here after ten years.

I was most terrified to see Poppy. Wondering whether she still blames me for what happened. Wondering what her true feelings are for me. And I'm still wondering about those things. Trauma and grief just have this ability to cloud judgment. It's like a fog that won't evaporate or burn off. Instead, it blinds you in this constant state of worry.

However, the longer I'm with her, the less the fog has a hold over me. The more I can see what's happening all around us. It's like this cataclysmic change is happening to us. But it's not just Poppy and myself. It's everyone.

Eventually, we turn north following the signs that welcome us to Phantom Ranch. The trail thins out, following a creek of lightly flowing water. It gives our ears a rest from the heavy moving flow of the river.

The closer we get, the more hikers and cabins we start to see. It's been ten years since I've visited, but the memories of being down here are still fresh. I remember my dad had us leave our phones behind. I was bored out of my mind at first, wondering what you do at the bottom of the Grand Canyon with no technology. Meanwhile, Dad was with us, but his mind was so distant and lost in his recently failed marriage.

Luckily, I had Nick to distract me from my sour mood. We ended up making friends and socializing with many of the foreigners that were down here at the time. We explored different trails like Ribbon Falls. Carved branches into walking sticks. We even went fishing. But we spent most of our time in the Canteen. It's a communal cabin where people go to eat, socialize, and play games. It's also where they serve a family-style dinner every night.

I was only 14 years old at the time. Nick and I were still coming to grips with our parents' divorce. It made things awkward for my dad. I remember him trying to spend time with us. But for the most part he wasn't really living in the moment. He had this destitute look in his eyes. It's like he was there physically, but on the inside, he was wallowing in his own depression.

"We're here!" Lettie shouts, unmounting from her mule and shaking me from my trip down memory lane. "You guys can take the one on the right," she says, pointing to one of the two cabins that sit 20 feet apart. "Chrissie can bunk with me in the Ranger's quarters, that is, if you two don't mind sleeping together."

I can see Poppy's cheeks pinken out of the corner of my eye. I feel the same blistering heat rise in my face.

I clear my throat before talking. "Um, sure."

"How many beds are there?" Poppy asks.

"One bed. I mean, a bunk bed. It's two twin mattresses. We don't do a whole lot of upkeep on the cabin. But there's a functioning sink, mini fridge, closet, and desk, so it's not too shabby. The communal bathrooms are just 20 yards up the trail. But you guys will be warm and cozy in there. We use the cabin for situations like yours when someone gets hurt and can't hike out."

I take another look at the two cabins. Ours definitely looks older because the color in the wood is more faded and dilapidated. The one with the Park Ranger symbol is also a little bit larger. It has a green metal slatted roof and the log structure has a rich reddish-brown color. Lettie tells us it was built two years ago to take the place of the guest cabin that we're staying in. Apparently, it used to be her old Ranger's quarters.

"It looks great. Thank you again for helping us."

"Yeah, this is incredibly kind of you all," I agree with Poppy.

"Of course. Can we help you down?" Chrissie asks Poppy.

The three of us help lower Poppy off her mule. She winces the second her feet touch the ground. Then she grabs onto my shoulder for balance.

"Ow! Ow!"

"I've got a first aid kit with fresh wraps and ice packs in my cabin," Lettie offers, smiling at Poppy. "And crutches if you need them."

Poppy's face lights up. "That'd be great. Thank you."

Lettie and Chrissie hook their arms around Poppy's waist. "Come on, Poppy. We'll get you taken care of. Zane, you're more than welcome to grab a shower. It's the next cabin about 50 yards down on the right. We can get Poppy all fixed up and meet you in the Canteen. It's where our visitors check into their rooms, grab a bite to eat, and get to know one another."

"Sounds good. You good with that, Poppy?"

"More than good," she tells me, still flashing a relieved smile.

After a quick shower and stretch, I follow the signs to the Canteen. Once I step inside, it's just like I remembered. There are four long tables that take up most of the space. People are mingling around and enjoying one another's company. And like before, I can tell that most of these people are visiting from other countries. One couple has shirts with the Switzerland flag. A couple of other people are talking in what sounds like a British accent.

It's amazing how things haven't changed. Everything is just like I remembered. There's a wall full of board games, many of which I remember playing with Nick. A front register where people can order snacks and drinks, and buy different Grand Canyon labeled clothing and souvenirs.

Since I'm still wearing rain-soaked clothes, I buy a brand new outfit and get changed in the bathroom. When I'm back in the Canteen, I meet a volunteer named Rick. Rick tells me how he helps with the maintenance down here. He's a self-proclaimed handyman for anything that needs fixing; from clogged toilets to electrical issues, he can do it all. He's been volunteering down here for the last 20 years with his wife, Sandy, who's working the front desk of the Canteen to check people into their cabins.

When I tell Rick I was here ten years ago, he explains how not a whole lot has changed with Phantom Ranch. They still serve a family-style pancake breakfast every morning and a family-style dinner of either vegetarian stew or steak every single evening. And for lunch they're still serving the same bagel and summer sausage sack lunch that we begrudgingly ate ten years ago.

"The only thing that changes is the people," he says, looking around in a reminiscing tone. "Every day I meet someone from a different country, with a different set of beliefs, a different perspective, different values, and different goals. But we're all not that different. The one big difference is your either here, or you're *really* here. You get my drift, son?"

"Yeah, I think so."

He pulls his coffee mug up for a sip. A smile cracks through his lips. "What brings you here?"

"Saying goodbye to my brother. I'm with a friend who's doing the same thing, but she's saying goodbye to her sister. We brought their ashes down here."

"Hhhmm, I'm sorry to hear that. But this place holds memories like no place on earth, so I'd say you guys picked a good spot to say goodbye. A hell of a spot," he says, glancing behind me like he's distracted. "Say, your...um...friend. Is she the girl on crutches with the green bow in her hair?"

I follow his eyes to Poppy. She's over in the corner reading through some books on the wall. Like me, she's changed into some fresh clothes. She must have gotten a shower, too. Her wet hair is tied back into a ponytail.

After saying goodbye to Rick, I spend the next couple of minutes just looking at her from across the room. In those couple of minutes, two women walk up to her, shaking her hand. Then a third one comes to get a picture on her phone. She even has Poppy sign a napkin, which brings a giggle out of both of us when we lock eyes from across the room.

"So, looks like you're still the woman of the hour."

"I guess so. I've yet to wrap my head around what's going on here." She huffs out a strained exhale. "I'm going to just keep smiling for now and playing the naïve card. Anyways, what year did you say you and your brother came here?"

"2016. Why?"

"Aahh, I think I found it," she says, reaching into a higher section of the bookshelf.

She pulls down a severely faded book with a brown cover labeled 2016. It takes a second for me to realize that it's a logbook. It's where past visitors leave their names and notes about their visit to the Grand Canyon. Most people write where they're visiting from and usually a little note about their trip.

"Hey, that's my note," I tell her, pointing to my handwriting.

Poppy starts reading it aloud. "Hi, y'all. Zane Armstrong here visiting from Phoenix, Arizona. I'm here with my brother and my dad. If you see this note, don't forget the name. One day I'll be a gold medalist. Just you wait..." Her voice fades into a regretful tone. Then she clears her throat before finishing. "Just you wait for the 2024 Paris Olympics. Here I come. Sincerely, Zane Armstrong."

Poppy turns to face me. Then she grabs the collar of my shirt, burning her eyes into mine as she speaks. "Hey, look at me. You'll be back. You hear me? You'll be back. All we have to do is make a quick little edit here."

She punches the back of her pen and crosses out the Paris 2024 part, replacing it with 2028 Los Angeles Olympics. "See! Now we're good."

Her lips curl up at the corner into a smirk. I realize how close our faces are as I look down at her.

"Flip the page. Let's read what Nick wrote," I tell her.

Poppy flips the page, taking a deep breath in sync with mine. We both read Nick's note in silence.

Dear Grand Canyon, thanks for bringing my brother back to me. This has been one of the best weekends of my life. And I can't wait to be back here soon. So thank you for making me feel like life's worries are nothing more than grains of sand in the wind. They come and go. Sincerely, Nick Armstrong. December 11th, 2016.

I read my brother's note a second time. My eyes linger on a certain collection of words. 'Life's worries are nothing more than grains of sand in the wind.' A part of me wishes I could get a deeper explanation on what he meant—or more so, what he was feeling on the inside the moment he wrote that note.

Poppy wipes her eyes a couple of times before turning to the next page. "Is this your dad's note?"

I look at where she's pointing to read his message:

As a father, I've never been more content than to see my sons smiling down here. It heals my heart. And my heart needs a lot of healing right now. But I'll get there because my boys are special.

This place is special. If you have children, bring them down here. It'll change you as much as it'll change them. Sincerely, Dr. Ryan Armstrong. Visiting from Phoenix, Arizona. December 11th, 2016.

I glance at Poppy after reading my dad's message.

"That's sweet," she whispers under her breath.

She looks up and our eyes lock again. I'm instantly tongue tied by the mix of pain and warmth in her smile. Then, the first thing out of my mouth surprises us both as I point to the green bow in her hair.

"I love your, uh, dipsey-doo-thingy."

We both laugh at the same time. It cuts the tension as her whole face lights up. She's flattered by my silly comment. After the day we've had, it melts my heart to bring her joy through a simple compliment.

"Still calling it a dipsey doo, eh?" She laughs again.

"This one's my favorite. I love the bow. The color also matches the hint of green in your eyes."

Her cheeks pinken. Our breaths hitch at the same time. She glances away for a moment—maybe to slow her racing heart or catch her breath. But if that's the case, it's nowhere close to the maniacal pounding in my chest.

I need her eyes back on mine so I lightly pull her chin back until our eyes are magnets.

"Can I tell you something, Zane?"

"Of course."

"Well, you know what's funny about the headbands—"

"Dipsey doos," I correct her

"Right, dipsey doos." She guffaws, her lips widening into an even brighter smile. "Well, what's funny is I brought more head—I mean dipsey doos on this trip than I did bottles of water. That's crazy, right? I just...had this weird premonition to bring a few of them. And I remember you complimenting it at your house. It was sweet. A little thing, but it was sweet."

"Can I tell you what I remember most about meeting you?"

I take her hand in mine, looking down as we interlace our fingers. Then she gives my hand a squeeze that sends my heart in a tailspin.

"Tell me," she whispers.

"I remember the way you protected Kitty. And I thought, this girl has some spunk. She's not afraid of a big guy like me trying to flirt. But when you smiled—like you're smiling at me right now...I was done for."

"Done for, huh?"

We lean in closer. All I see now are her lips. The pinkness. The warmth. The way they're begging to be tasted. I can even feel her chest, slowly pressing into my torso. Her heat melding to mine. Then I take control, tilting her chin up with my hand.

The second our lips touch, it's like falling back into that blissful rhythm. The give and take. The melding of our mouths. It's like time stops and nothing exists in this place but us. But it's more than just a kiss. It's letting go.

Ding! Ding! Ding!

The dinner bell has us both flinching backwards. I look over to see Sandy ringing a dinner bell that's the size of her head with reckless abandon.

"Attention! Attention!" she shouts. "Dinner will be out in 15 minutes. If you are eating dinner with the 5:30 group, we ask that you take a seat. If you're eating with the 7pm crew, we kindly ask that you step out and return at 6:50 so we can get you seated!"

Our eyes come back to one another at the same time. We both wipe our lips, flustered and a bit tickled by our untimely interruption.

"Shall we head back?" I ask, nodding to the exit.

"Actually, Lettie got dinner reserved for us at 5:30. She said we're on the list and that they'll meet us in here to eat with us."

"Really?" My voice squeaks.

Poppy nods. We're both still reeling from our kiss. I can see it in the way Poppy's face has this unbelievable glow. Then, it hits me. This isn't just dinner. It's something better.

I start laughing. It's unexplainable, the timing for this emotion. But it feels right. And for no other reason than being overjoyed with happiness.

"What's so funny, Zane?"

"Oh, the last time we had dinner with just you and I it was in a hospital cafeteria. And now here we are again. Just the two of us. But now we're in the most beautiful place on earth. May I?" I ask, giving her my hand.

Poppy hands me her crutches as I take her hand for balance. I guide her to the table and pull out the chair.

Once she's seated, I lean down to her forehead, planting a long kiss as I inhale the lavender and vanilla in her hair. Then I lean down to her ear to whisper.

"Welcome to our second dinner date."

CHAPTER 28

POPPY

I NEVER THOUGHT MY life was unique or interesting. I'm not an Olympic swimmer like Zane with looks that could put me on a billboard for Calvin Klein. Nor am I a park ranger working in the most beautiful place on earth like Lettie. And I'm not an ultramarathon runner like Chrissie. Yet, my story has these three people enthralled.

It's just weird to wake up each morning feeling ordinary and often saddened by life circumstances. Then one day you're eating a family-style dinner at the bottom of the Grand Canyon with 50 other visitors from all around the world. Not to mention people, complete strangers, that have been coming up to me to shake my hand and thank me.

I'm just not used to being the center of attention. And while I'm an open book with telling my story, it's funny how this one part of my story always grabs people's attention.

"Wait! You're adopted?" Lettie asks, leaning in closer from across the table.

"Did you ever meet your biological parents?" Chrissie chimes in, spooning a slice of pie into her mouth.

I hesitate for a moment, not knowing why this fact is the most interesting, given all the other things that Zane and I have shared tonight. But this isn't the first time I've faced this line of questions. It's just harder to answer knowing Nina's no longer here.

"No. Never really had an interest. I've only had my family. It's all I've known since I was like 4. It's all I can remember. I have no recollection of my biological parents. Plus, the adoption agency told me that I don't have any siblings and that my father was deceased before I was born."

A silence settles over our table. It brings a twinge of tightness in my throat—even as I take a deep swallow, the noose is still tightening.

"Would you ever consider looking down that path one day? You know, maybe if the time is right?" Zane asks.

"Of course, it just hasn't felt like a priority yet. I don't know if it ever will. But my sister, or my adopted sister, Nina, always wanted me to find my biological mom. In fact, one day she dreamt of her. The next thing I know, she's doing all sorts of research with Health and Human Services. She even found some different leads to where my biological mother may be living. For some reason it was always very important to her. And to be honest, it would be nice to be more in touch with my Mexican heritage, maybe learn her story, my family's history—stuff like that. But it's kind of scary, too. I mean, if I ever met her, I wouldn't know what to say...or do. I'd feel bad for her. And what mom would want anything resembling pity from their son or daughter? I mean, I'm not mad at her, but she did leave me at a fire station with only a birth certificate. No note. No reason why. Nothing else."

Their faces wilt. It's like everyone's taking a collective breath at the same time. I've experienced this sympathy many times before. But tonight, it feels different. Maybe it's because Zane is at my side, rubbing the top of my hand as it sits on my lap.

Eventually, the night wraps up because the next round of dinner is going to be served. Zane and I give each of the Ortega sisters a long hug, thanking them again for their hospitality and kindness. And while the one thing we didn't discuss was my Insta post during dinner, they both thank me again for making the video, saying how honored they are to meet me. Chrissie even reminds me again that I'm her hero.

All I can do is smile back at her. I don't know how to take her compliment, because I don't feel like a hero. And I still don't understand all that's happened with my video somehow going viral.

The walk back to the cabin takes a while because I'm still getting used to being on crutches. Luckily, I have Zane at my side, ready to catch me. It makes me feel like I'm learning to ride a bike and he's just prepping to catch me if I fall.

The closer we get, the more comfortable I get with the crutches. I'm also eager to see what it's like on the inside of our cabin. After I got my ankle wrapped in the park ranger's cabin, they let me shower and from there I went right to the Canteen to meet up with Zane. This'll be my first time seeing the inside.

The first thing I see walking in is a huge basket with a white ribbon. It's full of clothes, toiletries, fresh fruit, and snacks. There's even a sweet note.

It's such an honor to meet you guys and help you. This care basket was put together by multiple staff members, canyon volunteers, and even a few visitors. It's all on the house. When people found out that THE Poppy Rodriguez would be here this evening, they felt the need to do something. It's an honor to have both of you as our guests and be of help. "Fire the water!"

My hand slaps over my mouth. I can't believe they did this. The card has multiple signatures on it. I recognize Lettie and Chrissie's signatures, but the other 10 or so are names I don't recognize. It's people I don't know and may never meet.

"Fire the water," Zane's voice reads my brother's words over my shoulder.

"They're quoting Jet." I laugh to myself, not believing this can be real. "They don't even know those are his safe words. His way to comfort himself. It's just..." My throat locks up thinking about my brother. The breath of fresh air he gives my lungs by just saying those words.

How those words are always followed by him smiling or laughing or stimming around with his head on a swivel.

I take a quick wipe at my eyes to beat the first tear from spilling over. A deep breath later we're walking around the cabin. It's maybe a couple hundred square feet at the most, but it's got a cozy warmth to it. There's a tiny mahogany colored desk with a green lamp by the one window. A tiny fireplace sits next to it with logs already in there. There's even a mini fridge across from the twin-size bunk bed.

I run my hand along the white and blue comforters on the beds. The corners are tightly tucked in without a ruffle anywhere. There are even fresh white towels and linens folded on each bed.

It feels like we're at a hotel together. The only drawback is there are two beds when I only need one bed tonight.

"So, bottom or top?"

Zane's question has me smirking. Luckily, I'm looking away. For whatever reason, his question seems to be hanging out in the dirty part of my brain. It makes me want to go full Michael Scott on him and tell him, 'That's what she said.'

"Um, top, I mean, no. I like being on the bottom. Um, bunk that is," I stutter, clearing my throat.

He gives me a wry smile. "Suit yourself. Top bunk it is for me."

He climbs up the ladder, then weaves his body in between the ceiling fan and the bed to lie down. He looks like a giant sleeping on a bed the size of a coffee table.

The second he slithers in and goes fully supine, the entire bedframe comes crashing down.

The crash onto the bottom bunk is loud as I hear wood still splintering and cracking. Then an entire wood slat falls off the side and crashes to the ground with an echoing thud. We're both stunned in silence as dust particles float in the air all around us.

"Oh, fuck, Poppy!

His eyes are bugging out. I put my hand over my mouth as our eyes lock. Then, out of nowhere, we laugh hysterically—to the point where we're both doubling over in disbelief.

Zane's able to catch his breath first. "Oh fuck. I guess there's a weight limit."

"Ya think?" I tease, still giggling so hard my ribs hurt.

We're still laughing as we work together to pull the bed frame off of mine. He does most of the work because I'm still hobbling around.

His mattress ends up on the ground, perfectly parallel to my bed. Meanwhile, my bed is still intact on a frame that's a couple feet off the ground. It's not an ideal setup, but Zane reminds me that it's better than sleeping out in the below-freezing weather.

After brushing our teeth and changing into our jammies, we climb into our separate beds, wishing each other a good night. The second I shut my eyes, I realize it's a lost cause. There is no way I'm going to sleep right now. There's too much Zane on the mind.

The irony of it all is how our sleeping arrangement is just like the night I slept over at Zane's house. Thinking about how that night ended with a flashback dampers my spirits. But I try to remember how good it felt before the flashback—when I was able to touch him and bask in the way his hands lathered over my body. It was such a new experience because I didn't know if I was capable of letting a man touch me—let alone do it in such an intimate, loving way. But I remember how good it felt to just melt into him. To be free of scary thoughts. I was learning to live in the moment. And it was heaven for about ten minutes, until my PTSD heard the tearing sound.

My racing heart has me suddenly short of breath. I try to hone in on my breathing as I close my eyes to calm down. Deep inhales through the nose and long exhales through the mouth slowly bring me back.

"You sleepy?" Zane's voice cuts through the night with tender curiosity.

"Not at all, you?"

I hear a ruffling sound in his bed. Then his head peeks over my mattress. "Nope. I'm wide awake. What're you thinking about?"

"These women. They came up to me before dinner. They said there's a movement. All because of the video I posted."

"A movement?"

"Yeah, something like that. I, uh, I told them that I just needed to tell my story. Then one of them asked if I knew how many times my video had been shared. I told her I didn't want to know. Then each of them hugged me, thanked me again, and walked away in tears. But it wasn't just a hug, Zane. They...*held me*," I whisper, feeling suddenly out of breath as I recall the emotion in that lady's blue eyes. "And it didn't occur to me until now, but I'm afraid that I started something I don't have the strength to be a part of. I mean, I'd rather focus on Nina and Nick. And there's like this...beautiful distraction I never saw coming."

"Then let's just focus on them," Zane says, leaning in a hair closer to me. "How about tomorrow we release more of their ashes? Let's make it about them. I mean, that's the reason we're here, right?"

"Yeah, but I also feel like as scary as it is, I need to know what's really going on. Lettie told me her cabin has Wi-Fi and phone reception. I think I need to go there and get into my Insta account. But I don't want to do it alone."

Zane sits up taller, placing his elbows on the edge of my bed. Then he grabs hold of my hand. Our room may be pitch dark, but his face is close enough for me to see the beauty and empathy radiating in that face. And feeling his hand in mine helps me imagine the blue in his eyes—like the crystal blue waters of a Caribbean Ocean. The kind you can see right through to the very bottom. Those are the eyes that bring me peace and comfort.

"Tomorrow, we'll do it all together. Pour the ashes. Maybe give a eulogy if we're up to it. Then we can head to Lettie's cabin and watch your video. But one thing at a time. And Poppy, you have every right to be scared. But being scared is sometimes a good thing. Because when we work through the scary, we make it to the other end. That's how we find peace. Then it's onto the next scary thing in life—and finding more peace. Until eventually we become immune to the scary, because we find acceptance in it."

His words settle over me like a weighted blanket, soothing my soul to the core. The warmth and compassion in his words, the tenderness in his voice, becomes every fluttering feeling in my chest. All I want now is to jump back into his arms. I want to relive that night at his house, minus the flashback. But I don't know if I'm ready.

"Thanks, Zane."

"Goodnight, Poppy."

The second I feel him letting go of my hand, I squeeze back with a death grip.

"Wait." I gasp. "I can't sleep like this."

"Like what?"

The frog in my throat feels more like an elephant sitting on my chest. I want so badly to just tell him what I need. But my voice is rendered useless. My chest aches with a fire that is raging out of control.

I need him. And not just in the sense that I want to fuck his brains out. Make out for hours. Taste every square inch of his body. But more than anything, I want him to remind me of what it means to feel safe and free of nightmares. A place where I felt at home only one other time. His arms.

Please! Please! Read my mind!

Zane continues to stare at me in silence. I can't read his eyes because it's too dark. Then my heart skips a beat when he slides the comforter off his body. He scoots over to give room in his bed. *Room for me.*

I climb into his arms with my back against his chest. Then his arms envelop me—like a suction, he pulls me in.

His lips hover over my ear as he whispers. "You're safe. Always safe in my arms."

After a soft kiss to the back of my ear, he wishes me sweet dreams. My instinct may be to turn around and bury my lips into his. But the feeling of being spooned and held is too perfect to leave.

Exhaustion pulls me under, and I drift into a peaceful sleep. My last thought before everything fades is that if heaven exists, this is it. Safely at home in his arms. Worries drifting out of me like grains of sand in the wind. And I have Zane. I have his touch.

CHAPTER 29

zane

I GET TO THE last of my stream. It feels so good to pee outside even though it's freezing. There's something freeing about it that only guys would ever understand. Even watching the condensation from the heat of my urine float into the air is oddly cathartic.

Our room luckily has a sink, so after washing my hands and brushing my teeth, I slither under the covers to spoon Poppy.

"Ooohhh!" She squeaks the second my skin touches hers.

"Sorry, I was outside."

"I know, I saw you," she whispers, turning around to look at me. "I woke up a few minutes ago."

I take a deep swallow as she bites her lip, fighting back a grin. "Why were you peeing outside?"

"All three of the doors were occupied in the communal bathroom."

"Oh, ok. Must be nice to be a guy. Speaking of which, I need to use the little girls' room."

I snicker at her bathroom reference, feeling suddenly curious. How much of me did she see when I was peeing outside?

After helping Poppy out of bed, she insists on trying to move around on her own. It's hard to watch her limp around. However, she does look better. I also know with ankle injuries one of the worst things you can do is baby it. A little bit of movement to increase blood flow to the injured area can actually do more good than bad.

After Poppy brushes her teeth and gets dressed, we head out. The plan is to release the ashes before break-fast. I tell her there's a nice spot that's a little off the beaten path just north of the Canteen. It'll hopefully give us the privacy we need to say goodbye again.

When we get there, I feel a strong gust of wind in my face. It's just like I remembered. The memory of being here with my brother sends chills right through me. I can still see him sitting on that log bench, scraping bark off what would become his walking stick. Across from that is an old wrought iron bench with our secret red boulder still sitting underneath it. The bench sits right near the edge where there's a ten-foot drop in elevation that leads down to a creek of flowing water.

"This is nice," Poppy says, taking a seat with me on the wrought iron bench that sits under a towering Oak tree. "Been here before?"

"Nick found this spot. I'll show you something in a second. But should we pour the ashes out first."

Poppy nods.

We decided on the walk over here that I would go first. But now I don't know what to say as I twist off the top of the urn. The breeze picks up a little, which to me feels like a good sign. Nick wouldn't want these ashes in just one spot.

I tilt the urn. The ashes fall out like dust in the wind. It reminds me of what Nick wrote in the logbook ten years ago. I watch how his ashes flow away from me, but in different directions. Some of him will end up in the creek. And some will continuously explore the different parts of the canyon.

When the last bit of his ashes come out, Poppy's arm wraps around my waist. She pulls me tightly into her side, resting her head against my shoulder. Then she tilts her chin up to meet my eyes, flashing a smile—a smile that feels so extraordinary to the moment. It's a smile I've never seen, because it stretches higher up to those eyes, telling me so much of what she's feeling on the inside. And I feel it, too. She doesn't need to say a word because it's a living and breathing life force. This sense of pride—like she's proud of me—proud that I'm embracing my scary.

Her pride in me gives me the power to find my voice.

"Nick, I know this is where you want to be. And Nina's here with you. I'm sorry I was estranged from Mom and Dad for those couple of years. I thought about myself and never thought about how it affected you. But you need to know we're better now. We're talking. Mom has a new boyfriend. Dad finally told me how sorry he was for everything. And they both told me over and over again that they don't blame me for what happened to you guys. Apparently, they never blamed me. Even Poppy forgave me. And that makes me feel..." I pause to catch my breath. "Well, it's a freeing feeling. The best kind of feeling."

I stop to catch my breath right as a whipping gust ruffles my hair into my eyes. Poppy pulls me in tighter to her side. It's her way of telling me to keep going—to keep saying the things I need to say.

"Thank you for being my brother...My coach...My best friend...And thank you for always believing in me. You always saw me as more than just a swimmer. And most importantly, thank you for bringing Poppy back into my life. For talking me into coming to those Thanksgivings. It's like you and Nina found a way to bring us back together. And here we are in your favorite place. Together again." My heart aches as my voice begins to crumble. "I love you, Nick. And one day, I'll see you on the other side, with my ashes out here next to yours. I promise."

My vision clouds up. Poppy wraps her arms around me. The second she squeezes me, I fall apart. But it's more than just crying. It's heaves of pain falling out of me, all at once, like the weight of the world has been barricaded beneath my chest for far too long. But not anymore. This is the release of painful emotions I've held in since his death. It's pain and catharsis all in one. If not for this wonderful woman holding me, reassuring me, I don't know if I could handle the pain alone.

Poppy has the strength of three people in this hug. I can't explain it. I just feel it, living in the deepest parts of my soul, that Nina and Nick are truly here with us. *All of us. Together.*

It takes a while for the tears to flush out of me. But when I'm done, we both take a seat on the bench. I lay my head against her chest, feeling the soothing thuds of her heart as her fingers massage their way through my scalp. Each brush of her fingers is heavenly.

After a few minutes I sit up to dry my eyes.

"Thank you."

She smiles. "Always, Zane."

Her eyes go down to her urn. I watch as her fingers nervously strum along the lid.

"Are you ready?" I ask.

"No." She pauses for a moment, pursing her lips with a deep exhale. "I can't pour out all of it. I want to keep some of it."

Her hand is shaking, so I quickly grab hold of it. "Then don't. Pour out some of it. Pour out none of it. But say something. Talk to her while Nick is out here with her."

Poppy stands up, puffing her chest out with a deep inhale as I wrap my arm around her shoulder.

She looks straight out into the canyon as she speaks. "I get the feeling you saw us being here. Now here we are—on an adventure. And to be honest, I still don't feel brave, but I'm getting there." Poppy pauses to clear her throat, then lets out another deep breath. "It's funny how the rain brought us to Phantom Ranch. Well, that and a sprained ankle. It's like you planned that all along." I laugh at myself, realizing how odd these events are.

"I spoke about not knowing my biological mom last night. And even last night, it didn't seem like something worth pursuing. But for some reason, I feel different to-day—like maybe it's time to open that door and find her. You were always good at encouraging me but not pushing too hard. I loved that about you. Always so empathetic and loving. But I miss you, Nina. I think about you all the time. And I know it's a good thing to remember and miss you. But I'm hoping over time it won't hurt quite as much. But we'll see. For now, I give your ashes to this dirt so you can be down here with the love of your life. The man you told me you wanted to marry and make a hundred babies with." She quietly sniffles, laughing into her hand. "And I'll keep my promise to you. I'll be brave. I'll *always, always,* try my best to be brave...like you."

Poppy screws off the lid. We kneel down together. I rub my hand along her back as she pours a small amount of Nina's ashes into the dirt. My vision clouds the second she places her hands in the ashes, rubbing it into the soil as her tears drip into it.

After screwing the urn top back on, we stand up to-gether. I hand her some hand sanitizer and a bottle of water that she uses to pour over her hands. Then she wipes her eyes with the sleeve of her shirt and smiles at me.

"Should we head back?" I ask.

"No. Not yet. I love it here. Let's sit and watch the sunrise...*with them.*"

Those final two words send a chill up my spine. I put my arm around her. Together, with tears still brimming our eyes, we look up at the high canyon walls from the bottom of the Grand Canyon. It's not our home. Mother Nature was here first. But right now, it feels like she's making room for two more, because our Nick and Nina are home.

CHAPTER 30

zane

I SLIDE OFF MY gloves and begin feeling my way under the bench. The Sedona red, basketball-sized boulder is still here. But it's sunk its way further into the earth over the last ten years.

"Ah! Ah! I got it here." I grunt, finally pulling the boulder loose. Then I take my Swiss Army knife and delicately dig around the area. Luckily, there's enough moisture in the ground that I dig it out quite easily.

I take a seat next to Poppy. She pours water on my hands and the two treasures I just dug out. To my surprise, they're still in good condition, although now completely dull at the tip. One of them even has these speckles of white mixed in that I don't remember.

"What are those? Oh! Are those arrowheads?"

"Yep! Nick found them the last time we were here. He buried both of them here ten years ago. He called it a mini time capsule. He had the idea that each time we come back here, we can find it and maybe add to this spot if we found anything cool."

Poppy holds up the arrowheads in each hand. I put my arm around her and stare at them with her. The only sounds are the rushing water from the creek and a few birds singing their good morning tunes above our heads. The sun is just starting to bring its light upon the canyon. It's not fully peeking out, but it's painting the sky into a palette of lavender and orange that's majestic.

It's funny how she's enamored by these two arrowheads. Nick reacted the same way. I just can't believe how much they've changed in ten years.

I tell Poppy the story about finding them. We had just arrived at Phantom Ranch. Nick went off the main trail not too far from where we're sitting and found both of them lying next to an old ash tree. I didn't think much of it at the time, but Nick acted like he just found a buried treasure of gold. He couldn't believe there were two of them together.

"Should we put them back?" she asks, still rubbing her finger along the arrowheads.

"We could, but I think I'd like to keep one."

"Which one is yours?"

She hands me the arrowheads. They look nothing like the ones he found because now the ridges are more perforated. The sharp ends are almost completely dull. And the colors look way different than I remember. There are speckles of white on one, and the other has hints of purple and orange that remind me of a faraway planet.

"I'm not sure, Poppy. We never really took ownership of one. Why don't you pick one?"

"Why me?

"Because I want you to keep one. I'll put the other one back where I found it—so it stays with Nick."

"I don't know, Zane."

"It's okay, really. I'm giving you mine for a reason. Nick will still get to keep one down here with him. Now which one do you like?"

Poppy sighs. Then she goes back to studying them both. She flips one of them over and instantly gasps. "Huh. Look! Look at the white on this one." She traces her finger along the white speckles as she speaks. "It's like the white dots were painted into the shape of a little..." She pauses, shaking her head in disbelief. "It's a lotus flower. Oh my! I can't believe it! It's beautiful!"

She brings it closer to her eyes, still marveling.

"Then it's yours," I say, smiling down at her.

Poppy smiles back at me. "You will not believe this," she tells me, sitting up tall while taking off her gloves.

The next thing I know, her jacket is off. Then her long sleeve shirt. She grabs the shoulder area of her T-shirt, hooking her fingers underneath to her bra strap.

"What're you doing?"

"Um, just a strip tease," she quips, looking around to make sure there's no one around. "Well, not quite. But I want to show you something."

Poppy slides the corner of her shirt and bra strap a couple of inches down her shoulder until I see it. Three inches below her collarbone, at the crest of her left breast, sits a tiny tattoo directly over her heart.

"It's a lotus flower," she says, tracing her finger along the blossoms. "And behind it is a rising sun."

I don't know flowers. In fact, the only one I'd ever recognize is a rose. But the intricacy of the blossoms in her tattoo and how they're opening up to a sunrise is a sight to see. I look back at the arrowhead and notice how the speckles of white look almost exactly like the lotus flower on her chest.

"Why a lotus tattoo?" I ask.

"It's a symbol for rebirth."

"Rebirth?"

"Yeah. The lotus is the most resilient flower there is. It can grow in the muddiest, murkiest, sewage-looking waters. But it finds a way to blossom with each new day. It was Nina's favorite flower for that reason. It's why she also had it tattooed on her chest. About a week after she died, I got the same tattoo, but I wanted a sun in the background because it reminded me of her. I just love this tattoo. The blossoms. The sun rising behind it. I don't know if Nina's more the sun or more the lotus. But this is my homage to her."

Poppy closes her eyes, putting her hand over her heart with the arrowhead still in her grasp. The smile she's wearing is full of happiness. It's like the arrowhead and the tattoo are a vessel. A vessel to only the most perfect memories of Nina.

It's hard to not envy the feelings and emotions she's radiating in this moment. My memories of Nick usually make me feel dead inside. But not always. Sometimes, they can be good like this. But it's rare. I guess this is just the roller coaster of living through grief. It's nothing but highs and lows. And I know Poppy doesn't always feel this way, but seeing her like *this*, being able to bask in a perfect memory, heals my heart.

She's like a statue for the next couple of minutes, smiling with her eyes shut and her hand over her heart.

After a while, she lets go of the memory. She puts her clothes back on and rests her head on my shoulder. Her arms coil around my torso and I'm content.

Then it happens. The memory hits right as the sun creeps over the horizon. Goosebumps percolate right through me as I remember Nick's words.

"Do you know the symbolism behind the arrowhead?" I ask.

"I don't."

"Nick told me it symbolizes protection and strength."

I let my eyes linger on her. Her eyes sharpen into mine with wonderment. That's when I know without a shadow of a doubt. It's time. Now is the time for her to know the true depths of my feelings for her—because her pride in me will never match how proud I am of her.

Never!

My voice is already crumbling as I speak. "You know, when I saw your video about the guy that hurt you...Jonathan. All I could think about was how hard I would hit that guy. How, if I ever saw him, I'd pulverize his skull. I wanted to kill him for what he did. But then that thought completely went away. It went away because I realized how incredibly strong you are. How brave you are. How I respect the fuck out of you for standing up...and for just being, WHO...YOU...ARE!"

My voice gives out, wavering in a storm of emotion as I remember watching her video for the first time. The pain I felt for her was all consuming, raging like a wildfire that had to burn through the world, leaving only its scorched path behind.

Poppy's eyes slowly come up to mine. Our faces hover inches apart as I feel it. A gentle hand pressing over my chest, her other hand cradling my cheek. Like the arrowhead and the lotus, she's protecting me. Her touch gives me the air I need. The strength to find my words—words that feel like the culmination of everything I've ever wanted to tell her.

"Poppy, since the first day I saw you, I've been obsessed. All I want is you. *Every...fucking...second!* And you should know, Chrissie was right. You are a hero! You just don't know it yet. But you will. And you're right. You need to know what's really going on in the world—because of *you.* You did more than just tell your story. You started a movement. You are every bit the lotus on your chest and the arrowhead in your hand. And whether you want to believe it or not, you've inspired a generation."

"But I didn't ask for this, Zane. I made that video on a fucking whim of inspiration. I'm not built to handle this type of attention. Don't you get it. I'm forever scarred. Jonathan stole a piece of me I'll never get back. And without Nina in my life, it feels impossible to ever be normal again."

"Who says we have to be normal? Or healed? You're allowed to hurt. I'm allowed to hurt. That!" I raise my voice higher, trying to catch my breath. "*That*, is normal. What's not normal is everything that brought us here. I mean, think about it. Nick finding Nina. My dog finding you in a crowd of people. The visions your sister had as a kid. Her last words. These symbols. People coming up to you, strangers, who are survivors like you. In the bottom of the fucking Grand Canyon. This isn't fate, Poppy. This is bigger than that. And you need to know. You have to know...that I'm fucking in love with you!"

Her mouth is on mine. The pressure in our kiss is manic with desire. My lips try to match her strength. Her need. But it's all consuming, she's overwhelming me, and I'm fucking here for it!

I grab hold of her cheeks to take control. We open our mouths as our tongues intertwine. Everything slows as our kiss goes deeper. The need for more is never ending. It's a bliss-filled cycle that's every perfect dream we could ever fathom.

This kiss is everything I've ever felt for this woman—living and breathing with those luscious lips. Yet, it feels like something more. It's more than years of pent-up desire. More than hormone-infused adrenaline. It's satisfying our most innate need. The need for intimate touch that no longer feels stolen from her. Because now she's mine. And I'm irrevocably all hers.

We break apart. Her head falls into my chest while we're both panting and out of breath. When her eyes come up to mine, I'm speechless by so many things. Her beauty. Her smile. The glossy reflection in her eyes. But the part that leaves me speechless is the way she makes me feel whole on the inside.

We stare at one another as time stands still. Then Poppy says the thing I least expected. But she doesn't just say it. She begs for it.

"I want you inside of me. Make love to me...*please*."

CHAPTER 31

POPPY

HE'S YET TO RESPOND. It may have only been ten seconds since I asked him to have sex with me, but he's still a deer in headlights. Meanwhile, I'm lost in the sea, deeply entranced by his ocean blue eyes.

"Um, are you sure?" he finally whispers, tucking a few loose hairs behind my ear.

Am I sure?

"Y-yes."

"You hesitated."

"Because I, I—"

"Then we'll wait until you know for sure. There's no pressure. No rush."

Zane smiles at me while running his soothing hands up and down my arms. It feels so good, but I'm disappointed. It's not the response I wanted. He was supposed to carry me back and make love to me for hours on end in our cabin.

Being intimate with him is everything I want right now. *Everything!* I can't help it. I trust the goodness that is the very core of Zane Armstrong. And I want him! I need him! *Desperately!*

The only thing I don't trust is my brain. The horrid flashbacks that always come back uninvited. How being with him could be the best moment of my life, only for it to become the worst moment in the blink of an eye. But with the way he's looking at me right now, I know he'd support me no matter how terrible or great the lovemaking experience would be.

Is it worth risking? I don't know.

I let out a nervous giggle. It helps break a little of the tension rumbling in my tummy. "I can't believe what I just said."

I drop my chin into my chest. Embarrassment warms my cheeks. Then the fiery warmth in his hand quickly tilts my chin back up. All I see are his eyes fully absorbed on mine.

"What you said, is the hottest thing I've ever heard. I like what you asked for," he assures me, his voice oozing with confidence.

The deeper I get lost in his eyes, the more I can see it. He yearns for me just like I'm yearning for him. But I also feel like he's unsure about initiating.

But can I initiate?

I open my hand to take one more look at the lotus. It feels impossible that the lotus symbol has somehow imprinted itself onto this arrowhead that Nick found. But like the symbol of rebirth and the symbol of protection, it's here with me. Ever-changing with time. Evolving with the very soil it lives in. But more than anything, it's healing. It heals me in a way that makes me want to initiate—to take back the power that was stolen through innocence, and no fault of my own. To do what I *want!* What I *need!*

Fuck it!

I yank him down by his shirt collar, plunging into his lips. Then I pull back, still hanging onto him.

"Fuck it! Carry me back to the cabin. I want you inside of me. Right the fuck now!"

Before he can respond, I pull him back for a longer, more passionate kiss. Then he pulls out of it, scooping me into his arms. He leans down for a quick moment so I can grab both urns. Then we're off.

There's a pep in his step as he carries me all the way back to the cabin with ease. After opening the door, he kicks it shut and softly lays me on the bed.

I kick my shoes off. The second I hook my thumbs under my jeans, I'm quickly reprimanded.

"No!" He raises his voice while grabbing hold of my wrist. "I'll do it. Let me take your clothes off."

I nod. The confidence in his tone has me breathless. Not to mention the lower half of me is pooling in volcanic heat. I sit up as he comes around me to lean his chest into my back. Then he slowly undresses me—layer by layer while trailing soft kisses along my neck. It's not urgent or rushed. It's sensual and delicate, like he knows exactly what I need.

When I'm exposed in just my bra and panties, I turn around to him. "My turn."

I come around to his back while he sits at the foot of the bed. My breasts lean into him while my nose marinates along his neck. My light kisses along his neck include little nibbles and flicks of my tongue. He tastes like dessert as I rub my hands along his bare chest. I work my hands lower as he moans deeper into each taste along his neck.

Then he swings his body around. Our lips fall into each other while I undo his belt and frantically slide his pants down. One click later, my bra is off. Then my panties. I don't have time to slide his boxers off because his body overtakes mine. I'm on my back as we kiss and grind, leaving no part of our bodies unexplored.

I can't think. My mind is swimming in unabated pleasure and ecstasy. His lips begin working their way down. One slow, sensual kiss at a time until his head is between my legs.

I grab hold of his head, lightly massaging my fingers through his hair. My nails dig lightly into his scalp as he teases me with kisses that get closer and closer to my opening. I feel so exposed as his eyes look up from my pussy. But these eyes are unlike the ocean blue I'm used to. No, these eyes have a fiery intensity. A hunger that's dying to taste my center. And I want it so bad I'll beg for it.

"Please! Please!" I cry out.

Then my vision goes black. My head arches back as my clit goes into his mouth. His finger barely slides into my opening while his tongue lightly swirls around my clit.

It's an out-of-body experience. This unfathomable, overwhelming pleasure. The kind I can bask in, live in, and never forget for as long as I live.

I look down at him, seeing and hearing how wet I am. My arousal is overflowing with the way he's teasing his tongue along my slit. And I want more, so I pull him in, arching my hips into his mouth for more mind-bending pressure on my clit.

Then his finger goes deeper inside, curling up as I feel my clit swelling over his tongue. The pressure inside me quickly builds to the brink. There's no turning back. My legs shake. My hands dig into his scalp. I scream out.

"Don't stop! Don't stop!"

I push him off because it's too much. The orgasm pulses out of me as I roll onto my side, shaking all over. The shivers run through me, jolting me with wave after wave of pleasure. The orgasm keeps going as I scream out with moan after moan.

I'm still shaking intermittently as he comes up to spoon me from behind. The pressure as he pulls me in helps me drift deeper into what's left of the orgasm.

"Oh my," I pant, still unable to catch my breath or control my body.

Then his lips hover over my ear, leaving light kisses as he whispers. "You taste amazing. I could do that all day. Watching you cum like that was unreal."

I swing around to find his lips, tasting my pussy off his mouth. Then I pull back. "I want more."

"More?"

He watches intently as I climb off the bed. I lean down to grab his pants and dig out his wallet.

"What're you doing?" he asks.

When I find it, relief washes over me. I look at him as my throat opens up. *I have my voice. I have control* of this moment—a confidence in what I want, and more importantly, what I need. *I need him.*

"This," I seductively whisper, holding up a condom wrapper. His smirk gets wider as I crawl on my hands and knees to his engorged cock, tenting underneath his boxers. I stop with my lips a couple inches from his to whisper again. "I want you inside of me. Make love to me."

Zane puts his hand on my chest. He leans back a little before speaking. "Just wait."

"I don't want to wait. I want you now," I beg.

"I know, but can we talk about it first?"

I lean back and sit up with my arms crossing over my breasts. There's concern in his eyes and a tenseness I can see by the muscles straining in his neck.

"What is it?"

Zane's cheeks puff like a blowfish as he blows out a long exhale. Then he grabs my hand.

"I've read a couple of books."

"Books?"

I'm so confused.

"Yeah. I just thought if I ever had sex with you, I should do some research on how to ease into it and make you feel comfortable. Make you feel safe."

My mouth opens, but I'm too shocked for words.

"Um, so, is it okay I did that?" he whispers with a tentative tone.

I'm still too shocked for words. All I can muster is a slow head nod up and down.

"Okay, then. Is there anything I can do to make this more comfortable for you?"

It's a question I never saw coming. But it's also the sweetest, most thoughtful thing I've heard in my life.

"So, let me get this right, Zane. You bought books and read them. So that I'd be comfortable...if we ever had sex."

His Adam's apple goes inward. "It's just that um, the last time we almost did it, you, uh, you—"

"I had a flashback," I finish his words with a confident tone. Then I try to reassure him. "But things are different now. I know you. I want this. I want you," I beg, gliding my hands along the erection outlining his boxers. "But, uh, since you're asking. I'd like to have control when we start. Maybe I can be on top."

Zane nods. "We can do that. What else?"

"Maybe just be patient with me. It's been a long time since I've had sex. And it..." I pause, looking at how girthy he is as I stroke my way up to the tip of his cock. "Well, uh, maybe just check in with me a lot. See how I'm doing. It might hurt a little."

Zane scoots closer to me. He cradles my cheeks in both hands as he leans his mouth into mine. The kiss is slow but deep with pressure. Then he slowly pulls back and seductively whispers into my lips. "Of course, Poppy. On top. Take it slow. And check in. Just remember you're safe. *Always* safe with me."

I've never felt more instantly horny. I'm practically orgasming to all the things he's just told me. His level of sensitivity and caring has overwhelmed me with desire.

My hands forcefully push him down until he's flat on his back. I pull his boxers down and get ready to straddle him. But I can't do it just yet. The way his cock stands tall with precum already beading out the top has me suddenly hungry for a taste.

There's no hesitation. I position myself between his legs. He needs to see my eyes before I taste him. Then, with those oceanic eyes begging to be sucked, my tongue glides up slowly from the base up to his tip. Then my mouth inhales the tip of his cock. The salty taste of his seed and the sound of his moan has me in heaven.

His hands dig lightly into my hair. The soft moans grow louder as I swallow him deeper. The smell and taste of him has me overwhelmed with pleasure.

Then I begin stroking with my hand while using my mouth over the tip. His moans get louder and louder until he pulls his girth out of my mouth, leaving me drooling.

"No more. I'm ready."

I frantically rip the condom wrapper open with my teeth. I glide it tightly over him and quickly straddle over his hips. His hands guide my hips down as I reach back to guide him inside me.

The second he sinks inside, I pull up a bit.

"You okay?" he asks, palming his hands over my cheeks.

"Yes, I just have to go in slowly. Really, slowly."

I reach back to grab hold of his cock and slowly guide it back in. The feeling of being stretched while fully lubricated in wetness and warmth is unreal. Further and further I sink into him. Then I gasp when he's fully inside me.

"Oh my god!"

"You okay?" he asks again.

"Yesss!" I say, slowly riding into him.

My hands window wash over his chest and shoulders. My body begins to let go. I drive deeper and deeper. Each time it's pain and pleasure mixed together. But pleasure is winning. My inside is opening up, melding perfectly over his cock.

I could die a happy woman with how good it feels. And just seeing the pleasure in his eyes has my heart fluttering in ecstasy.

"Oh my God! Don't stop!" I scream, leaning my chest into his.

Our arms wrap around each other as I feel the sensitivity in my clit come to life. It overwhelms me as I ride deeper, finding new spots of pleasure. It feels so good to be in control. To know the angle and pressure I need over my clit. It's all consuming and overwhelming me with pleasure until I scream out.

My legs and hips are no longer mine. I'm living outside myself in a place of rapture I never knew existed. I'm shaking uncontrollably as I keep screaming and scream-ing the orgasm out of me.

I roll off of him, still shaking in pleasure. Then I feel his weight come on top of me. My legs spread wide to invite him back in. The orgasm is still living inside of me, but I'm already hungry for more.

"Is this okay?" he asks.

"Yes."

I hone in on his eyes as he waits to push inside of me. The anticipation grows. His smile is all pleasure as he slowly leans down for a long kiss that steals my breath. Then his lips glide up my face, lightly caressing along my skin until he plants an endless number of forehead kisses.

Then his lips glide across my forehead and down to my ear as he whispers. "You're still safe, Poppy."

"I know."

"You're loved, Poppy."

"I know."

"But do you really know?"

Zane leans his head back. I hold his cheeks in my hands as we kiss some more. Then I nod my head, unsure of what he's really asking. My voice is gone. All I have is his full smile warming over me. His eyes serenading mine while my heart is fluttering with anticipation.

"Poppy, I love you so much. Always have. And I don't take this moment for granted. You are my...*everything*."

We kiss, falling into the perfect rhythm of light tongue and sensual tasting. Then I feel his girth slowly push inside me. When he can't go any further, he pulls back, doing light thrusts as my pussy slowly opens back up for him. He keeps going a little further until he fully slides inside me, filling me whole.

The pressure has me gasping again.

"You okay?"

I nod, unable to speak for a moment. Then he starts pulling out, until my hands slap down on his rock-hard glutes. I dig my nails in like a pair of talons, not letting him leave.

"I'm good. I'm good. Just go slowly. And please don't stop," I beg.

Everything that follows is how I would've dreamt it, but somehow better. The way his eyes meld into mine, manic with desire. The panting breaths. The neck kisses. Endless head kisses. The whispers in my ear, telling me how much he loves me. How he's the luckiest man on earth to be in between my legs.

The communication doesn't stop. He asks what feels good. If something hurts. What I like. How my clit needs to be touched.

"Like this," I tell him, guiding his fingers down to my clit.

There's an intentionality in how he wants to bring me pleasure. Even with the way he thrusts into me. The different pressures and angles along my clit have my head spinning. It's like he's finding new spots inside me that take me to new worlds of ecstasy.

The longer we go, the wetter I get. The warmer I feel all over. Then we both get louder. But not just our moans. It's the sound my pussy makes, lubricating over his cock with each thrust.

Then a wave of warmth floods through me. All at once I'm a tidal wave reaching the apex—to a point of no return I come apart. Pussy throbbing. Hips and legs spasming. White dots in my vision. Carnal screams of pleasure.

He cums right along with me. Our arms squeeze tighter and tighter into a perfect embrace. All while I imagine his seed filling my insides.

The orgasm keeps pulsing through me, even after he rolls off me. I don't want it to end. But I know it will be the first of many.

Zane eventually swallows me back into his arms. I'm left with the rhythm of his heart as I lie on his chest.

My mind begins to ruminate. I don't want to ever forget this moment. Zane holding me as I fall asleep. The feeling of post-orgasmic bliss. And falling deeper in love with him.

What we shared was more than just sex. It was more than just allowing him inside my body. It was a release. An unleashing of chains. A way of finding my newer, better self. A freeing of my soul. And a way of taking back a part of me that was once stolen. It was just as he perfectly, and so eloquently put it.

It was *everything!*

CHAPTER 32

POPPY

ALL I HAVE IS the ground level view, like I'm lying flat on my back. Nothing else. It's just my eyes staring up into a pristine, crystal blue sky. There's cheering going on all around me. I can hear it. I can't see it, but I feel the energy. It lives in each goosebump, electrifying its way through my body.

I wish I knew who was here. Why are they here? What are they chanting? But it's just me and the sky, until I see it. The water cascading up into the air. It flows up and up until gravity lets it rain back down. The mist coats my body, leaving an invigorating chill. I let it soak me because it feels cleansing. Fortifying. Life-altering.

Then I see remnants of something else. A rainbow, perhaps. I'm unsure at first. Then it slowly becomes clearer until it becomes a part of the sky. The sequence of hues living in the mist has me awestruck and wondering—is there a beauty more transcendent than this rainbow?

The mist gives way to a fog flowing upward. The fog becomes thicker, darker, until it feels more like smoke. Then I see the orange embers popping their way through the air like little orange lightning bugs competing with the mist.

The smoke thickens into a darker grey, but the mist persists. I'm not hot. I'm not cold. Instead, there's this high of adrenaline flowing through my veins. It's as if the smoke and water are coalescing with my body, making me feel whole.

A flash of light blinds me. I suddenly can't see a thing, but I hear it. So many different sounds at once. The cheering gets louder until all I hear is a celebration going manic with energy. But the energy now lives inside me, right where I want it to be. It makes me so happy I could cry, and I don't even know why.

Then the chanting suddenly stops. Quicker than a blink of an eye, I'm living in a dark, foreboding world of silence. The kind that's uncomfortably quiet, until I hear her whisper in my ear.

"See the movement. Be the movement. Fire the water."

I open my eyes up to the logs in the ceiling. Zane rolls over, wrapping his arm across my bare chest. He nuzzles his face deep into my neck. Then he hooks his leg around my hips to pull me even closer.

He's still asleep as my sense of reality comes back. It's the morning after the most mind-altering night of sex. We're still completely naked. I want to obsess over everything that happened last night—maybe play it all back in my mind a thousand times. Then I could straddle him and let it all happen again this morning. But right now, I know I can't.

The dream was more than a dream. It felt like a message. A message I can no longer ignore because it's time.

It only takes a few minutes to slither out of bed, get dressed, and brush my teeth. Then my body becomes a statue at the doorway. I need to leave, but I also need to drink in the way this man looks.

Zane is only wearing a thin white sheet around his hips and upper thighs. I can see the outline of his morning wood underneath it. I also love how the sheet sits extra low on his hips, highlighting the "v" in his rock-hard abs. Every bit of this man has me salivating. But he's more than just an insanely beautiful, kind man. He was all mine last night. And he'll be all mine when I get back.

I round the corner of our cabin and almost careen into Lettie from walking so fast.

"Oh, sorry."

"It's okay. How did you guys sleep?"

My cheeks flush. "Um, great. Thanks." I clear my throat, praying my cheeks aren't as red as strawberries. "I was just heading to your cabin actually. I need a Wi-Fi connection. Do you mind?"

"Not at all. Here, it's all yours," she says, handing over a key. "The Wi-Fi code is 'that's what she said,' but no apostrophe. And yes, I'm a big fan of *The Office*."

I giggle, wanting to start a conversation about my favorite TV show. But I don't have time for small talk.

"Thanks."

After a wave, I walk past her only for her to call out to me right away.

"Oh, and Poppy! We'll get that bed of yours fixed. I saw you guys broke it," she says, biting back a laugh.

My throat locks up as her smirk widens.

"Oh, um, about that. It's not what you—"

"I know. I know. Sorry, that's none of my business. It's just, you two are the cutest couple I've ever met. If you're a couple...that is."

I smile at her, not knowing what to say but liking the sound of that.

"Well, have a good time in the ranger cabin. I won't be back for a couple of hours so make yourself at home in there."

"Thanks."

Once I walk inside, I take a seat at the desk because it's the closest thing to the door. There's a tight pressure in my chest as I turn my phone on.

The request for my passcode pops up on my screen. Then the anxiety rolls through me like the shock of a cold plunge into an artic river. My hands start to tremble. My breathing speeds up. Everything I'm feeling is over-whelmingly fearful.

My phone slips from my grasp. The echoing thud leaves my mind paralyzed. Confounding thoughts begin to take me over. The biggest being the people—all of the strangers that have approached me in the last cou-ple of days. The things they've said when it comes to connecting with my story and how it inspired them. I've been called brave. I've been called a hero. But the most touching sentiment is how people want to hug me.

Strange people want to give me affection. Each time it's happened, I've felt touched by the sentiment, but I don't think it's truly been able to touch me until now.

That's when I realize it—none of these people were ever strangers. They're my peers. Victims like me. Survivors like me. *They are like me.*

"Like me," I whisper to myself, closing my eyes.

They lost the power like me. Now, we're all trying to get it back in our own way. *That,* is why I'm here. That's why I posted the video. I'm here for them. And for myself.

After retrieving my phone, I type in my passcode. Then I connect to the Wi-Fi. The second it shows me connected is when I realize the full force of what's going on.

Each beep from my phone is a notification. It's not a surprise, given my prolonged absence from my Insta account. I was expecting this. What I wasn't expecting is for the beeps to be endless—or how each sound sends a sharp tingle of adrenaline through my body.

The next hour is nothing but tears—from tears of joy to tears of sadness. But more than anything, it's tears of hope.

There are too many videos to watch. In just a couple of days, there have been over 200 million views of my video. I thought I deleted it, but apparently I never did.

It also blew up when Lonny shared the video to her large following. She did it with the hashtags: fire the water and I choose fire. Those words, my words, are a part of every single video I watch. Little do people know how those words share a deep connection to Jet. Instead, these survivors are using his words as a part of a movement. A movement I accidentally started.

Most videos don't have the victims setting fire to a picture of their perpetrator. For some it's setting fire to an article of clothing or something that was symbolic to the night they were assaulted. And most don't set fire to anything. Instead, they do what's most important, they tell their story.

My biggest fear when finding out my video went viral was retribution. Not just from Jonathan. But I thought if others called out their accuser in the way I did, it would create a chain reaction of retaliation and put victims more at risk. I only set fire to the picture of Jonathan because in the moment it felt like the right thing to do. And I don't regret it, especially with so many people getting their stories out of them.

Of all the videos, there's one that stands out the most. It has over half a million shares and over 8 million views. I watch it again because I can't believe it.

"This coward no longer holds any power over me," the woman confidently asserts, holding up the picture with her head held high. "This is a serial sexual as-saulter—check that—was. His name is Jackson Reagan. I was victim number three. There could've been more. But my testimony stood in court. I got lucky. And now he'll be gone for a long time. I set fire to this picture for the two girls before me that were not believed. I also do it for Poppy Rodriguez. The girl whose Fire the Water movement is changing the world." Her voice fades into whimpering and tears. "It's why I stand united with all the victims. Especially those that were never believed. Or heard. Or had the chance to be heard. It's why...with every ounce of my will...every thread of my being...*I choose fire.*"

The lighter clicks. The picture crinkles up as the flame engulfs it. The young woman then drops the picture in a metal trash bin. She watches it burn while the fire's light dances against her brown eyes. Then her eyes square off with the camera, like she's looking directly into my soul—sitting across from me— speaking to me.

"I'm Janelle Morse. I'm a survivor of sexual assault. And today I fire the water. I choose fire. I win."

The tears roll down her cheeks as the video keeps going. Her eyes look up, she blows three kisses, then flashes the brightest, tear-filled smile I've ever seen. To say she looks relieved doesn't do it justice. There's something more in that smile. She's at peace.

I spend another hour scrolling through comments and watching other videos. It's amazing to see how it's not just women participating. There are men making videos. People of all ages, all backgrounds, ethnicities, and people from all over the world. And every single video ends the same way. People are taking the power back. All from telling their story and encouraging others to believe.

Eventually, the emotions of everything have me completely exhausted. All I want is to just hug every single person and tell them how proud I am. But there are too many people, which makes me feel inspired, but also sad.

After using the restroom, I wash my hands and splash some cold water on my face. Then I take a moment to dry my face in the mirror. I lean in close to take in the pink rings around my eyes.

Then my body spasms to the sound of my phone ringing, scaring the living shit out of me.

"Hello."

"Poppy? Poppy? Is that you? You fucking cunt bitch!"

Like a flash of blinding light, I'm there again. Panicked. Trembling. Terrified. Paralyzed.

He keeps screaming obscenities, but I can't hear anything. All I feel is my heart sinking into the void—my phone falling from my hand. I look at my hands, shaking uncontrollably. I'm completely paralyzed by the fear of *this* voice. The one voice I never wanted to hear for as long as I live.

It's Jonathan.

CHAPTER 33

zane

THE SECOND I CRACK the door open, I notice her phone on the ground in three pieces. I swing the door open in a panic, and my heart drops. She's crying in the corner in the fetal position.

"You okay?!" I beg, quickly huddling at her side.

She shakes her head, looking dazed and comatose.

"What happened?"

When I don't get an answer, I slowly peel her hands off her face. Her eyes and cheeks are pinkened and wet.

"Are you hurt?"

Poppy just shakes her head, still refusing to speak, refusing to look me in the eye. All I know is what Lettie had told me a moment ago. She came in here to get a Wi-Fi connection on her phone. But now her phone is in pieces.

"Did you see the reaction from your video?"

She gives me a gentle nod up and down, but still no words. I lean down to look deeper into her eyes, noticing more than just the pinkened rings. There's this desolate look in her eyes, like she's lost in a blinding fog with no way out.

Tears begin to trickle out. Her lips tremble. She's whispering words under her breath. But I can't hear what she's saying.

I take a deep breath and sit shoulder to shoulder with her. She quickly grabs my hand, cradling it in her lap. Then both of her hands become entangled in mine.

Her affection means the world to me. To show how much I love it, I begin tickling my fingertips along the back of her hand. Then her chin slowly tips up until our eyes lock. A smile barely cracks through those lips, but then it's gone in a split second. I drink in her eyes because they're the perfect shade of honey brown with that subtle hint of green. The residual tears give them an emphatic shine that's breathtaking.

I could look at her all day, even in moments like these with extreme despair. The problem is I don't know what to say. She's overwhelmed. I know I'd be with such a personal video going out to the world. But on a grander level, I can't relate to how she's *truly* feeling.

I've never been sexually assaulted. I've never been drugged. I never woke up feeling violated. Poppy's scars run deep. Emotionally. Physically. Sexually. I've never known any of it, and I hope I never will.

All I can give to her is my love. The kind she needs. The one that lives and breathes in patience and empathy.

And right now, she needs me to sit here while we hang on together, for as long as it takes.

The minutes pass. Our hands become clammy, but I don't let go of her for a second. I've traced my fingers along the smoothness of her skin so many times I've memorized every mark, mole, and ridge. We're still at an impasse with talking. She hasn't even told me why her phone lies in three pieces on the floor. But I'm at least thankful her breathing has slowed down.

"I had a dream last night."

Her words cut through the dead of silence. The most shocking part is not what she said. It was the profound calm in her voice.

"Good or bad?" I ask.

She huffs out a loud breath. "I don't know. I think good. It was very, very..." She pauses, squinting her eyes as she shakes her head. "Beautiful. Yeah, it was so beautiful."

I lean in closer to her face as she looks up to me. "What do you mean, Poppy?"

"All I could see was the sky. A perfectly pristine, aqua blue sky. I couldn't see anyone, but I heard so many people. They were all around me. Then the water shot up in the sky, and it rained down on me. It felt so good. The chill on my skin. I even heard chanting and cheering. It was like my sister's vision, in a way. But then there was smoke rising, fighting against the onslaught of water. But I wasn't scared. I wasn't hot at all. If anything, I felt at peace."

I'm left in awe at her dream. It's a dream that makes no sense. But it feels important, given how parts of this dream have a connection with her sister.

"I don't know what to do, Zane," she says, looking away.

I take a contentious, deep swallow before speaking. "Maybe you don't have to do anything. I mean, you've done enough already. What's left to prove?"

"No! No, goddamnit! I didn't do enough. Not nearly enough!" She raises her voice in contempt, shaking her head.

"What're you talking about? You told your story and challenged others to do the same. Millions of people are being heard. Being believed. You chose fire and—"

"I burnt a fucking picture of an asshole! That's it, Zane!" Poppy screams, her teeth gritting with tension while her whole body shakes. "It did nothing. NOTH...ING! You don't get it. That piece of shit just called me."

"What?! Who?"

"Jonathan. The man who drugged me and raped me. He threatened me with a defamation lawsuit. Says he was already fired from his job. Then he said...he said..."

Poppy can't finish. Her eyes are bugging out, staring away like she's fallen back into the nightmare. Then I feel my hand cracking in her grasp, like she's desperately hanging on for dear life.

"What else did he say?" I coarsely demand.

Her voice trembles, pausing between words. "He said...I got...what I... d-d-deserved. Then he called me a pathetic bitch. And I, uh, I, uh, didn't know what to say. I couldn't speak." Poppy pauses to let out a loud, quivering breath. Then she takes a deep swallow, finding the willpower between panicked breaths. "I would've never answered if I knew it was him. Oh, Zane! I can't! I can't!"

Poppy falls into my arms, sobbing uncontrollably. I squeeze around every part of her, making her absorb every bit of my touch. It only makes her scream louder. Cry harder. The pain continues to pour out of her. Everything that hurts inside of her has been opened back up. It's suffering that makes me not want to live—because her pain is every bit my pain.

I've never felt more hopeless. Maybe it's because all of my empathy and sadness for Poppy is slowly evolving into rage. There's this dire need to inflict violence—do anything for revenge. But is that a means to an end? I've been down that road before.

Fuck it!

All I know is this fucker will suffer. One way or the other, I'll find a way to get retribution. There's no other option.

Poppy cries on my shoulder for the next hour. It's so taxing she eventually falls asleep in my arms. When I'm sure she's out like a light, I carry her to the open couch and lay her down. I cover her with a throw blanket, dry her tears, and kiss her forehead.

The whole time she was crying, I was planning. It's not fully fledged. What I'm thinking right now cannot be done without help. A *lot of help.*

I quietly step outside to make a couple of phone calls. Each of them is successful. Then Lettie stops by, and I chat with her about supplies. She tries to talk me out of it at first, but when I tell her my grander plan, she's quickly on board.

"Anything for Poppy," she tells me with tears brimming her eyes after we share a long hug.

The way I see it, I have about 36 hours to get this done. It's the right thing to do, and the only thing to do. I will help finish what Poppy started.

CHAPTER 34

POPPY

I WAKE UP RIGHT as Zane walks back into the cabin.

"Oh shit. I can't believe I fell asleep." I rub my eyes, yawning as I find my words. "You know, if crying were an Olympic sport, I may have just won a gold." I huff out a self-deprecating laugh. "How are you doing?"

"I've been better. Lettie just let me know that we'll be stuck here at least another night or two. The rim's getting another snowstorm. She said no mules in or out."

"What about hikers?" I ask.

"She said both the Kaibab and Bright Angel Trails are completely closed coming down into the canyon. No hikers heading down but she said some of the visitors and more experienced hikers may be heading out. Chrissie's heading out early tomorrow morning to try and beat one of the storms rolling in. I was thinking I might go with her."

"What? Why?" The pit in my stomach is instant—as is the noose strangulating my throat. I can't imagine being alone down here. Especially after Jonathan's phone call.

"Um, I'll be back. I have some business I've got to take care of. I'll only be gone a day and a half. After I handle what needs to be handled, I'll hike back down here to be with you so we can hike out together."

"But," I pant, already out of breath. "But what if the trail doesn't open back up?"

"I have a backup plan. Don't worry, I'll be back in a day and a half. I promise."

He's concealing something from me. I don't have patience for it. Not now. Not when I need him now more than ever.

This is fucking bullshit!

"Zane, what's going on?" My voice is hanging on by a thread. "What business do you have to handle? And why are you acting so weird?"

Zane takes a bite down on his bottom lip. Then he purses out a long exhale. "Um, I'd rather not tell you. Just know that I'll be safe. I have a plan, and you're just going to have to trust me. It'll make sense later. Besides..." Zane takes a step closer, placing his hand on my shoulder as he crouches down to my eye level. "We still have the rest of today. Let's make the most of it."

I flinch my shoulder out of his grasp, raising my voice. "No! What the hell is going on! I know I freaked out earlier, but it doesn't mean you have to leave." I grunt under my breath, looking away because I know he's not going to tell me.

"Come on, Poppy. Trust me."

The begging cadence in his voice gets me this time. Then I stick my hand out for a handshake. "Just promise me you're not going to try and hurt someone. Or do anything stupid."

He shakes my hand, giving me a smile with no teeth. "Okay, Poppy. I promise not to do anything stupid."

After we both grab a shower and get changed, we meet up in the Canteen. I look across from him as he works way too hard trying to decide his next chess move. He doesn't know that I've already won.

"Why are you giggling?" he asks, clearly annoyed.

I didn't realize I was giggling under my breath. "Oh, I'm just about to beat you for the third time in a row. That's all."

I smirk at him as he shakes his head, whispering expletives under his breath. He's an Olympic athlete, so there's no doubt he's competitive. But it's cute to see him get all worked up over a board game he never had a chance in hell at winning.

My childhood neighbor, Miss Penny, is the one who taught me chess. Every Sunday evening I'd play with her, and every time she'd beat me. Even when I got close, she was probably just toying with me. But I love the way this game always has you looking ahead. It's in many ways a metaphor for life. We try to be steps ahead on things to make life easier and more in control. But some things are just impossible to foresee. Maybe that's the beauty in life. Releasing control. Accepting what is. Planning ahead, but being open to the surprises we'll inevitably not see coming.

"Fuck!" Zane shouts, covering his mouth instantly. He glances across the room to a group of giggling young tweens who thought his f-bomb was hilarious. I'm laughing right along with them. He's so fucking cute when he's got those perturbed wrinkles in his forehead.

He shakes his head, running his hand down the back of his neck as he talks. "You're like some secret master at chess. Aren't you?"

His shit eating grin only makes me laugh harder. "I'm pretty good. I had a neighbor that made me play with her growing up. Never beat her, but she made me pretty good."

"Excuse me, miss."

I turn to a young girl with red hair. The girl couldn't be much older than 13 or 14-years-old.

"Hi." I pause, noticing how the girl is twiddling her fingers while she looks down at her feet.

"Everything okay, sweetie?" I clear my throat when her eyes lock with mine. "I'm Poppy. This is my friend, Zane."

"I know who you are," she murmurs with the smallest crack of a smile hanging on the corner of her lips.

I shake her hand. Then I watch Zane warm her with a full smile as they shake hands.

"What's your name?" Zane asks.

"I'm Isabella. But people call me Isa."

"It's so nice to meet you, Isa. Can we help you with anything?" I ask with a softness in my voice.

She stiffens her neck. I watch her eyes peer around her head before she speaks. "I, uh, my mom didn't want me to bother you. But, um, I wanted to tell you something."

Her hands begin to shake. I quickly grab both of them, sliding my chair to get closer to her.

"You're okay, sweetie. What's going on?"

Her eyes stay on her feet as she speaks. "My mom showed me your video. She told me she was hurt when she was in college..." She pauses, tilting up her wilting, tear-filled eyes on me. "She was hurt like you were. She told me to always remember that consent is everything and that no is a full sentence. You see, today is her birthday. And she's too scared to ask, because she doesn't want to be a bother, but all she wants is one thing..." Her voice gives way to whimpering tears.

My hands pulsate through hers with tight, tender squeezes. Each time I squeeze, it's like our eyes are sponges full of tears.

"Oh, honey. Let it out. It's okay. What does she need? You can tell me," I cry.

Isa wipes away the tears, letting out a shuddering breath as she finds her words. "She just wants to hug you and say thank you. That's all she wants for her birthday. Can you give that to my mom?"

We dive into each other's arms. We're both crying incessantly, tears soaking one another to the bone. Her body is shaking as I rub my hand along her back, telling her it's okay. To let it out. I keep trying to soothe her with my words. But she just cries harder, and so do I.

I don't know this little girl. I don't know her mom. But I feel in my heart how there's a deeper story here. A shared pain between both of them. And it's not my place to ask. However, it's my place to comfort. To console. To make the most of this moment. *To give love.*

Eventually, we lean back. I'm hanging on to her shoulders while she sniffles back more tears. My voice hangs on by a thread as I speak. "Thank you. Thank you for telling me. Your mom is a brave woman to speak up and tell you. Just like you are. And you can tell your mom; I'd hug her a hundred times. Heck, I'll hug her a thousand times. Whatever she wants. I want to give it to her."

It's in that moment, with tears still running wild between the both of us, that I notice it. The pin drop silence all around us in the Canteen. Not a soul is speaking—let alone moving. It's like 30 statues staring at myself and Isa. Some people even have their phones out to record.

Then a bell rings as a young woman in her forties with strawberry blonde hair walks in. My eyes lock with hers from across the room. The second she sees me, her lips start to quiver. Her eyes wilt with a mix of sorrow and hope that I feel reverberating in my chest. The intuition in my gut is knowing who this woman is without a shadow of a doubt. It's Isa's mother.

So, without a second thought, I kiss Isa on the top of the head. Then I lean down to her ear.

"What's your mom's name?" I whisper.

"Maddy."

"Can I go hug your mommy a thousand times?" I beg.

She frantically nods with eyes still soaking in tears. "Please."

I stride across the room. It feels like I'm floating all the way to Maddy. She's still frozen at the door, looking at me like I'm a ghost. Then I stop, barely a foot away, looking into her brown eyes. The levees between us have already broken. We are a dam overflowing with emotion. It's tears that only a survivor can *truly* understand. But these don't feel like tears of trauma or weakness. They're tears of retribution. Tears of healing. She is like so many survivors, the lotus of hope.

Through quivering breaths, I find my voice that's barely hanging on. "Happy birthday, Maddy. May I hug you? Please."

She nods as the tears drip off her chin. Our bodies fall into one another. The embrace feels timeless. It's in this moment, in her arms, I realize Zane was right. But only partially.

I have done enough—for myself. I chose fire to the memories of Jonathan until he was nothing but a pile of ashes. I told my story to the world, unbeknownst to the wildfire that would ensue in the world of social media. It was all done because of Jet's words and Nina's visions. They gave me the hope I needed. The courage. The push. And the will to do something so different from myself and who I am. Now, here I am as some type of symbol in the world.

However, after getting the call from Jonathan, I know I'm not done. Not even close. There's still more to this fight. A fight I plan on continuing, until I'm six feet deep in the earth. I'm doing it for people like Janelle Morse. People like young Isa. And for people like Maddy. For EVERYONE!

I fight at their side, to do what I've always wanted—to give a voice to the voiceless.

While hugging Maddy, I close my eyes. The first person I imagine is Jet. He's wearing his exuberant laugh and sour looking expressions that always warm my heart. He's telling me to "fire the water." He's been saying it his whole life. But what he's really telling me, *really, truly saying*, is never to stop fighting.

That's why today, the movement begins.

CHAPTER 35

POPPY

I DON'T HAVE A ring light, but luckily the desk lamp in Lettie's cabin has enough wattage to light up my face. There's no time for makeup. No time for planning. Like the first video, I'm going in without a definitive plan in mind. All I have is an idea. An idea fueled by inspiration and adrenaline.

I position my phone against a coffee mug sitting toward the back part of the desk. Then I pull my bag onto my lap to dig out the red bracelet. Once it's in my hands, I bump my leg on the desk, sending my phone tumbling down behind the desk. The second my phone clanks to the ground, the sound sends me back in time.

Thanksgiving 2023

"Here, take my phone," Nina says. She leans her body up to the front seat and slides her phone into the phone holder so Nick can see the GPS to the restaurant. The second she leans back, a speed bump knocks the phone loose. It falls into the crack of my passenger seat. I reach down to dig it out, but I can't reach it. It must've slid under my seat.

"Yo, Nick. Where is this place again?" Zane asks, with one hand on the wheel and his eyes giving me a brief glance.

"It's in Nina's phone. Let me grab it," Nick says.

"I can get it, you don't need to unbuckle," Nina replies.

All I remember next is staring at Zane as a bright white light spotlights the side of his face. Everything from that moment on is a blur.

The sounds are what I remember the most. The explosion of glass. The sound of metal crunching inward. My body becoming a rag doll as a human body is sucked out of the front windshield. Everything else is a haze of confusion as our car continues to roll over and over—like I'm living in a kaleidoscope of horror.

When I wake up, Zane is dragging me along the road. All I see are the stars in the sky. The only sound is my body sliding along the pavement. It's surprisingly silent as I slowly come back to full consciousness.

He sits me up against a light pole and quickly assesses my injuries. Other than a small cut on the back of my head and a possible concussion, I tell him I'm okay. Then he runs back to the car. I watch for a moment as he keeps running past the mangled vehicle. It confuses me for a moment. Then I hear him screaming out for Nick.

"P-P-Poppy," a quivering voice calls from behind me.

I quickly crawl on all fours to my sister. "Oh, fuck! Nina! You okay?"

Nina is flat on her back. Her chest is erratically bouncing up and down, like she's gasping for air. The panic in her bulging eyes has me so terrified I snap out of my daze. I quickly assess her body. Her head. Her neck area. All I see are minor cuts and bruises. Then I remove the jacket lying over her right leg.

The second I see a bone popping out above her knee, I almost vomit. My hand goes over my mouth as I fight back the bile in my throat.

"Poppy, where's Zane? I saw Nick, but where's Zane?"

"He ran to get Nick...I think."

"No. No. No. No. Nick pulled me out. Where's Zane?"

My mouth hangs open. I'm unable to put together words because I remember a body being sucked out of the car. I don't know how I remember it, but I know it wasn't Zane.

A blood-curdling scream echoes through the night sky. It's so loud it overtakes the sound of approaching sirens. All I hear next are the begging pleas from Zane. It's the worst, most nightmarish sound I've ever heard in my life.

"T-T-Tell me..." Nina stops, gasping for air. "Everything's okay, right?"

The desperate cries and screams from Zane keep echoing and echoing. He's screaming the same words over and over again: 'Nick, *please!*'

I'm confused how Nina doesn't hear it or even seem bothered by it. It's like she's in her own world. A world where we all survived a wretched rollover car crash. But the pit in my stomach is knowing that miracle will not happen. And each time I try to bury the reality, Zane's heaves of pain become the never-ending ice pick piercing through my heart.

The paramedics arrive on the scene. They quickly tend to Nina while I sit there, feeling helpless. I hear things like compound fracture. Possible internal bleeding. A potential collapsed lung.

I feel helpless because there's nothing I can do to help her. I also don't know where Zane is. His screams have ceased. Everything around me is suddenly disorienting—especially all of the flashing blue and red lights. Every direction is shattered glass, pieces of medal, paramedics, and cops. So many of the cops keep trying to ask me questions. But my mind can only process so much amidst the chaos—let alone the screams from Zane that have stopped, yet I can't get them out of my head.

Once I arrive at the hospital, I refuse treatment and run to my sister as she's being stretchered in. The nurse tells me she's prepping her for surgery and that outside her leg being severely broken, she may also have internal bleeding.

Nina is awake but still in a state of shock. It's hard to know if she can even register the fact that I'm standing at her side as we enter the elevator. But when the elevator doors close, her hand snatches mine. The grip is so tight that it feels like she could break my hand.

"Where are the boys?" she pleads with panicked eyes.

"I don't know."

"Yes, you do. Yes, you do." She raises her scratchy voice. "Nick dragged me out. Right?"

She poses the question to me like she's suddenly questioning her own recollection. I don't know what to tell her other than I'm sure that Nick *did not* drag her out. It had to have been Zane. But there's no point in arguing.

"They said one…" Nina coughs up a lung, grimacing with each cough. Then she leans her head up a little bit and tightens her grip around my hand as she speaks. "They said one d-d-deceased. Was it Zane or Nick?"

My chest caves in on itself. I can't breathe because the tears are already spilling down the side of her cheeks. And I don't have a definitive answer for her, but I know in my heart that Nick didn't make it. I'm sure that he was the one I saw sucked out of the car because I remember him taking off his seatbelt.

Nina's tears become a steady stream. Her question hangs in the stagnant air as the elevator doors reopen. I have to answer her question, but it's an impossible question to answer when her own life is hanging in the balance. And I've never, ever, lied to my sister—until this moment.

"Nick's okay. I promise, he's okay. Remember, he pulled you out, so he's going to be fine."

Nina smiles at me. It's a peculiar looking smile—unlike any smile she's ever given me because it's not *her smile*. There's no teeth. No dimples. It's the smile of a person who's trying to stay strong in light of receiving the worst news in her life.

Nina looks at her wrist and quickly pulls off her favorite red bracelet. She hands it to me with a smile that's now wilting at the corners.

"Liar," she mutters quietly. She forces the red bracelet into my hand. "Keep it, until you're ready to wear it."

"No, no, no, no. I'll give it right back to you when you wake up."

I squeeze tightly through her hand. It's paramount that she believes my words. She needs to know she'll be okay.

"Liar," she whispers again.

"Sweetheart, you're going to have to let go," the nurse says, giving me a stern look.

"Wait," Nina says. She looks dazed as she motions me with her finger to lean in. I quickly bury my face into her ear as she faintly whispers. "Be brave. It's a celebration to change the world. Just follow the bright angel to the gardens. Bright angel to the gardens," she repeats, clearing her throat. "It's so beautiful. The water shooting up into the sky. Coming down on so many people," she breathes, gasping for air. "And the four of us with so much red everywhere. On an adventure. To celebrate. To change the world. All while letting the water rain down. You got this. Just f-fire...fire the water."

The nurse pulls me off of her. I collapse down onto my knees as she's wheeled away. Then I scream and beg for her to live. People in scrubs rush to my side to comfort me, but it's hopeless. I knew when the doors closed I'd never see her again. And I was right. She died on the operating table 30 minutes later due to severe internal bleeding.

Zane and I lived through that horrid day with just cuts and scratches because we were both buckled. If not for a bump in the road and a phone falling in between the crack in the passenger seat, Nick and Nina might still be alive. Still be in love. Heck, they could be married with their first kid on the way. But instead, they're gone forever. It's all because a drunk driver recklessly pulled in front of us that night. There was nothing Zane could do.

I wipe the beading perspiration off my forehead. Deep breaths through my nose and out through my mouth slowly bring me back to the bottom of the Grand Canyon.

Lettie bursts through the door with heavy breaths. "I found one!" she shouts, giddy with excitement.

"I need a minute!" I shout at her with my hand in the air.

Calm breaths.

Calm breaths.

"You okay?" she asks.

"Is it red?"

She pulls out a red headband from a bag. "Yes. I hope it fits. Why does it have to be red?"

"You'll see. You mind if I have the room back?"

"Of course." Lettie smiles as she hands over the red headband, or as Zane would call it, a dipsey-doo. Then she gives my shoulder a comforting squeeze. "Thanks for letting me help."

"You're welcome."

Before closing the door to leave, Lettie freezes in the doorway. She looks over her shoulder at me. Her eyes well up as she speaks. "I'm like you, Poppy." Her lips begin to quiver. She wipes her eyes. Then she puffs out her chest, standing tall after a deep breath. "I'm a sur-vivor...just like you...but I feel brave now...thank you."

Lettie rushes out, giving me no time to respond or em-pathize. My heart sinks into the pit of my stomach, know-ing what she's telling me. It kills me that a kind-hearted soul like her had to experience a similar trauma. But I also felt a power in her words. The strength in her tone. The willingness to speak up and tell her truth is the reason why I'm going to continue this fight. And it's Lettie's bravery that gives me the final push I need.

After tying up the red dipsey doo into my hair, I prop my phone back against the coffee mug. It's an odd feel-ing—the déjà vu to do what I did just a couple of days ago. But this time it feels different. I'm wearing red. I'm wearing the color I've been afraid to wear since that night. But today I don't revere the color. I don't blame it on what happened to me.

No more!

I prepare to press the red record button on my phone. But first, I close my eyes to find the last bits of courage. The first person I picture is Nina. She's wearing red from head to toe with her blonde hair fluttering in the wind. Red lipstick. Red heels. Red headband. Red sundress. Red jewelry. It's all red, accompanied by her angelic smile.

Then I imagine Nick coming into her world to put his arm around her. His smile of love and admiration only brightens her spirit. Seeing them together is the final piece of the puzzle. They're home. They're happy. And I feel them here with me.

One deep breath later, I press record.

CHAPTER 36

zane

WE MAKE OUR WAY up the final switchback of the Kaibab trail.

When at the top, Chrissie and I take a moment to catch our breaths. We both look down into the canyon, feeling a profound sense of accomplishment.

It was a treacherous 4 and a half hours of hiking, but we made it out safely in spite of the last mile putting us ankle deep in snow. It's no wonder they closed the trail going down given the dangers of slipping.

I give Chrissie a hug goodbye and thank her for being my guide out of the canyon. Then she wishes me luck.

After using the restroom, I take a seat at an open bench and turn on my phone. It'll be another thirty minutes until Trey picks me up. It gives me some time to see what's been going on lately. I've been mainly cut off from the outside world for the last three days. The only time I used my phone was to make the couple of phone calls I made yesterday.

I'm not sure if I'm ready to go back to my normal routines of training and working after this trip. Luckily, I still have today and tomorrow to take care of some unfinished business.

Once my phone is on, I text my parents that I made it out safely. Then I jump into my Insta account. The first thing I notice are the endless notifications. To my surprise, Poppy posted another video and tagged me in it. I play it right away.

Poppy:

"I don't know where to start. The response to my video has been amazing. It's made me feel so many things. Overwhelmed. Happy. Sad. Hopeful. So many cathartic, heartfelt emotions. But I feel like I'd be doing a disservice to everyone who watched my video if I didn't tell more of my story."

Poppy rubs her hands together by her lips. There's a sudden discomfort and tenseness I can see in her jaw.

"First off, I set fire to a picture in my video. Do I regret showing that monster's face...no. Not for a *single, fucking, second.* But, and this is a big but...for some survivors there's a risk of retaliation. I'm saying this, because there's so many videos out there, and taking part in this movement doesn't mean we need to name our accuser or show their picture. That was my choice. And more than anything else, I just want us, victims, survivors, whatever it is we are, in this moment of time. I just want all of you to be safe, however you choose to share your story.

Because in my mind, you're all heroes. You're all so brave. You're taking part in this movement because you have the power. And the greatest power is your voice."

Poppy pauses to catch her breath. She's so far away from me, but I feel the heaviness in her words, sinking deeper into my gut. Everything about her, I feel it. The emotion in her eyes, so lost in her thoughts. The pain she feels that I may never be able to eradicate. I feel it all. And I *want* to feel it. I'm here for her. Always!

Poppy takes her time to collect herself. Then she leans in closer and continues speaking.

"When I was drugged and sexually assaulted, I wore the most beautiful, gorgeous, out-of-this world, halter neck mini dress. I looked so sexy in it. Felt so confident. And it was the same shade of crimson red, just like the headband I'm wearing right now. I used to love red. It was my favorite color. I'd wear it all the time, and I loved that dress...*soooo much*."

Poppy looks down, shaking her head while rubbing her eyes. Then she tilts her chin up, looking lost in a memory as she speaks.

"I haven't worn the color red in a *really, really,* long time. It's been about 2000 days. I stopped wearing that color because it made me remember things. The kind of things I didn't want to relive. Things like the sound that red dress made when the fabric ripped. How that dress looked tattered the next day. It even had smears of my own blood on it. I remember feeling used. Destroyed. Destitute. Void of a soul. And more than anything, I remember no longer feeling beautiful. Or even feeling like myself. And that lasted a long time. A long...long time...I just...I couldn't ever wear that color again."

Poppy takes a tissue to her eyes. Then she bows her head for a brief moment. She takes two deep breaths. Then her eyes come back to her phone.

"You see, tomorrow is my sister's birthday. Her name was Nina." She smiles with glowing tears in her eyes as she remembers her sister. "She's no longer alive. But before she passed, she gave me her red bracelet. It's beautiful, right?"

Poppy holds her wrist up, moving it closer to the phone so I get a zoomed in look. I've never seen the bracelet before, but it has a gold chain and these polished stones the size of marbles. Each stone has a different shade of glossy red.

"I remember how she'd always compliment me any-time I wore something red. And she meant it. She said it was my color. And on her death bed...with her last breaths...she told me to wear red again—when I'm ready." Poppy pauses, pursing her lips as she blows out a heavy breath. Then she leans in closer and closer until all I see is her face. The intensity and glow in those hazel eyes have me waiting on bated breath for her words.

"I'm ready!" The screen shakes to the sound of her fist pounding the desk. "I'm ready because my red dress is not the reason I was drugged and raped. It was just a beautiful color, a beautifully designed dress, on *my*, beautiful body. *My body!* What it never ever was...was an invitation. It did not give that monster consent. And yes, Jonathan Christopher Reilly, the man whose picture I burned in front of millions, is a monster. But he's not worth my time anymore. He can no longer control me, or haunt me, or make me afraid of a color. Because tomorrow, on my sister's birthday, I'm in the one place Nina always dreamed of visiting. The *Grand...Fucking...Canyon!* And I'll be hiking out of here wearing nothing but red. I'll be wearing it for her, for myself, and for all of you brave souls that believe in this movement. For all the bravery we've shown in speaking up—standing strong against the people that hurt us and, most importantly, for believing and empathizing with one another's story. This is for all of you."

Poppy's voice teeters out to sniffling and tears. She takes a moment to collect herself by looking away. I do the same because my vision is fogging up. My own tears are making it hard to see the girl that I'm in love with. A girl who's not only the most beautiful woman I've ever met, but by far the bravest.

"I'm Paulina...Poppy...Rodriguez. I started the Fire the Water movement. Now, it's my life's mission. My greater purpose. And I will never stop fighting with all of you. So all I ask, all I beg of you, is to wear your red with pride tomorrow. Keep telling your stories. Keep choosing fire. And as my brother would say, let's 'fire the water.'

Poppy closes her eyes. She blows two kisses to the camera. The mix of smile and tears on her face has me awestruck. She didn't just start this movement, she's carrying it on to make it her life's mission.

The second the video ends, I feel an electricity inside of me. It's alive and flowing through me like an adrenaline rush I've never felt before. It almost feels unreal, like an out-of-body, spiritual awakening.

The video has only been out a few hours but already has over 5 million views and over 30,000 comments. The most liked comments at the top grab my attention first.

It quickly occurs to me that the plan I developed yesterday may need to be altered because of this video. It'll also make things more difficult to pull off than I expected. But it can still be done with help.

Two honks have me turning my head to Trey. He just pulled up in his red Jeep. While walking to his truck, I call Lonny.

"Hey, long time no talk," she answers.

I cut to the chase. "Did you see the second video?"

"Ha! Of course! Social media is my job."

"I know, that's why I'm calling. I need you to do me a favor. It's for Poppy. I need you to pull off a miracle. Do you think—"

"I'm there," she cuts me off with a commanding tone. "If it's for Poppy, I'll do anything. Just say the word."

Chapter 37

POPPY

One Day Later

Lettie came by a few minutes ago with the good news. The weather has cleared up on the rim, and both of the main trails are fully open. It means hikers and riders can head down or out of the canyon at their leisure. She even said that the mules will be ready to head out at 1p.m.

I already texted Zane that I'll be leaving at one, but he hasn't gotten back to me yet. We spoke briefly last night. He sounded a bit distracted. I didn't dig deep because I know he'll keep his promise to be back on time and hike out with me.

I take a little extra time in the mirror to get ready after my shower. It feels weird to see myself like this. I'm wearing red all over except for my navy-blue jeans. I have a red long sleeve shirt Lettie got from a fellow hiker. I'm wearing the same red headband she gave me last night.

I've even painted my toenails and fingernails red thanks to the red nail polish that Lettie gave me.

I also got a surprise this morning. Someone left a spool of red ribbon at my door with a note that said, "I choose fire." There was no name with the note, and I didn't know what to do with it at first. But in the spirit of wearing all red, I tied a ribbon off into a bow and clipped it in my hair. Then I made more red bows and clipped them into the zippers on my backpack. The remaining red ribbon I tied onto my shoes.

Once I'm ready, I check the time to see it's exactly 7 a.m. "Early bird gets the worm," I tell myself. Then I give myself a few more looks in the mirror before heading out.

My ankle is feeling a little better, so my plan is to head back to the spot where Zane and I poured ashes a couple of days ago. There's been something on my mind since we were last there. I figure since it's my last day down here, I'll need to tie up a few loose ends of my own.

"Poppy! Poppy!" a voice calls out.

I turn around to see a girl running towards me like her hair is on fire.

"Isa?"

Isa puts on the brakes and slides to a stop. I catch her wrist just in time so she doesn't fall on her ass.

"Whoa! Whoa! You okay?"

Isa's cheeks are pink. Her hand feels like a block of ice as she works to catch her breath. If not for a smile full of teeth, I'd be worried. But she's the opposite. She's beaming with excitement.

"I—I, sorry," she says, panting for breath. "Sorry. I wanted to give you a present."

"Ah, you don't have to do that."

"I know. But I wanted to help. My mom and I watched your other video last night. And I want you to know that you're not just helping her, you're helping me too. If you know what I mean."

Isa's brown eyes quickly have tears brimming on the edge. But her smile is unmoved. My heart aches for her, but it also senses that this young girl is on a path to healing—a path to bigger and better things that I can feel in my bones.

"Anyhow." Isa clears her throat, nervously fidgeting her fingers. "After seeing your last video, the two of us stayed up til 3 in the morning to make you this."

Her hand is shaking with excitement as she reaches into a brown paper bag. The second I see the red scarf, I slap my hand over my mouth in awe.

"It's handmade," she shyly admits. "We knitted it for you."

I squeeze my hands through it, feeling how plush and soft it is in my hands. Then I wrap it around my neck and tie it off. It fits like a gem.

"What do you think?" I ask, giving a fun look over the shoulder pose.

"I think it's the greatest thing we've ever knitted. And we've knitted so many things. It's always been me and my mom's thing. But to get to do this for you, well...like my mom said, 'it's an honor. An honor of a lifetime.'"

After a long hug, I let Isa know that I'm leaving today at 1. She's sorry to hear the news. Her and her mom are planning on staying one more night, but she promises to see me off.

The rest of my walk to the spot where we poured ashes has me on a high. I've never felt an adrenaline rush like this. It's like there's this electricity that's constantly buzzing through my body.

It's hard to identify the feeling because I've never felt this surge of goodness in my body. Whether it's the people on social media telling their story or the people I've met down here—I don't know. But what I do know, is my life has been given purpose. My purpose is to serve others and be a catalyst for change. To help those stuck in the prison cell of silence and fear. To *give a voice to the voiceless.*

When I get to the bench, I go down on one knee. After removing the boulder, I reach into my pocket to pull out the arrowhead. The tip of my index finger begins tracing along the calcified little dots. I still can't believe these white dots connect into the shape of a lotus blossom.

I remember learning about the lotus symbol and Buddhism in my world religions class in college. There are many concepts behind the religion that were of interest to me. However, what intrigued me at the time was the goal of Buddhism: to find enlightenment and end human suffering.

The construct of religion has always been something I've found interesting. They're interpreted like a game of telephone over their long histories. Interpretations change with the times just as humans evolve. But for some reason, learning about Buddhism made perfect sense to me. Especially now. In this place I've found my path. I'm living in my own nirvana because I've accepted my suffering.

My sister died at far too young an age. I even watched her die. And yet, even in the years after her death, she still feels so present inside of me—like she never *truly* left.

Then there's everything Jonathan took from me. I'll have to live with that trauma for the rest of my life. There's no going back from it. It was a part of me then. And it's a part of me now. It was one of the worst moments of my life, and yet, it's carved the path I'm on now. And because of it, I know what I want to live for.

My eyes look to the sky right as a beam of light shines through the hundreds of flowing branches and leaves. It catches my eye for a brief second, blinding my sight. Then a chill runs up my spine. The birds get louder, singing like they're speaking to me. Perhaps asking me why I'm back. Even the sound of the wind passing through the branches puts me in a melodic, zen-like state of mind. I've never felt more present to the beauty of nature.

I look down at the arrowhead in my open hand as I speak to them one more time in this place.

"So, I've said my goodbyes to Nina. But not you, Nick. Nina always spoke so highly of you. You were like a god to her. She thought you were perfect. In fact, she wanted a hundred babies with you. Her words, not mine." I giggle to myself. "You guys were perfect as life partners. She loved you, unconditionally. She loved sharing the outdoors with you. It's why I thought you should have this arrowhead back with you. After all, you found both of them. This one wasn't ever meant for me. Besides, I don't need the lotus on here. I already have mine on my chest." I pause to rub the lotus on my heart. "I want you to share this arrowhead with Nina. It's meant to always bloom with the both of you."

A strong gust of wind comes out of nowhere. It tickles across my face. I move a few loose tendrils as I take a panoramic look around.

"Anyhow, I just wanted to thank you for loving my sister and making her happy. You see, growing up she was the brave one. Taking care of me. Taking care of Jet. Older siblings sometimes have no choice. They have to be brave for their younger brother or sister. And I know I'm brave because I had Nina. Zane's brave because he had you. And now, we have to carry on without you guys. To be brave and keep moving forward."

My hand closes over the arrowhead. Then I delicately lay it back into the divot of dirt where the boulder was. After rolling the boulder back in place, I sweep the area with my hand to make it look untethered and natural.

For the first time in a long time, I'm not crying as I think about the two of them. Maybe it's because it feels like they're closer together now.

All I know is I'm happy. This place brings something out of me. After blowing them two kisses, I stand up to say my final goodbye.

"Well, guys, I gotta go. And Nina, don't you worry, I did exactly as you said. I'm on one hell of an adventure. And

I'm wearing red. It's my own kind of...celebration, I guess." I stop to look up. "No rain in the forecast or fountain of water coming down on me. But it feels like everything in my life is just getting started. And I'm happy. Zane's happy too. Hopefully that brings you guys peace because we love you. Always and forever."

The door squeaks open. Lettie pokes her head in again. I look at my phone to see it's exactly 1pm.

"It's time. You ready?"

I hesitate at her question, taking a deep swallow before muttering a quiet whisper back. "Yeah."

My tone is as reluctant as my urgency to leave this place. There's a heavy pressure in my chest for two reasons. One, I'm scared to leave this place and get back to a life that, while feels exciting, still has uncertainty. The second part that has me anxious is Zane's text from an hour ago.

Zane

> There's a small chance I may not make it back to you by 1. If you can't wait, I'll meet you on your way up Bright Angel. So sorry. But you'll understand why soon.

We were supposed to do this together. Not part of it or half of it. The whole way out. That was the deal upon him handling whatever business became so urgent.

I limp my way out of the cabin with a heavy heart and boulder-sized lump in my throat. There are no delays because we only have so much sunlight for the mules to get us out of here. Lettie takes my backpack as we walk to the loading area for the mules.

It'll just be me and her for the next five hours. Her mule connected to mine as we head out of the canyon, feeling like we're living in a 60's western. It'll be beautiful, but not the same without Zane.

The second we turn the corner to head up to the mule area, I do a double take. It feels as if I'm suddenly walking down a parade. Up ahead of me there are at least 50 or 60 people in two lines. The two lines of people part like the seas all at once. They're all wearing red. The procession leads to two mules with magnificent red bows tied to their saddles.

My legs give out as I grab Lettie's wrist. The sight ahead freezes me in place, leaving me numb and unable to move. They're all staring at me. Every last one of them.

"What's going on?"

"Everyone's here to see you off."

I can barely sputter out a reply. "Every...one."

"Yeah. They all know why you're wearing red today. And they're here to support you."

"They're all wearing red..." I stop because my voice is suddenly overwhelmed with emotion. "For me?"

Lettie's all dimples with her smile. She takes a ribbon out of her front pocket and ties a bow around the base of her ponytail. Then she wipes the corner of her eye and grabs my hand. "Come on. Today's your sister's birthday. Let's make her proud. Let's get you home."

We walk through a parade of spectators on both sides. Every single person is wearing red in one way or the other. Red ribbons in hair. Red ribbons tied around people's wrists. Red clothing. Red lipstick. Red fingernails. It's all I see. The color I once revered is now the color of triumph and hope.

It's a slow limp to get all the way through the procession of people. Some people wave. Some people smile. And some even walk up to give my hand a quick squeeze. But the majority of them are crying.

I'm able to keep my emotions in check until I see Isa and her mother, Maddy, at the end of the line. The second our eyes lock, I'm a blubbering mess of tears. If not for my handy little scarf, I wouldn't be able to see through all these tears and sniffles.

When I make it to the mule, I rub my hand along the mane. Then I kiss the red bow. Once I'm assisted onto the mule, Lettie peers over her shoulder at me.

"You ready?"

I give a gentle nod to Lettie. Then I wave goodbye while blowing kisses to everyone.

When the mules start their trek, a wave of sadness washes over me. My eyes take another panoramic look around. I'm going to miss everything about this place. The invigorating smells. The sound of wind whipping around cliffs and cutting through the trees. The sound of the creeks and rivers all moving at different speeds. Even the colors of this place. How they evolve so quickly in descent or rise. It all has me speechless and wanting to be back soon.

But I'm also lonely, starting the ascent without Zane. I know I'll see him soon. But selfishly, I want to be with him every single second—especially while down here.

My journey to the Grand Canyon started as a way to say goodbye. But it's turned into so much more. I found myself. I fell in love. I made love. I made peace. And I learned that saying goodbye is not an ending. It feels more like a segue to a new chapter with new beginnings.

When I get to the top, I don't know what's next. All I know is I'm excited. I'm ready for what will be the best chapters in my story. Because my story is just getting started. And I feel more than just ready. I feel grateful. I'm grateful for the next beginnings of my beautiful life.

Chapter 38

zane

The Previous Night

WE HEAR HIM COMING. Trey and I tighten our gloves and pull down our ski masks.

"You ready?"

"Let's fuck this shit up," Trey quietly replies in a cocky tone.

The lock unlatches. I wait in the recliner while my heart feels like it's about to explode in my chest. The door squeaks open. When it shuts, I hear Trey knock him to the ground.

I slowly rotate the recliner around right as the piece of shit cowers, putting his hands up in surrender. "F-f-f-fuck," he stutters, freaking the fuck out.

Trey raises his aluminum bat in the air, readying to swing as he speaks in an eerily calm tone.

"One fucking scream and I splatter your brains. Don't test me, motherfucker."

My legs cross as I lock eyes with him. He's every bit the coward I imagined. His body is shaking like he's ready to piss his pants. If he hasn't already.

"Who the fuck are you guys?"

"Have a seat," I calmly tell him, gesturing my hand towards the couch.

He staggers to his feet and sits at the edge. Right away he pulls out his wallet. Then he unclips his watch, speaking a mile a minute. "Take it. Take it. Take it all. Whatever the fuck you want. Just don't hurt me," he pleads, trying to hand it all over.

"I don't want it," I tell him in a calm, cold tone.

"Then what do you want? Just say it."

"All I want is to talk to you. And let me first just say that if you scream for help, try to run, or even worse, if you lie to me, that bat is going to go across your face once. Then, when you're lying dazed, coughing up your own blood like a half-conscious sack of shit, you'll get the best part of that aluminum bat. You see, my friend, that there is a world-class baseball player. And the next swing he takes will be into your balls until it's a bloody fucking crepe. You understand?"

He frantically nods. "I'll do whatever you say. Just don't kill me."

"That's right. We're not going to kill you. I'm not even allowed to hurt you. But like I said, my friend here has different ground rules. Well, technically he goes by no rules. He'll do what I say. Or what he wants."

"Okay. Okay. Okay. Just tell me what you want."

"What's your full name?"

"J-Jonathan C-Christopher Reilly," he stammers.

"Did you drug and sexually assault Poppy Rodriguez on May 24th, 2020?"

His eyes widen. It almost looks like his pupils are going to fall out of his face. Then he extends his arms to me with his wallet and watch still in his hands. "Come on, man. Just take it. Take everything I have," he begs, crying like a pathetic little bitch.

It only takes a gentle nod to Trey. Trey's aluminum bat tomahawks down on both of his hands. The bones in his hands snap like twigs.

"Aaaahhhhh! Fuck! Fuck! Fuck!" he screams, falling to the ground, rolling in agony.

I quickly grab him by his hair and gag him. Then I throw his dead weight back on the couch. He rolls into the fetal position. He's still writhing in pain, but at least the sound is muffled.

Slobber and snot begin dripping off his chin and nose as he cries. His hands have already ballooned into a pinkish-purple color. He looks absolutely pathetic.

I don't want to find joy in this. I really don't. But for a split second, I wonder, is this overly vengeful? Are we going too far? And then I remember how Poppy looked at me a day ago, telling me she didn't do enough. Then she repeated the words this monster told her.

He had the gall to call her a pathetic bitch after committing the most evil act imaginable. But now he's the one looking like a pathetic bitch. *That*, is why I'm here.

That, is why I find solace in seeing him suffer. After all, his suffering is only a microscopic crumb when compared to the pain he's inflicted on Poppy—only to have zero remorse.

The rage against everything he's done begins to burn inside of me. I feel reckless with this need for revenge. This need for closure. And I know in the furthest depths and threads of my soul, that this'll be it. It's my time now!

"Do you think it's hot enough by now?" I ask Trey.

"Oh, it's fucking fire, my man. I'll be right back."

I pull off the gag with a shushing finger over my lips. Trey throws me his bat and heads outside. I take a step closer to stand tall over him. It's like he's bowing to me with the way his spine curls in like a hunchback. Then he slowly tilts his teary eyes up to mine as a thick string of mucus hangs out of his nose.

"What's fire? Where's he going, man?" he cries.

"Don't worry about him. He'll be back. But let me ask you an important question, Jonathan. Have you ever watched *The Matrix*?"

"What?"

"It's a movie! Answer the fucking question!" I shout, tightening my grip on the bat, raising it above my shoulders.

His hands shield his face as he stumbles over his words. "Y-Y-Yes, Wuh-Why?"

"Well, it's time for you to make some life altering choices. Some real red or blue pill type shit, if you get my drift."

He watches me as I place two paper cups in front of him. They both look identical. Same Dixie-style white paper cups. Both with a clear liquid.

"These two cups are your little red and blue pills. You're going to drink one of them. But you better choose the right one. Or else…" I shrug my shoulders, watching his mangled hands start to shake violently.

"Or else what? Fuck!"

I raise the bat higher, like I'm ready to pound his face. But I stop myself.

"Answer my question."

"About what?"

"Did you drug and sexually assault Poppy Rodriguez on May 24th, 2020?"

"Yes! Yes! I slipped a drug in her drink. And we fucked. I didn't think she would remember it. The guy that sold me the drug said they usually don't remember it."

The fire inside me comes alive. The burn of anger is now volcanic with hatred. My hands go clammy as I try to re-tighten my grip on the bat handle. All I want is one big swing to splatter his brains. But I have to rein it in. I have to keep my promise. And more importantly, I have to ask an even bigger question.

"How many girls have you done this to?"

I raise the bat higher with both hands, coiling my grip tighter and tighter around the handle. I'm a baseball player with my eye on the ball. The ball being his pathetic face that I could pulverize into a thousand pieces.

His shaking becomes manic. His crying morphs into a desperate weep. I watch as he slides off the couch and falls to his knees, begging and pleading for mercy.

"Th-Th-Three girls. I've done it to th-three girls. All the same way as Poppy. Drugged them and fucked them."

"Tell me their names, Jonathan. Their full names."

"Stacy Hansen, Bridget Kirkland, and Mia Johnson. I know, I know, I'm sick in the head." He starts slapping the side of his head. Harder and harder he keeps slapping himself, knocking the spit out of his mouth while wincing in pain. "So. *Fucking. Sick. In. The. Head!*"

The sound of my aluminum bat hitting the ground has his eyes and mouth gaping at me in shock. He stops hitting himself as the pinging noise echoes in his pathetic shithole of an apartment. I reach into my pocket to press stop on my recording device. Then I cross my arms over my chest—finally ready to show him what real pain looks like.

"Here's what's going to happen." I pause, hearing the door open back up. Trey walks back in with a new weapon—a better, more appropriate weapon for the occasion. "You're going to choose one of those cups and drink every last drop. But you better pick the right one. Because one is going to ease the pain. The other isn't going to do jack shit for the pain."

"No, man. Come on. Come on. I told you everything. Please. Please, show me some mercy. They're onto me. I'm already fucked. I'm so fucked."

"Who's onto you?"

"The police. Private investigators. They have my DNA already. From that Mia chick I fucked. Look, man. I'm not lying." He shoves a bunch of papers off a nightstand with his elbow. They float in the air, dirtying his already crusty living room. The papers aren't worth my attention. Especially when I just added more fuel to his case. It also won't change what's about to happen.

"You have 3 seconds to drink a cup, or else you're dead."

I pick up the bat and cock it back, ready to swing. Using his wrists as hands, he quickly takes the cup on his right and downs it. The look on his face is suddenly full of confusion.

"Water? That was just water, right?"

"You'll never know, will you?" I go down on one knee to grab the empty cup. Then I look at the bottom to see the words I wrote with a black sharpie.

"What did you put in it? Did you poison me?"

His breathing panics. I stand up tall, while his eyes begin to look around the room. "I feel normal. Come on, man. What did you put in there?"

I slowly lean my face down to his until our noses are practically touching. He's shaking and paranoid. The second his eyes look away, I quickly slap my hand along the scruff of his neck, digging my fingers into the scalp of his shaggy black hair as I scream. "Look at me! Look at me!"

The tears pour out of his brown eyes as he cries out for mercy. But he's too late. It's time to *brand this motherfucker!*

I lean back from Jonathan's face and hold the empty cup in front of his eyes so he can read what I wrote on the bottom.

"Read it," I demand with gritting teeth.

"I, ch-choose, fuh, fuh, fire. What? What? What does that mean?" he begs.

Using every bit of anger in my body, I lean into his face until our foreheads collide. Then I whisper the letters at an agonizingly slow pace. "H...Two...O...You drank water, you pathetic fuck." I lock my eyes with Trey. "Trey! Now!" I call out, feeling the greatest rush of adrenaline I've ever felt in my life.

It's time for Poppy's retribution. But it's no longer just for her. It's for the three other girls this man hurt. I do it for all of them. And like Poppy, I *choose fire!*

Trey turns the corner, walking out of the kitchen with a sizzling branding iron in his hands. The coals and fresh embers smoke off the top as he throws it to me. I catch it with one hand as the embers float off and onto Jonathan. Trey quickly gags him right as he screams out. Then he puts him in a full nelson, locking his arms behind his back while his legs wrap around his torso.

"Do it!" Trey shouts.

I hold the branding iron up with two hands. The X on the molten hot end of it steams into the air. His muffled scream gets swallowed by the gag. His eyes bulge out of his head as I get ready.

"Balls...or face?" I ask.

He desperately tries to wriggle free from Trey's hold. I stall a moment longer, taking pleasure in his suffering. This coward hurt and scarred the woman I love. He branded her in a way that is, and always will be, unforgivable. And he got away with it, only to do it three more times. All while never feeling an ounce of remorse. He deserves the X I'm about to melt into his flesh. He deserves what he chose. He chose fire.

The branding iron flies into his flesh with every ounce of my weight and every last bit of hatred I have for this prick. I dig it deeper, and deeper into him, smelling the scent of skin melting away. It's ten seconds of pressure while he screams into the void of helplessness. He's not heard. He can't be saved. He is living the nightmare he inflicted on four innocent women.

I pull it off as he passes out, mumbling under the rubber ball. Trey pushes him off, and he rolls onto his side. All I see is the large X engraved into his left eye and cheek. The smell of his melted, mutilated skin permeates his apartment. Then I go down on one knee, removing the gag from his mouth as he mumbles the words 'please stop' over and over again. Trey hands the other cup of water to me. Then I lean down to his ear.

"You chose fire," I whisper in his ear. Then I get up, taking a look under the other cup to read the words out loud. "It says, I choose fire. Looks like you were fucked either way," I calmly say, holding the cup of water over his head.

His eyes open back up. He's dazed, but hopefully conscious enough to hear my final words. "You ever threaten Poppy Rodriguez or hurt another girl again, my friend and I will be back. But next time we won't brand your face. We'll brand your balls until you don't have any. Have a nice fucking life in prison, asshole."

I spit on his face. The cup tilts in my hand. I watch the water slowly pour onto his melted, dismembered looking face. The sizzle it makes as he groans is my final act of retribution. I'm done.

No more.

CHAPTER 39

zane

I'VE BEEN RUNNING FOR thirty minutes straight. It's weird to be faster than the endless line of cars that have all pulled over along the I-40.

The sound of a helicopter brings my eyes up to the sky. It's the third one I've seen in the last ten minutes. There are even a couple of drones whizzing above my head. They're all going the same direction I'm running.

People are all starting to get out of their cars since the interstate heading north is nothing more than a parking lot. I see all kinds of people: men, women, seniors, kids, babies in strollers, and even large families. It's people of all ethnicities. Many of them have signs and pictures. I wish I had the time to take it all in—truly see what's happening with all the red before my very eyes. But I can't. I'm running out of time.

My legs are burning. My lungs are fighting for breath in the thin air. I need to rest, but I can't. If I do, I'll be really late. So, I push harder, determined to keep my promise—to finish this hike with her. To celebrate a moment she'll never forget.

The last message I texted her was that I'd be late coming back down. But now I'm unsure about where I'll meet her on the trail. To make matters even worse, there's no reception on my phone.

Then I see it. Hope. A silhouette of a canyon peeking out through the thick pine trees. The next sign tells me I'm only a hundred yards from the trailhead. Everything around me is suddenly changing. But it's not just the fact that I've made it back to the Bright Angel Trailhead. There are crowds of people getting in my way. It feels like I'm at a concert. Then I see the fire trucks parked ahead. There are even firemen rolling large boulders into a circle.

I finally stop when I see the sign: **Bright Angel Trailhead.** I'm panting for breath while my eyes look at everything happening all around me.

"Holy fuck. We pulled it off," I mutter under my breath.

I asked Lonny for a miracle, and she pulled it off. I asked Trey to help me deal with Jonathan, but he did even more with his connections to the Fire Department. Together, we all did this. But more than anything, this is all Poppy.

The closest water fountain allows me to refill my CamelBak. Then I head to the start of the trail, where it's roped off with two police officers and two park rangers blocking the path down the trail.

I quickly jog up to them, and right away a police officer holds his arm out to stop me. "No one's going down, sir."

"Why?"

"We've got too many people trying to get on the trail at the same time. It's not safe, so we had to close it down temporarily. It should open back up tomorrow."

"You don't understand. I'm with *her*. That's my girlfriend down there. Please! Please! You have to believe me!"

The police officer just shakes his head at me, not willing to budge an inch. Then a park ranger steps in between us. "What's going on?"

I look at her name tag and my stomach somersaults. "Mia?" I ask.

She nods with a bright smile. "I'm sorry we can't help you. If we let one in, it could create a bit of a situation. We need our special guest to make it out first. We can't overcrowd the trail."

I plead my case one more time. "Look, Mia. That's my girlfriend. Poppy Rodriguez is with me. I promised her I'd hike out with her, and I'm late. But you need to let me down there. Please."

The static noise from her walkie-talkie distracts us both. I instantly recognize the voice. "Just leaving Indian Gardens."

"That's Lettie! I know her! I know her! Lettie Gallego! She works down there. Please get on your walkie and tell her that Zane Armstrong wants to come down and hike out with Poppy." I fall onto both knees, interlacing my hands as I beg. "Please, Mia. I'm a part of this. I need to keep my promise. I promised Poppy I'd hike out with her."

Mia furrows her brows at me, angling her gaze.

"Wait, are you the one who gave her a piggyback ride?"

"Yes! Yes! That's me!"

I watch as she pulls out her phone and begins scrolling. Then she holds her phone next to my face. "Oh my god. You're the one." She lifts her walkie to her lips with eyes as wide as saucers. "One second, Zane."

I watch with bated breath as she walks away. She's having a conversation on her walkie, but I'm too far away to hear it. All I know is she looks frustrated. When she turns her back to me, I contemplate making a run for it. The two cops are easily in their late forties or early 50's. There's no way they can catch up if I get past them. They also would have to man their post to prevent others from going down.

"Zane," Mia calls out for me, waving me over.

I walk up to her. "Did you reach them? Are they close? Can I go down and see them?"

She extends her hand out in a stopping motion. "Look, our reception is crap right now. Now, if you're really her boyfriend, why are you up here while she's down there?"

My mouth hangs open for a moment. Then I chuckle under my breath because there's no way she can know about my visit to Jonathan last night.

"Well, Mia. Let me ask you this. Do you have a boyfriend or girlfriend?"

"I do."

"Well, if someone hurt them, what would you do?"

"I don't know, but I'd make sure that it can never happen again."

"Well, that's what I was doing." I pause, clenching my teeth as I lower my voice. "I was making sure that the prick that hurt Poppy can never hurt anyone again. You get my drift."

Astonishment stretches her eyes wide. I watch her mouth fall open. Her lips twitch like the words are hanging on the tip of her tongue. Then she lets out a loud breath while turning her eyes to the two cops.

"Okay, look," she lowers her voice. "I believe you. But those guys have authority over me. Let me go talk to my colleague, and we'll distract them by bringing them over there." She points to a picnic table about five yards away. "Once they step over there, my colleague will let you through. But make it quick. And discreet."

I extend my hands to her, shaking them with both of mine. "Thank you. Thank you. You're a lifesaver."

I inch my way towards the roped off area of the trail while keeping my gaze off in the distance. I make sure not to get too close. Then, out of the corner of my eye, I see Mia and her park ranger colleague pointing at the picnic table.

I wait for my opening, and the second the officers walk away, I quickly walk under the rope. Once out of sight, I sprint down the trail. After a minute or two, I look back and see I made it without being noticed.

Everything from that moment on is pure adrenaline. I sprint down the trail as it zigzags with switchback after switchback. Each time I turn down a new switchback, I imagine the feeling of holding her in my arms. Inhaling her sweet scent. Kissing her incessantly.

It's ironic to think when I was here four days ago, I was a broken man. Now, the paradigm of my world has shifted. I'm rebuilt. Reinvigorated. Inspired. All of it is because of Poppy and what she's done for me and so many others.

It also feels different because I'm no longer on the sidelines. This time I'm on the frontlines, fighting for her. To protect her. To protect people like her. And to see her dream, her sister's visions, and her brother's words, become a reality.

Chapter 40

POPPY

I never knew it would be this slow. Don't get me wrong, the views are pristine. But these mules are in no rush even though their legs are about as tall as me.

Nevertheless, there's so much to take in with my senses. The earthy smell of damp soil. The melodic sound it makes crunching under hooves. The creosote bushes, still dripping with moisture, make my lungs feel brand new. Anything that's in the shade still has a thick coating of snow. But most of it has melted away.

The flora is now a richer shade of evergreen from all the moisture it's gotten. It mixes beautifully with outcroppings, cliff walls, and boulders that have a mix of Sedona red and beige. It feels like I'm moving through the backdrop of a priceless desert landscape painting.

It's warmed up enough that I've been able to strip down to just my red long sleeve shirt. It's a little tighter on my bust area than I'd like, but the crimson red matches perfectly with my headband. Or as Zane would call it, my dipsey-doo.

We approach the first of what Lettie says will be many switchbacks on our mules. I look up while trying to pull out the wedgie that feels impaled into all my private bits.

"Close?" I ask her.

"Oh no. This is the part of the Bright Angel Trail that lies to you. You think you're right there by the top. But we've got a good 90 minutes worth of endless switchbacks. You doing okay?"

I nod back with a smile. Lettie and I haven't spoken much over the last hour. My mind is just ebbing and flowing through all the emotions over the past few days.

I also miss Zane. Lettie said she heard from one of her park ranger colleagues at the top that radioed down. But all she heard was a quick mention of Zane, then they lost reception. According to Lettie, it can be normal for this area of the canyon. They call it the dead zone for radio communication.

I'm no longer disappointed he couldn't hike out with me. There's a good reason why. I just know it.

The next hour is exactly as Lettie said it would be. The trail just zigs and zags its way up. It's deceiving because you feel like you made it out, just to see higher cliff walls and more trail going up in elevation.

Our mules are suddenly faster than all the hikers. We keep passing them by, and their lethargic looks tell us that the canyon is winning. They all look beat to a pulp by this never-ending staircase of a trail.

When we pass one group of hikers who look even more out of breath, I start feeling empathetic. To the point where a wave of sadness washes through me. I look at my right foot, lightly kicking it into the side of the mule to keep the blood flowing. Then I slowly rotate it around. The range of motion feels pretty good. The pain level is surprisingly minimal. It doesn't even hurt when I wiggle my toes.

When I walked on it this morning, I still had a noticeable limp, but it was quite a bit better. It's still nowhere near hiking shape, but significantly better. The vast improvement from a couple days ago gives me an idea.

It suddenly feels wrong to be sitting here on this mule. Yeah, I need it to get home. But do I need it the whole way? Is this really how I want to finish this adventure?

My mind wanders to the memory of sitting on Zane's shoulders. The view was unlike anything because I had the intimacy of his closeness. The sound of his laugh. The strength of his broad shoulders supporting me. It was heaven. A heaven so inexplicably perfect, a moment so beautiful, I wish I could relive it one more time.

"Stop!" I shout.

Lettie's face crinkles into concern as she looks over her shoulder. "Everything okay?"

"No." I shake my head and let out a long sigh. "I need to get off this mule. My back hurts. My panties are impaled into my ass crack. And I just feel bad seeing everyone else struggle while I'm riding out like some fucking queen. Aaahhh!"

My grunt of disgust brings out a chuckle from Lettie.

"Oh, sweetie. You have a high ankle sprain. There's no way you're hiking out of the hardest stretch on one leg. That's not possible."

"I don't care. Can you stop these things? I want to at least try."

Lettie begrudgingly helps me off. The second my foot touches the ground, the pain is a ten. "Fuck, fuck, fuck," I mumble under my breath, grinding my teeth.

I try walking on it, but there's been no blood running through it for the last four hours.

It'll get better. It'll get better.

I keep telling myself this mantra while I try to walk on it. It's incredibly hard to go up the steps built into the trail, but the more I walk on it, the more I find a rhythm up the steps.

"See, I got this. Look, Lettie! I can do this!"

I look back at Lettie, who's still giving me a look like I'm full of shit. She's probably right. But the more I walk, the more I feel this surge of adrenaline. There's so much pain, but there's meaning behind it. A reason to hurt. I can't articulate why finishing this hike on my feet suddenly feels so important, but it does.

Eventually, after some persistent enticing, Lettie reluctantly agrees to go ahead. She says she'll stop every five minutes and wait for me to catch up. It slows her progress quite a bit. However, she agrees to roll with my plan since we should have enough sunlight.

It takes a while, but I find a rhythm on my own. If I lead with my good foot onto each step, I can then drag my bad foot up behind it. It lessens the pressure dramatically. It may not do much for speed or efficiency, but I'm getting the hang of it. In fact, I'm really starting to get a move on.

The trail has little tunnels built into the cliffs. When I see the first one up ahead, I get another surge of adrenaline as I gasp for breath. This is the second tunnel, which means I'm getting closer to the top.

While walking through it, I hear a funny sound. It's hard to articulate the thudding noise I hear. It's less the timbre of the noise echoing inside the tunnel and more the way the sound moves to a consistent beat. There's a distinct and discernible rhythm. Is that a drum?

I slow my breathing down so I can hear it better. And I'm right. I just know it. It's most definitely the beat of a drum.

The second I step through the tunnel, I look up, seeing something else whizzing in the sky. "Drones?" There are three drones about a hundred feet above me. They look like mini white helicopters but with a distinct buzzing noise.

Then the echo of a voice has my heart bouncing out of my chest. It gets louder and louder as it echoes off the cliff walls.

"Poppy! Poppy! Poppy!"

For a split second I wonder if it's just Lettie. But the louder it echoes and the closer it gets, the more I recognize it. There's a familiar power and masculinity in that voice. It's undoubtedly a man. But not just any man.

Zane turns the corner around a large outcropping. Our eyes lock, and I freeze. He continues his mad dash down the trail while shouting my name. When he's past the last switchback, I limp my way forward until he crashes into my arms.

The second his arms go around me, I'm weightless. He lifts me in the air, swinging me in circles while kissing me along my neck. My legs lock around his hips right as he finds my lips. Every last bit of pain and lethargy disappears.

If this were heaven, I'd want to relive this exact moment for the rest of my life. The way our lips move with such desperate intensity. The way the warmth of his body engulfs me with desire. It's perfection that's been irrevocably redefined.

The longer we kiss, the more it feels like I'm melting into a puddle of bliss. It's like I've been starving myself of the only thing I'll ever need. And he's back. He's safe. He's embracing me in a moment so perfect, I could die a happy woman.

He slowly pulls his lips off mine, setting my feet on the ground. His hands go lightly through my hair.

"Nice dipsey doo," he whispers, his lips still within kissing reach.

"It's a headband," I correct him with a smirk.

"No. It's not. It's a dipsey doo. Forever a dipsey doo." He quietly laughs, letting out a relieved sigh. "Man, I missed you."

Zane flashes a smile that just gets brighter by the second. It feels like a mirror to my own smile. Then he brings his lips to my forehead, leaving so many head kisses I lose count. But each kiss is slow and sensual. And each time he kisses me there, it's followed by three perfect words.

He repeats the words over and over again. Each time with such depth and meaning in his tone. When he's finally done, I tell him the only truth I know.

"*I love you more.*"

CHAPTER 41

POPPY

I GO DOWN ON one knee, gasping for air. My tank is completely empty. My body feels beat to a pulp from head to toe.

I'm regretting my decision to tell Lettie to meet us at the top. We just passed through the last tunnel. It means we're close, but at my current pace it feels like forever. The burn in my lungs mixed with the throbbing pain in my ankle is becoming too much. But I have to keep pushing. I have to dig deep.

"Come on. Let me help you," Zane insists, squatting down and handing over his water.

I guzzle it down and emphatically shake my head for the hundredth time. "No. I got this. I've made it this far." I shoot another squirt of water in my mouth. Then I wait for my breathing to slow. "There's no looking back. I can do this."

"Come on, Poppy. Let's compromise." Zane's gaze sharpens into mine as he gently squeezes my shoulder. "Let me give you a piggyback ride up to the last few switchbacks. Then you can finish it out from there."

"Let me think about it," I tell him, slowly standing upright while I use his shoulder for balance.

The second I'm upright, I feel Zane suddenly behind me. Then I feel the back of his neck go up between my legs in one quick swoop. Before I can protest, I'm ten feet tall on his shoulders. *Again!*

"Really?" I sigh. "Come on, put me down!"

"No. You're walking like a zombie. I can't have you die on me. You're precious cargo."

I scoff at his joke. There's a breeze now flying into my face. It feels weird because there's not a hint of wind in the air. It takes me a moment to realize it's not the wind. It's the rapid pace at which he's moving.

"Holy shit! Slow down, turbo. We got plenty of daylight."

Zane ignores my comment. If anything, he starts moving faster.

The drumming noises have stopped, but the drones are still overhead. Zane says it's nothing. But it feels weird that they're hovering just above us.

Zane's pace continues to pick up. Meanwhile, my fingers begin massaging through his fluffy, golden-brown hair. I know just the way he likes it, with just a hint of nails gliding through his scalp.

"I saw your latest video."

"You did?"

"Of course I saw it. You tagged me in it."

"And?"

Zane stops. I curl my head down until my eyes are swimming in his ocean blues.

"Poppy, I'm in awe of you. I, I uh…" Zane's smile stretches higher and higher. He seems lost for words, shaking his head. "I'm so proud of you. And I respect you so much. I mean that. *I respect the fuck out of you.*"

I'm shell-shocked by his words. It's more than just what he said. It's how he said it. The confidence. The belief in his tone. Even his smile speaks of genuine admiration. And all of it, every last word, has me melting on the inside.

"Ditto," I tell him, leaning down for an upside-down Spider-Man kiss.

When I slowly pull off his lips, I give his chest a playful slap. "Where's your red?"

Zane tilts his gaze. "Oh shit. I forgot."

"Don't worry, baby. I got you," I tell him, pulling some extra red ribbon out of my back pocket. Once I've tied it into a bow over the top of his head, it's absolutely perfect. It is every bit the girliest looking thing on the manliest of men, and I'm all for it.

I pinch his cheeks while speaking to him. "You're so fucking hot."

He tilts his gaze back up to me with a smile. "Thanks, Poppy. Red is a hell of a color on you. Speaking of which, are you curious to know where I've been for the last 36 hours?"

"Yeah. But I know you're not going to tell me."

Zane stops walking again. Did my reverse psychology actually work?

He goes down on one knee and helps me off. After standing tall, he takes a long look over his shoulder before burning his eyes back into mine. "Well, you're wrong. And we only got a few more switchbacks. So, I uh, I need you to know something. I kind of broke your promise...a little."

Both of my hands go to my chest. I'm instantly aching because there's so much disappointment in his face.

"What happened?"

"Well, um, after you told me what Jonathan said to you, I had to do something."

I raise my voice. "What did you do?"

"Calm down. It's okay. Let's just say, he got what he deserved."

"But..." I stop myself, trying to wrap my mind around what he could be telling me. Then the worst outcomes begin to play out in my head. Each breath is cut short by panic. But I have to know. "Did you k-kill—"

"No, no, no, no. Of course not. Did I want to? Maybe. But either way, a message had to be sent. So, I got a little help. You see, I don't want you to ever worry about him calling you, threatening you, or doing anything at all to you or anyone else. And that's what I did. I took care of *that*."

My breathing shudders through more panicked breaths. I take a deep swallow, trying to find my voice. Then I ask the question I may regret. "How did you break my promise?"

Zane's chest rises up. The inhale keeps inflating his broad chest as I watch his shoulders raise up. Then he lets out a long exhale, pursing his lips. "I kind of hurt him. But I hurt him in a way where he'll never hurt another woman again. And it looks like he'll be going away for a long time. He's a bad person. You know that. I just had to…I had to, Poppy…I had to protect you and make sure he never comes back."

My mouth hangs open. His words have me utterly confused, while his eyes have me transfixed. I watch as the brimming moisture slowly builds behind his pinkening eyes. Then the tears quietly roll down his cheeks. I can't tell if he's sad, regretful, or happy. Or maybe he's feeling all those emotions at once.

"Can I just ask you some things? You don't need to get specific. But I need you to be honest with just a couple of things."

Zane nods, taking a step closer to me. "Go ahead," he whispers.

"Does he know you're the one who hurt him?"

"No."

"Okay. You said you got help. Does that mean someone else may have hurt him?"

"Trey helped me. But we both had ski masks."

"How do you know he'll never hurt me or anyone else ever again?"

"He's going to prison."

"Really?"

"Yes. You weren't the only one he hurt, Poppy. There were others. But the evidence on him should put him away for a really...really...long time."

A bone-chattering chill runs through my body. I watch in awe as the tears keep trickling down his face. I'm trying to understand what's really going on as his words play back in my mind.

You weren't the only one he hurt? Prison? Long time?

I feel sad and happy at the same time. It's a weird juxtaposition of emotions. Maybe one day it'll all make sense. But processing news like this will take time. And all I hope is one day I'll be less hard on myself. One day, just maybe, I'll believe I've done enough to fight against assholes like this.

For now, I'm just going to trust Zane's words. Jonathan will never hurt me, or anyone else, ever again. *That*, is what matters most. *That*, means everything.

"Well, Zane. I only have one more question."

"What's that?"

"How good did it feel to hurt that motherfucker?"

Zane flashes a relieved smile while laughing under his breath. Then he wipes his tears away. "Pretty fucking good. Actually, really fucking good."

Zane takes the back of his hand to my cheek. I didn't even know I was crying. But he's gently wiping away my tears as he speaks to me in a tender tone. "I did it all for you, baby. You're my ride or die, Poppy. I love you. I fucking love you so much."

I bury my face in his chest as our arms engulf one another. His squeeze suctions me tighter into his body.

It's so tight I can feel the beat of his heart as if it's living in my ears. And if that wasn't enough to make this moment perfect, he plants kiss after kiss on the top of my head.

The realization of missing this place and missing home suddenly has a new meaning. Maybe it's because I'm already here. The only place I'll ever need to be—feeling safe and loved in his arms.

I'm home.

CHAPTER 42

POPPY

THE THUDDING DRUM NOISE picks back up. Zane stops suddenly. The rhythmic sound is closer than it's ever been. I can even feel the vibrations, throbbing and rattling around my rib cage.

"What's going on, Zane?"

He gets on one knee to let me off his shoulders. When I'm standing upright, I feel nothing but butterflies swimming inside me.

"This is it," he says, putting his arm out for me to lead the way. "Last two switchbacks and we're at the top."

Then I hear it. It's more than just drums. It's commotion. It's cheering. It's so many sounds that I can't make sense of it all. The only thing I know is it's getting louder and louder.

"Are you going to tell me what's really going on up there?"

His smile widens. "Absolutely not."

"Come on, Zane."

"Well, first off, this was just as much Lonny's doing as it was mine. Trey was a big help, too. As was Lettie. But you'll need to see it with your own eyes. Come on, they're waiting. *Your people*...are waiting for you."

"My people?"

"Yeah, you do know that between the two videos you posted, you had over 500 million views. And if I'm re-membering right, in your last video you told everyone where you'll be today. Did you not?"

I furrow my brows at him, thinking about everything I said. It all feels like a blur as the commotion above rattles around in my brain. Then it hits me. He's right. I did say I'd be hiking out of the Grand Canyon today.

"But I don't understand. Why are they here? And who's they?"

Zane laughs. His smile widens while my eyes trace along every perfect feature—from the bulging muscles in his shoulders and neck, to his razor-sharp jawline, to the radiance in his blue eyes.

Zane takes a step closer, grabbing me by my hips. He pulls me in tightly until my breasts are flush against his torso. I look up as the back of his hand traces from the base of my jaw up to my ear. Then he threads a few loose strands behind my ear, speaking with candor and affection in his tone.

"Well, it is your sister's birthday. And they're here for all the right reasons. Because, like you, they chose fire. They've found a way to fight back. A way to be free. And they found a symbol of hope. *You*, Poppy Rodriguez. *You*, are that symbol. They're all here because of *you!*"

He plants a soft kiss on my lips. When he pulls away too quickly, I moan for more. My hand grabs hold of his collar. I yank him back down as our lips meld back together.

When our lips part, my head falls into his chest. We're both out of breath. His heart is even beating like a machine gun. It's a perfect match to my heart and the nerve-racking excitement rumbling in my tummy.

"Just breathe," he whispers softly into my hair, soothing a hand across my back. "We got this. Just breathe."

We walk together through the final two switchbacks. The closer we get to the top of the staircase, the louder it gets. All I feel is adrenaline. The rapid breaths. Sweaty hands. But amongst all the butterflies, there's not an ounce of pain in my body. My ankle feels healed by the sheer adrenaline of being at the finish line.

I take my final step to the top and can't believe what my eyes are seeing. It's a sea of red in every direction. People as far as the eye can see are on both sides of a rope line. The two lines of ropes lead to a cul-de-sac of boulders surrounding a fire pit. The fire is raging some thirty or forty feet in the air. It's silhouetted by two fire trucks with ladders fully extended into a sky of blue.

My hand rests over my mouth. I oscillate my gaze over the crowd. Believing what I'm seeing just doesn't feel real.

SO. MANY. PEOPLE. ALL. WEARING. RED!

Some people are holding pictures. Some are holding clothes from the night they were assaulted. Others are holding signs with the words 'I choose fire' or 'fire the water.' But what I notice most is how so many of them have their arms around each other. As a survivor, I get it. They're all healing together. They're all hanging on to hope for a better tomorrow. A tomorrow where they're no longer victims being ignored, but survivors with a powerful voice. And a voice that *will be heard.*

Zane pulls me tighter into his side. Did he also just kiss the top of my head? I don't know. What I do know is all my senses are in overdrive. He keeps telling me to breathe. He's right, I need to breathe. But it's less about slowing my heart and more about breathing in this moment—letting it marinate in the deepest parts of my soul. Because everything I'm seeing is a core memory I don't want to ever forget.

My lungs slowly start to breathe it all in. The sharp, earthy scent of soaked dirt. Creosote bushes and boulders still dusted with melting snow. The sweet, smoky aroma of mesquite wood from the fire ahead. The low hum of thousands of murmurs and whispers. Many people are smiling, some are crying, but it is the way they look at me, full of adoration and awe, that leaves me breathless and inspired.

It all brings a sharp chill running up the back of my neck. Then the breeze blows harder, filling my body with more goosebumps. It's followed by a strong gust that pushes at my back so hard that it feels like a sign. A sign to keep going forward. To follow the rope lines that lead to the fire.

Then I'm tackled with a hug from out of nowhere.

"Lonny!"

She pecks my cheek and gives me a playful smirk.

"What the fuck is going on? What are you doing here? What did you do?"

"Ah, ah." She wags a finger at me. "This was all his idea."

"She's a liar. You think I could organize all of this?" Zane contests, holding his hand out to the crowd. "I got Trey to help me get the fire department out here. He pulled some strings for the fire pit. Then Lettie notified the Park Ranger's Department. They needed to be prepared for the largest onslaught of visitors this place has ever seen. And Lonny blew everything up on social media. She's the reason there's four local tribes out here playing drums. She's the reason every non-profit, every service for victims of sexual assault, and every supporter of yours is out here today."

"But you started this, Poppy. This is you," Lonny chimes in, grabbing me by my shoulders. "And believe it or not, there's more surprises coming."

The second I see him over Lonny's shoulder, I'm a statue. My vision, once clear as day, is now blind to weeping tears. He's 50 yards ahead, but it's impossible to miss that smile.

Jet slowly pivots into my line of sight on his forearm crutches. He's in between the rope line, waiting for me as the fire rages right behind him. Without a second thought, I let go of Zane's hand and run, screaming his name.

"Jeeeeet!"

People all around are hollering and cheering as I whiz past them. I'm running so fast it feels like I'm floating. As I get closer, I can barely see through my tears. Then I hear the drums from earlier come back to life. They beat in perfect rhythm as I run into Jet's arms.

We hug each other so hard we both fall to the ground laughing. Then I quickly help him up and hug him harder while we're both on our knees.

"Poppy! Poppy! Poppy! Fire the Water! Fire the Water!" He keeps shouting into my ear, nuzzling his face into my neck.

I cry profusely into the crook of his neck as I speak. "I know. I know. I know, Jet."

I lean back, cradling his cheeks in my hands. His head starts bobbing intermittently with excitement. I've never seen him look so alive and happy.

Everything going on around us feels suddenly non-existent—like we're living in our own little bubble. There's no fire raging next to us. Nor are we amongst thousands of cheering people all dressed in red. It's just *us*, celebrating our sister. And celebrating each other.

Another voice begins shouting something behind me. I crane my neck around to see Trey of all people, dressed to the nines in his firefighter gear. He's waving his hands frantically in the air. It looks like he's trying to signal someone.

"Do it now! Do it now!" he keeps screaming.

I follow his eyes to a firefighter who's at the very top of the fire truck ladder. He's so high up in the air he looks like an ant with a fire hose. Then I see a second firefighter on the opposite ladder.

It's hard to process what's happening—or why Trey is screaming incessantly at the top of his lungs, waving like a madman. Then, it makes sense. All at once, the crowd erupts in awe. That's when I see the impossible. Two firemen, each at the top of their ladder, shooting a rainbow of water into the air.

The water cascades so high up into the air. Then it's like two fountains colliding in the sky. All I can do is be mesmerized by the beauty as the water comes down like a mist on my face.

I tilt my chin up to absorb this invigorating chill. It's heaven on earth, the way the mist just keeps tickling its way along my skin. But the mist isn't just for me and Jet, it's for everyone.

My eyes breathe in the moments happening all around me. Every morsel of it becomes mine to bask in. Then I settle my eyes on the fire as it slowly dies down. People keep throwing things into it from all angles. They're turning their worst memories and moments into ashes. They're doing it not to forget, not to forgive, but to take back the power that was stolen.

That's when I realize my deeper truths. I'm living my life's greatest purpose. Right now. This moment. It's all happening. I'm going to change the world. I'm going to help those who feel like a piece of their identity was stolen. It's everything because it's symbolic to my own life. That's because I am the lotus. This is my rebirth. This is my blessed, beautiful new life.

But this moment is more than my experience. It's more than videos on social media going viral. It's Jet's words, '*fire the water*,' playing out in real time as the firemen shoot the water onto the fire as the mist touches all of us. It's Nina's visions that not only foresaw this moment, but saved my life. And it's my dream, playing out before my very eyes and the eyes of so many brave survivors. It's as if everything that's never made sense finally becomes crystal clear.

The rest of the day becomes a collective rejoicing for all. My parents are here. Zane's parents are here, too. Even Lonny and Trey's family are all here. Together, we all celebrate with the thousands of people who came—many of whom took the challenge and chose fire in speaking out and bravely telling their own story.

Little would I know the significance of this day: January 21st, 2026. How it would become more than just my sister's birthday. Or how I'd be back here annually and for years to come. Nor did I know that in a month from this day I'd open my own non-profit organization. It would aptly be called Fire the Water. And it would go on to become one of the most predominant charitable organizations in the world, fighting on behalf of sexual assault victims.

The organization would be built on the tenet that all victims deserve to not just be heard, but *believed.* We'd provide free legal services as well as free mental health services. This would include a 24/7 call-in line with licensed counselors and social workers available 365 days a year. And we'd fight beyond the victims, getting to the many roots of the problem—like archaic statutes of limitations and laws that only serve to silence victims.

But more than anything, Fire the Water would become a driving force in changing our culture, where abusers are brought to justice and victims can bravely report without fear of retribution.

That's what January 21st means to me. It's a tribute to my sister. It's the day I truly found myself because of my experiences in the Grand Canyon. And while I may only be one person. I'm someone. I'm someone who made the choice to be brave. I chose to fight back. And more than anything, I chose fire.

Fire the Water.

EPILOGUE ONE

ZANE

August 2028

I walk down a tunnel as we're escorted towards the main stage of the stadium. The other two swimmers trail behind me while a young lady in a black blazer guides us. She's speaking into her headset, but I can't hear a thing. All I hear now is a raucous crowd. The cheering and pounding of feet are so loud it feels like I'm living through an earthquake.

"Wait!" she commands with her hand held out.

The three of us stop behind a large black curtain. But now I can see it. Up ahead are three podiums. That's when it slowly starts to sink in. This isn't a dream. This is *really* happening.

When she gives us the signal, the three of us walk past the curtains. We all wave as the crowd goes nuts. The rush of adrenaline is unreal. The waving of flags is all I see in every square inch of the crowd. It feels like I'm floating in a dream all the way to the podium.

Once on the center podium, I look out at the crowd. It's hard to see with the blinding flash photography. I'm frantically searching for them, but the spot they were at earlier is now vacant.

Then I see all of them at once. They're being guided into the front row by the same lady in the black blazer. Every last one of them now has a front row seat to my dream playing out in real time.

I wave at them with both hands while jumping up and down. Then I'm interrupted by an older gentleman.

"Congratulations, Mr. Armstrong," he says, opening a black case with Olympic rings on the top. "Your country is proud of you, son."

My eyes light up, seeing the gold up close for the first time. I lean my head down as the gold medal is put around my neck. It's heavier than I thought. My fingers guide along each intricate engraving as I read the center.

2028 Los Angeles Olympics.

My eyes lift to my cheering section in the front row. I hold up the medal for them all to see. I even take a playful bite out of it for good fun. They're all crying and blowing kisses, so I do the same back. Then the National Anthem starts playing.

The last thing my coach whispered in my ear before my race was "one minute and forty seconds." It's not the time I needed for a gold medal. One minute and forty seconds is the approximate length of time for the national anthem. It seemed like a presumptuous thing to tell me before I was even on the starting block for my final race. But I guess he just knew it was my time.

I didn't just win a gold medal for my country in the 200-meter freestyle, I broke the world record by 1.33 seconds. When I got out of the pool, it didn't set in right away. I was elated, but it just didn't feel real yet. But as I watch my flag rise in the air, I realize it's all happening. Years of my life have been devoted for this one moment, and I finally did it.

The joy I feel watching my flag get raised into the rafters of the stadium has me also a bit saddened. After winning the race, I announced my retirement from swimming. It's been an amazing run, but I'm ready for the next chapter in my life.

My eyes flash down to a teary-eyed Poppy in the front row. She has her arm around Jet, who's crying along with her. She keeps mouthing the words *I love you* while blowing me kisses.

I look further down the line of people, seeing my best friend Trey and his fiancée, Lonny. The two of them started dating after we hiked out of the Grand Canyon. I was a little surprised they got together since Trey wasn't looking for anything serious at the time. Apparently neither was Lonny. But according to Poppy, seeing a man in their firefighting garb can do something to a woman.

Poppy and I aren't engaged—yet. It's only a matter of time. We're both just at points in our careers where we're getting our footing. I'm transitioning from my career as a professional swimmer into coaching and athletic training. My plan is to work six months out of the year as an athletic trainer. The other half of the year I'm looking to devote my time to supporting Poppy's foundation.

Her foundation, Fire the Water, takes up a lot of her time as the CEO. However, she's gotten better at delegating responsibilities for what's slowly becoming one of the largest charitable organizations for sexual assault victims in the United States.

Every single day I tell her how proud I am of her. I also remind her every second I can of how much I'm in love with her. And right now, with the way she's smiling up at me, I couldn't be prouder and more in love than in this exact moment.

But there's something different about her today that's more than just this momentous occasion. She has this glow in her face. This sense of pride I feel her emulating. Even the way her arm cradles around her stomach is peculiar to me. It's like she's holding something in there.

Wait!

All at once the hair stands up on my body. Poppy was throwing up this morning. She assured me she was just nervous for me. I believed her at the time. But right now, there's this proud sense of ownership in the way her arm caresses its way across her belly. Then she starts rubbing it, and I know it without a shadow of a doubt.

Pregnant!

I wrap my arm around my stomach to emulate her. Then I feel my mouth fall open, unable to hide my own shock. Poppy angles her face at me with admiration. Her hazel eyes begin to gleam through every snap of flash photography. It's as if suddenly, there are only three people in this stadium. Me. Her. And the baby in her belly. *Our baby!*

"*I'm pregnant.*" She keeps mouthing the words to me. But I knew it before she said it. I felt it inside of me. The kind of elation that makes you feel like you're floating in the air. The kind of happy where all you want do is cry and laugh at the same time.

I frantically nod my head up and down while mouthing the word "*pregnant*" back to her. Then the last notes of the national anthem play. I watch Poppy turn to our families. She's delivering the news with her hand still held around her belly. Then she's quickly swallowed up in hugs by everyone around her.

Every single person in the 90,000-seat stadium is still standing on their feet, waving their flags. The National Anthem may be over, but the cheering is getting louder. The love and admiration from the crowd has me soaking up the moment.

The reality is the people cheering know my story. They know I made an impossible comeback to swimming after serious shoulder injuries. They know I use my platform as a professional swimmer to advocate for victims of sexual assault. They know that my girlfriend is a hero to so many. And they know I'm competing on behalf of my late brother.

The sense of pride and gratitude I feel from this ovation is beyond words. Then my eyes glance up to the big screen. The word pregnant flashes as Poppy is being shown with tears in her eyes and people still hugging her from all directions. It's at that moment I know. My place on the platform, while an honor for my country, is no longer where I need to be. What I need is the love of my life. I need Poppy in my arms. *Now!*

Without a second of hesitation, I jump off the podium. The crowd lets out an audible gasp. I'm supposed to stay on the main stage until I'm escorted, but fuck that! I'm about to be a dad!

I'm sprinting to her. Poppy ducks under a rope and runs towards me. I can feel the manic energy in the stadium growing as I get closer. Then we collide into each other's arms.

My hug is gentle, yet tight. We hang onto each other as the tears pour out and the sounds around us reach deafening levels. The swelling affection in my chest is the need to hold her, hold onto this moment, and never let go.

It's a surreal moment. I just won a gold medal. I'm going to be a dad. She's going to be a mom. And we're madly in love.

Together, we arrived at the apex of this moment through so many impossible events. And I still wonder, was it some grand plan by God with the help of my brother and her sister? Or was it just fate? We'll likely never know. But all that matters is we are in love, and this is just the beginning. The beginning of our happily ever after.

EPILOGUE TWO

POPPY

10 Years Later

The banners, balloons, streamers, and confetti were all *her* ideas. As was the huge sign out front that says "Celebration of Life! No Crying Allowed!" Even the idea to have a jazz band and mariachi band there at separate times was her idea. The confetti cannon for each guest, well, that was nixed by us moms. We couldn't risk a kid losing an eye.

I still remember telling my mom and dad about it. They didn't believe me at first when I shared the details. They thought it was the morphine talking. But after speaking with her kids and confirming that the party plans and monetary donations were written into the will at the last minute, I had no choice.

When our longtime neighbor, Miss Penny, went into hospice, it was a gut punch for my whole family. She was the grandma I never had. Yeah, she was my neighbor, but always something bigger than family—bigger than life to all of us. And she lived a full life, dying on her 100th birthday surrounded by her family.

I visited her every day for those last two weeks of her life. She was always sharp as a tack, telling me many times that she wasn't afraid to die. If anything, she kept saying how excited she was to be with her husband, Benny McClain.

I learned during those last couple of weeks that she wanted to donate half of her money to my foundation, Fire the Water. I laughed it off at first, told her it wasn't necessary. But after talking to her son, Benny McClain Jr., it was a done deal. "Already added into the will," he told me the next day, without batting an eye. Then he told me, "It's an honor to support such a beautiful cause." And he thanked me again for the years of caring for and looking after his mother.

It was also during those final two weeks that Miss Penny planned her own funeral reception. But she never used those words. It was always a party or celebration. She wanted it at my house so that it could hold all of her children, grandchildren, and even great-grandchildren. She also wanted me to invite as many of my own family members as well. "A big McClain, Rodriguez, and Armstrong party!" she called it.

The conversations on music at the party were interesting to say the least. She wanted lots of it. It had to be loud and boisterous to fit the mood of a party. Nothing could be too sad.

Since she loved jazz, we hired an upbeat jazz band for the first half of the party. And since she got to know Rosita so well, she talked me into hiring a mariachi band for the second half of the party.

I learned so much about Miss Penny over those last couple of weeks of her life. I had already known that she was a retired special education teacher, but I also learned more about her philanthropy. She donated much of her time and money to the Special Olympics because her brother Jimmy had autism and was one of her greatest inspirations growing up. She told me many times on her deathbed how Jet always reminded her of Jimmy. How both of them have a never-ending supply of love that's always ready to be shared. And she told me many, *many times*, to never take that special kind of love for granted. And I never will.

It wasn't until my last couple of days visiting her that I also learned how she was adopted like me. Apparently, she met her biological father later in life and was able to rekindle a relationship with him similar to Rosita and myself.

The timer rings on the oven, snapping me out of my reverie. It takes me a couple of deep breaths until I'm ready. Then I slide on my oven mitts, praying I got it right this time.

Mom promised not to intervene. To my surprise, she kept her promise even though she's been lurking in the dining room for the past twenty minutes to take a few extra peeks into the kitchen.

"Confía en tus instintos," she's been telling me all day.

It's Spanish for trust your instincts. I can trust my instincts when it comes to feeding my family. But serving an authentic Mexican-style chile relleno to 30 guests of a funeral reception, or celebration, is a whole new ball game.

One by one I check each of them. They're all the perfect shade of light brown and melted to cheesy perfection. Even the two I cut into had that perfect texture that has my mouth already watering.

"Mija! Perfecto!" she admires over my shoulder.

I turn around to her grand smile, holding my spatula up like it's a trophy. "I did it! I did it, Mom!"

We hug in the kitchen, refusing to let go. It's the one thing I've learned since reconnecting with my Mexican culture and meeting my biological mother. There's no limit on the number of hugs you give your family. And the hugs need to be the kind that crack your back and leave your ribs feeling sore the next day.

I didn't meet my biological mother until Fire the Water became an international non-profit organization five years ago. We had just opened a small satellite office in Mexico City to support victims of sexual assault. That's when my biological mother, Rosita Lucia Rodriguez, saw a video on social media that Lonny created. Rosita told me the second she saw my face on the promotional video, she knew it was me without a shadow of a doubt.

She now lives two houses down from us for six months out of the year in the Kensington suburb of San Diego. She's been married for over twenty-five years to her husband, Marco. They're both retired elementary school teachers. The two of them have two daughters, Isabella and Ana, who are only a couple of years younger than me.

I'm so busy with work and family that I only get to see my half-sisters once a year when we travel to Mexico City for vacation. But it's been such a blessing to reconnect with my family down there as well as my Mexican heritage.

I never asked my mom why she left me at a fire station when I was four years old. One time she wanted to tell that part of her story, but for some reason I stopped her. An explanation just wasn't needed. It may sound ridiculous to most, but I'm glad she left me there. I know her well enough now to know she made a selfless decision that day. And likely the hardest decision of her life.

What matters most are all the blessings that came from her choice. I now have two sets of parents, three beautiful daughters, the perfect brother, and two new half-sisters who each have children of their own. The perfect best friend in Lonny. And the best part of all, a *husband*, like Zane.

Fire the Water became what it was destined to become shortly after I posted those videos over ten years ago. It's a movement that keeps moving forward to do more for victims. The expansion into 30 other countries and locally to almost every state in the US means victims have support and love from all over the world.

It hasn't always been easy as the CEO of my foundation. Especially now since I have young children. Shortly after Zane won a gold medal, I gave birth to my now nine-year-old daughter, whom we proudly named Nina.

A couple of years after that, we gave birth to fraternal twin girls named Isa and Jettie. They're now seven years old and idolizing big sister Nina just like I did at that age, and *still do*!

It takes a village to raise three girls and run a foundation—all while always putting Zane and my relationship first. Luckily, Rosita's here for half the year, and my adoptive parents recently retired and live right down the street. Most days we wing it as parents typically do, but we find a way to make it all work. I'm just eternally grateful that my kids get to grow up alongside their grandparents. It's like growing up with four Miss Penny's looking after them.

Zane plops his weight down on the couch next to me. Then he falls into my arms, using my bust as a pillow for his face.

"We did it," he says, the words muffled by my breasts.

"We did it." I sigh with relief. "Thanks for helping with the dishes."

"Of course, my love."

Zane repositions himself so he's lying on his back with his head in my lap. We stare in silence at one another while I massage my fingers through his scalp. We're both exhausted by a long day of saying goodbye to Miss Penny. Luckily, all the girls are asleep. All the guests have left. And the house is clean. It's just us again.

"Anything going on tomorrow morning?" I ask, forgetting Zane's schedule.

"Let's see." Zane yawns. "I've got to prep for my presentation next week. Then I have a training session with this new hotshot named Theo. He's supposed to be the next...Zane Armstrong."

I slap his chest, giving him a playful smirk. "There can't be another Zane Armstrong. No one's ever going to be a better swimmer and man than you."

Zane smiles up at me. I smile back, wondering if I could be prouder of him. Aside from being a tremendous father and coach, he travels twice a month to give motivational talks at seminars and conferences.

He initially used his platform as a gold medalist to be a spokesperson for my foundation, which he still does. But over time, it's evolved into him also giving talks on overcoming grief. It's still hard for him to do it, but after every speech he tells me how it heals his soul. He also tells me how it brings him closer to Nick because it helps keep his memory alive.

It makes perfect sense to me. Every milestone Fire the Water reaches brings me closer to Nina. I still think about her constantly every day, just as I know Zane goes through the same emotions with Nick. It's as if we both devote a part of our lives to doing things that make us feel close to the people we lost.

However, our work and our grief are just a part of our life. More than anything else, we stay grounded in our marriage. We make our relationship and our children always top of mind.

"How about you? Any plans for...tonight?" Zane asks with a sensual smirk.

His smile paired with those translucent blue eyes still holds an incredible power over my libido. And when his tongue lightly traces along his upper lip, I can't wait a second longer to taste those lips.

"Yum," I whisper, lifting off his lips.

"Can I show you something, Poppy?"

An eager, giddy nod has Zane rolling off my body. Then he scoops me into his arms to carry me to bed. We giggle at one another and kiss all the way to our bedroom. Then we make love.

After he rolls off my body, we're both gasping for air. The long party and multiple orgasms have us both exhausted. But I summon the strength to crawl into his waiting arms. Lying on his chest with a warm embrace is my favorite place to be. There's not a safer, more loving hold than the one Zane gives me every night before bed. And it comes with head kisses for as long as I need them.

Tonight, I don't need many head kisses. My heart is already full. I'm blessed with this beautiful life I get to live. Every day I fall deeper in love with Zane and my beautiful daughters. I get to live a life of purpose where I make a difference in the world. It may not always be a fairy tale, but it's pretty damn close. And what it truly is, more than anything else, is pure *happiness*!

The End

A Message from the Author

Thank you again for giving my book a chance. I sincerely
hope the message in this story lives on through the kindness and good deeds *you* put forth into the world.
Writing is my passion and I'm truly honored to share
it with the world. If you'd like to learn more about my
author journey and upcoming book releases, please subscribe to my mailing list by visiting
http://timothykylebooks.com
Lastly, I'd greatly appreciate your support by leaving a review on Amazon and Goodreads. For new authors like me,
it helps us grow our readership and improve as writers.

**Continue reading for a sneak peek of
*The Girl in the Red Wig!***

PROLOGUE

DAVID

I LOOK OUT INTO the backyard as the water runs down our sliding glass door. The multiplying water droplets make everything outside so blurry and distorted—the full moon, the light post by our shed, even the stars look different when the water trickles down the glass in the middle of the night.

The crash of thunder has my whole body flinching. The wrenching pain in my stomach spreads upward, slowly creating a suffocating pressure over my chest and throat. It's like an incurable flesh-eating disease, devouring what's left of my insides. Luckily, there's not much left.

Everyone else is asleep. I only know because I've checked multiple times. Sleep has felt impossible lately. I can close my eyes for prolonged periods of time, but falling into a bliss of unconsciousness only feels like a fantasy.

How does a twelve-year-old boy sleep into a dream or alternate reality? That's what I want—to blink and wake up in a new life. The kind of life where people aren't unfairly taken away from you in the blink of an eye.

"The roads were slick. Six inches this way, and we're looking at a totally different outcome," the police officer said to my father.

The words keep playing back in my head. Each time, it's like barbed wire slowly scraping through the inside of my chest. Then I hear the screams of a grown man as he collapses to his knees, begging. I wasn't meant to hear those words preceding his screams, but I did. I'm glad I did. It showed me the true evils of the world.

"Twelve, twenty-one, eighteen, thirty-six. For emergencies only," my dad told me when I was younger.

The numbers to the safe click as I rotate the knob. I grab hold of the metal handle, surprised by how cold and heavy it is in my hand. I'm sure this qualifies somewhere under the umbrella of emergencies—no longer wanting to live. But if I left this world to escape the pain, would I even find her? Perhaps that's a risk worth taking, albeit selfish to Dad and Angela.

I walk back downstairs, feeling the weight of my world in my right hand. I close my eyes and lean my forehead into the sliding glass door. This sharp, cold sensation sends a shiver down my spine and may be the last feeling I experience.

The Glock 19 goes up to the side of my head. My index finger becomes clammy as it traces along the trigger. I close my eyes. Then, my countdown begins.

Five, four, three...

Our aluminum trash can clanging to the ground has my attention. I put the gun on the counter to take a closer look outside. All I can see is a shadowy figure. The figure then walks under the light post by our shed.

It's a girl!

I know this girl. I rarely ever see her, but I know her. But there's something off. She's huddled under the thin eve of our shed roof.

A white light flashes, giving me a split-second vision of the girl. Another thunderous roar from the sky follows the lightning. I watch the young girl shiver in her pajamas, soaking to the bone.

Millions of questions run through my head. The first is why a girl my age is in my backyard in the middle of the night. Or why her lips move to a conversation she could only be having with herself. But those questions are suddenly unimportant. The intriguing part is the way the light post shines down upon her fiery red hair. It's odd how it doesn't look damp despite the rain coming down harder. In fact, it has a translucent red glow that has my eyes transfixed. It's *so red.*

It takes another minute or two before I gather the courage to head outside with my umbrella. The closer I get to her, the more I feel the need to slow my approach. She's huddled against the shed siding with her back to me. All I hear is the indistinct mumbling of words and water pelting the shed.

"Hey! Hey! Are you okay?"

The wind kicks up. The rain goes sideways, pelting the shed harder. There's still no response. She won't turn around, and her shivering worsens. I take another tentative step closer while positioning the umbrella at an angle to keep her dry.

"I know who you are," I tell her as I peer around to see her face. "Can I help you?"

The girl slowly turns around, looking at me like she's lost. But she's not lost in the physical sense. She couldn't be. She's my neighbor. It's her mind. She's here in front of me, dripping wet and wide-eyed with fear. But she doesn't seem to recognize me or even see me. Her line of vision goes over my head to an alternate reality. It's like she's lost in a dream.

"I'd like to help you," I tell her again—still nothing.

I'm running out of options. Talking to her is going nowhere, and the temperature is dropping by the second. The only option is to lead her into the shed to dry her off and see what's happening.

My trembling hand slowly extends out to her shoulder. I know a boy is not allowed to touch people like her. But I just don't care. All I feel is the innate need to help her. It's what Mom would do without a second thought.

The second my hand touches the sleeve of her shirt, she flinches and lets out a loud gasp. Then, her other hand slams down on my wrist, squeezing it with an ungodly amount of strength. Her entire body begins to shake violently.

"She lives! Go find her! She lives! Go find her!" Her whisper is loud and raspy. *It's terrifying.* But more than anything, the pleading tone in her voice has my whole body chilled.

The same words keep pouring out of her. Each time, it's a more desperate plea than before. Her hand continues to dig into my wrist as I feel her panic in my chest.

The need to no longer live becomes a distant memory in this moment. And to think, I was two seconds away. Mom was only six inches away from living. It's ironic how something so small and minute can be the threshold between living and dying.

Eventually, she lets me guide her into the shed. Once we're in there, I take stock in my situation. It's the middle of the night. I have no way of helping her or understanding the meaning of her words. All I have is a gut feeling. A feeling that's overflowing with clarity. It's a resounding truth I feel in the marrow of my bones.

I will live a little bit longer. Maybe to help. Maybe to just listen. But most importantly, I'll do as Mom would have done.

ACKNOWLEDGMENTS

GETTING TO THE FINISH line with any book is an arduous journey. This book was no different. My wife got extremely ill and was hospitalized halfway through the writing of this story. For three months, life stopped for me. I stopped writing and was convinced this story would never see the light of day. But, like Poppy Rodriguez, my wife is a fighter. She made a full recovery, and this book made it to the finish line. I couldn't be more grateful for her health, and for the person that is my everything in this world. Love you, Emmy!

This story came to my mind when I learned that one in three women will experience a sexual assault in their lifetime. As a father of three girls, the thought of this kills me. But sometimes the harsh realities of the world we live in become the fuel that drives our creativity. Hence, I wrote the most challenging, and the most gratifying story I've ever written with *Fire the Water*.

This book is written for <u>all</u> the victims of sexual assault. All of you! Women. Men. The LGBTQ+ community. The differently abled community. Everyone that's been hurt, both directly as a victim, or as a family member or friend to a victim.

I want to particularly mention the victims of sexual assault that were never believed or taken seriously. And even the ones that have yet to tell their story. I hope all of you find your voice when the time is right. I hope you find your healing journey and get the help you need. I'm a firm believer that we all have a little Poppy Rodriguez in us. And when it's your time to 'choose fire,' you'll do it in the way that best fits your healing journey.

To the differently abled community, <u>I see you</u>. All of my books have represented you in some form because of my experiences as an educator and an advocate. Jet may be a fictional character, but I've had the privilege in my life to meet and befriend so many talented people like Jet, Jimmy, and Sasha. It's because of all of you that my heart will forever be overflowing with gratitude.

I'd like to next recognize the team of people that made this book publish ready. First, I want to recognize my editors: Danielle, Ramona, and Nicole. For formatting services, a big thanks goes out to Brittany for her patience and diligence in putting the final touches on this book. Next, I'd like to recognize my beta reading team: Margret, Kathi, Lynn, Demi, Kat, and Keasha. The attention to detail and feedback that all of you gave to this story means the world to me!

I'd like to next give a special thank you to my hype team. This includes my entire street team and my team of ARC readers. I want to specifically give a special thank you to my PA's: Nicole and Bailey. I appreciate everything the two of you did to support the release of this book. I couldn't imagine doing this alone and I'm forever in debt to you both. Truly! Thank you so much!

Lastly, I save the best for last. The biggest thank you goes to the readers that made it through this book. It's an emotional journey to get through any of my stories. How you feel after reading my books should be subjective and unique to each person. But if I'm being honest, I sincerely hope you leave this book feeling inspired.

ABOUT THE AUTHOR

Timothy Kyle is a longtime native of Phoenix, Arizona. He's a proud husband and father to three rambunctious pre-teen girls. When he's not writing or making ridiculous social media content, he's pursuing his other passion in life as a tennis coach.

Timothy received his master's degree in exercise science in 2009. He worked for the next decade in the non-profit and education sectors that support individuals with *special* abilities. He's a proud advocate of the special needs community and of women's rights.

Fire the Water is his third book. His other books are *The Tree House* and *The Girl in the Red Wig*. If you enjoy his writing, he'd love for you to leave a review on Goodreads and Amazon. He'd also love for you to visit his website: https://timothykylebooks.com. There you can subscribe to his mailing list and purchase special edition signed copies of his books that directly support future writing projects.

www.ingramcontent.com/pod-product-compliance
Lightning Source LLC
Chambersburg PA
CBHW032031120726

47901CB00001BA/205